PRAISE FOR

# THE MOTHER OF CENTURIES

AND

# JOHN S. MCFARLAND'S WORK

"While ghosts and goblins and their human foil can be fun, I enjoy horror that is far more personal, stuff you suspect isn't just written but bled upon the page. Stuff that is more exorcism than entertainment, where the writer is tacitly saying it is either the notebook or the noose. The stuff that, when you read it, you feel as though you just stumbled upon a scene that you shouldn't have seen, that you should not be seeing, and that you should forget about as quickly as you can (a feat that often proves all but impossible).

"John McFarland is one of those writers. His stories put me in mind of Thomas Ligotti and Robert Aickman (fine company for sure) whose work reveals bits and pieces of the world-weary psyche behind them. He takes as grist for his creative mill the plight of the lonely, the psychological malaise of the alienated, the deception of love, and the general cruelties and absurdities of mankind; and churns out tales that hit you right in the heart as the best fiction should... McFarland wields his pen with confidence and an artistic vision rooted in the ordeal of living."

~ Evan Romero, Reviewer

"Excellent work."

~ John Padgett, *Vastarien, a Literary Journal*

"John S. McFarland wrote with poetic brilliance while creating intriguing and sympathetic characters. A truly masterful story."
~ Nella Warrent, Author of *Sin Full* and *Time Thief*

"Masterfully written with the perfect blend of historical setting, folklore, suspense, and horror. I couldn't put it down."
~ D. L. Andersen,
Author of *Across Unstill Waters* and *That Far Distant Country*

# THE
# MOTHER OF CENTURIES

by

John S. McFarland

From

Dark Owl Publishing, LLC

Arizona

Cover image by Marcus Propostus
Cover design by M.Y. Cover Design
Cover layout by Dark Owl Publishing, LLC

Author photograph ©2020 Cindy McFarland.

Visit us on our website at:
www.darkowlpublishing.com

# ALSO FROM
# DARK OWL PUBLISHING

**Novels**
*The Black Garden*
The beginning of the dark mysteries within the town of Ste. Odile
by John S. McFarland

*Carnivore Keepers*
Sci-fi adventure where humans and dinosaurs collide
by Kevin M. Folliard

*The Keeper of Tales*
An epic fantasy adventure by Jonathon Mast

*Just About Anyone*
High fantasy comedy from the twisted mind of Carl R. Jennings

*The Malakiad*
A hilarious mythological misadventure by Gustavo Bondoni

*The Wicked Twisted Road*
A gritty, grindhouse sci-fi thriller by D.S. Hamilton

**Anthologies**
*A Celebration of Storytelling*
The anthological festival of tales

*Something Wicked This Way Rides*
Where genre fiction meets the Wild West

**Collections**
*The Dark Walk Forward*
A harrowing collection of frightful stories from John S. McFarland

*The Last Star Warden:*
*Tales of Adventure and Mystery from Frontier Space, Volume I*
The first in the series of the Star Warden's adventures
from Jason J. McCuiston

*The Last Star Warden Volume II:*
*The Un Quan Saga*
More chronicles of the Last Star Warden by Jason J. McCuiston

# PREFACE:
# A WORD ABOUT
# THE GULLAH LANGUAGE

The Gullah culture and language may never have come into being if not for rice. The West Africans, the Angolans, the Senegambians, the Windward, and the Gold Coast people whom the slave traders were purchasing for use on the North American coastal plantations ranging from North Carolina to Florida were experts in the planting and cultivation of African rice. By some estimates, they'd had three thousand years' experience at this difficult type of crop production. When it was discovered that the grain thrived in the American coastal lowlands and Sea Islands, landowners quickly saw a whole new dimension could be added to the South's agricultural economy, consisting mostly, at that time, of cotton, sugar cane, and indigo.

The problem with rice was malaria. It is uncertain whether the Africans brought the disease with them to the New World or if it came from some other source, but the inundated fields needed to grow the crop were perfect breeding grounds for sickness-carrying mosquitoes. The enslaved people were generally immune to the disease. The whites were not.

Because of this, the presence of whites on the islands and coastal rice fields faded over time. More and more, black workers became overseers and gained some measure of autonomy. The Civil War nearly eliminated any remaining white presence in the region, and invading Union soldiers found the Gullah or "Geechee" people welcoming of their liberators and more than willing to fight for their freedom if called upon to do so. And many did.

Mitchelville, located on the northwestern coast of Hilton Head Island, became the first self-governing black community in the United States. After the war ended, and the remaining whites left the area, the Gullah people became more completely and effectively cut off from the rest of the country, both culturally and linguistically.

The Gullah language has been compared to the creole tongues of the Caribbean and to Jamaican patois. Although it is classified as English creole, as much as twenty-five percent of the vocabulary consists of words surviving from the people's West African origins. The language was dismissed as derivative and primitive by scholars until the early twentieth century. In 1949, linguist Lorenzo Dow Turner published his exhaustive study of the language after years of fieldwork. *Africanisms in the Gullah Dialect* triggered a complete revision among scholars regarding the complexity, beauty, and pedigree of the language, which is now estimated to be spoken by only about 5000 people.

I have been interested in Gullah culture for years. When I resolved to set parts of *The Mother of Centuries* in that culture, my wife Cindy and I traveled to Hilton Head and Daufuskie Island in South Carolina to do research. We visited Mitchelville and the plantations and met with historians and preservationists of the Gullah language and way of life. I wanted to make my treatment of it as accurate and respectful as I possibly could.

Boundless thanks go out to Irvin Campbell of Hilton Head and Dr. Louise Miller Cohen, who met with us at the "Little House" on Hilton Head. Her stories and tutelage in the Gullah language have been invaluable. Also instrumental in representing the "Island Talk" was Virginia Mixon Geraty's phrasebook *Gullah Fuh Oonah*. I have done my best in this work to do it all justice.

John S. McFarland
2022

# CHAPTER ONE

*December 12, 1894*

The dark air breathed around her. It had substance and a weight that oppressed her, held her fast against her thin mattress, and made movement or escape impossible. It had sentience, voracious and malevolent, that seemed to accrete then dissipate, moment to moment, only to reform itself elsewhere in the room and seep back to her bed—behind her, above her, below her, all at once. It was, finally, more terrifying than her solitude, as it had grown and fed upon itself over the last few nights. It had forced her into a universe inhabited by no caring or empathetic being, but rather by specters and shades populating dreams of horrors she could scarcely imagine.

"It's nothing," she whispered to herself. "My imagination moving shapes around in the dark. Waking dreams. I just need rest."

The night before, and the one before that, there had been moments like this one where, in a dream, she saw herself as a child twelve years before, confronted by a dark presence in her garret room at St. Perpetua's school for girls. As the faceless figure advanced upon her, the form of her sainted protector, Perdita Badon-Reed, materialized from nothing and intervened, pulling down the bricks and plaster of the room onto herself and the dark figure, crushing them both. It was a dream she'd had, in one form or another, during those twelve years since the terrible news had spread across the town of Ste. Odile of the deaths by fire and cave-in of Perdita and the fearsome Orien Bastide in a mine tunnel.

Even then, she had seen it all coming.

As a child, her mother, Sweetwater, a Tamaroa Indian, had recognized the second sight in her daughter. "It is a curse of the women of your consanguinity, Anatolia," she said. "I did not inherit it from your grandmother, so I hoped you would not have the sight, but you do... and stronger than anyone before you. I swear, by God, I will drive it out of you." But her mother had not driven the sight out of her, and Anatolia had predicted she would fail. Her father stole her away as a very young child from her obsessed mother, and probably saved her life. Yet he had not saved her from the presence that had flickered at the edges of her awareness for years and was now pressing in on her.

It could happen on any night, but it was worse on nights when Set was gone.

It would always be solitary, her suffering. She knew it even back then, and now every night confirmed it.

Most of the room was impenetrably dark, beyond the pattern of windowpanes the moonlight made on the floor. As she lay, half-awake, she sensed that she was not alone in the room.

The night before, as she was walking from Mrs. Heugyens's house, she'd been startled by something running across the path in front of her. It was a rather large, fluid mass that she could not identify as a fox or raccoon in the darkness. She wondered if the creature was now somewhere outside her window, or worse, if it had found a way to get inside.

After a few moments, she lit her bedside lantern. She examined every corner of the small room and the wardrobe but found nothing. She thought briefly about exploring the rest of the house but decided she was alone, and there would be nothing to find. She returned to bed and tried to put the terrible discomfort out of her mind. She drifted off into a light sleep.

An odd dream about pious medieval heretics trapped in a mountain sanctuary by the soldiers of the seneschal and Archbishop soon troubled her. In a room of whitewashed stone, a small congregation, archaically dressed in black ceremonial robes, medieval jerkins, and homespun skirts, were seated or standing quietly, calmly, as if they were all resigned to some great doom. There was a table, or altar, covered in white linen, upon which lay several white napkins and a book of the Gospels. A minister, flanked by two assistants, was preaching to the crowd, instructing them about the sacredness of the sacrament, the *consolamentum*, which, under these special circumstances, they were all about to receive.

Anatolia suddenly understood that these people were the heretic Cathars about whom Miss Badon-Reed had told her as a student back in her days at the Academy of Perpetua—a pious community that had challenged the doctrine of the Church and the authority of the Archbishop of Narbonne in 1244.

The minister, or *perfectus* as he was called, assured the congregants that by accepting the sacrament and therefore the death by fire at the stake that awaited them on the meadow below, they had chosen the right course, and that soon the dual nature of God would, at last, be known to them.

Anatolia slowly roused herself from this dream. She awakened, she knew, because she again had a sense that someone must be near, watching her. She meant to sit up in her bed, but she could not move. To her horror, she became aware that, as she laid on her right side, the hairs of her head and neck were moving in waves, as if there were a great breath upon them. She could feel warmth against her back from a form, a body, that seemed to extend beyond both her head and feet.

She heard the guttural snarl of a voice, perhaps behind her, perhaps reverberating from some other plane of being altogether—heard it growl something that sounded like "*You.*"

And she realized that pressure on her shoulder was turning her over.

Anatolia's eyes closed as she was forced onto her back, and soon a weight pressed over her that nearly crushed the last of the breath she had left. Her thighs were forced savagely apart, and she felt sudden, sharp pain in the space that was her own As if far removed from herself, she heard a faint gurgle of air in her own throat.

"Bastide...?"

# CHAPTER TWO

Anatolia gradually became aware of the room around her. It was morning, and she was in her bed and on her back. Her entire body was swathed in fiery pain. She moved her right leg and felt a stickiness against the sheet. Painfully, she raised her head to look down at herself. Her upper thighs were bloody, and her groin area was the epicenter of the pain that radiated to the rest of her body. Her head swam, and she felt for a moment that she was losing consciousness. She breathed deeply. Her ribs hurt as if they had been crushed. She thought one of her ribs might be cracked.

She knew she would have to raise herself by degrees. Slowly. She lay still for a moment. Her memories of the night just past were dark and confused. She remembered waking in the night and sensing a presence in the room with her and a form behind and then on top of her, that she could not make herself open her eyes to see. She remembered a crushing weight, a sense of suffocation, and the rough and savage violation that had left her bloodied that didn't seem real even as it was happening.

As she righted herself, she felt her gorge rise and thought she might vomit, but the sensation passed quickly. She sat still on the edge of her bed. As she breathed slowly, she began to comprehend how severely injured she was. She peeled the sheet from her thigh and stood. The room spun, and when she suddenly realized that she was next to her bed, not on it, she knew she must have lost consciousness and fallen.

The pain radiated from her groin, up her back and torso and down through her legs. She thought it foolish to try to move. She decided to lie still for a while.

Anatolia awakened to a knock on the door.

"Miss Anatolia! Miss Anatolia, are you there?" It was Rebecca Wallace, the nine-year-old daughter of Euphemia, one of Anatolia's new followers who lived in a boarding house across the street. Rebecca checked with Anatolia most mornings at her mother's insistence to see if their seer needed breakfast or housekeeping or any other errands run for her. Anatolia insisted to Euphemia many times that she did not require these attentions, but there were few mornings that Rebecca didn't appear.

"Rebecca..." Anatolia's voice was weak.

"Yes, miss...?"

"Come in Rebecca. I need you."

Rebecca pushed the front door open with some difficulty. She struggled into the house with a crock of fresh milk. When she saw her seer bloody and helpless on the floor, the child gasped and dropped the crock.

"Miss Anatolia!" Rebecca burst into tears. "What has happened?" She ran to Anatolia's side. Anatolia struggled to sit up.

"I'm not sure, Rebecca. I was attacked last night. Calm yourself, child. I think I will be all right. Run home and get your mother... please."

Euphemia Wallace had been a nurse in Baltimore and New York City. Unable to make sense of Rebecca's frantic wailing, she rushed to Anatolia's side.

"Good Lord, good Lord, what has happened to you, Miss Anatolia?"

Anatolia's vague memory of the assault had few specific details but was convincing enough to Euphemia. "Your gifts are a threat to the Evil One, and he is out to destroy you and end your good work." She helped Anatolia up and onto the divan. "If ever there were proof of the holiness of your mission... this is it!"

"I don't know, Euphemia," Anatolia muttered. "I don't know about that."

"This mattress is ruined," Euphemia said. "I have one in the cellar at home. I will clean you and tend to your injuries. We should call a doctor."

"Doctor Caton doesn't care for colored patients," Anatolia said. "He told me once it is bad for his reputation. Pressman will, but he is ten miles away."

"I can take care of you. You are not bleeding now and are able to walk. I will take care of you!"

As Euphemia washed Anatolia and treated her wounds, Rebecca ran from house to house in the neighborhood, spreading the word of the seer's injuries. By late morning, twenty or more adherents had brought food and linens and other gifts to Anatolia, and most were in agreement that her injuries were the work of a vengeful Devil.

Mrs. Heugyens arrived by carriage early in the afternoon. She seemed exceptionally distressed by Anatolia's condition and promised to insist Dr. Caton come and examine her.

"I am in very good hands under Euphemia's care," Anatolia assured her patron. "I feel better this evening. I am sure I am on the road to recovery."

"If my affairs hadn't kept Set away like they have, I must wonder if this would have happened. I feel I am to blame!" Mrs. Heugyens fretted.

"No, ma'am, "Anatolia said. "Somehow, I am glad he was gone. I had the sense as it was all happening, a sense I feel even stronger today, that whatever came for me last night would have killed Set to get to me. Nothing... *nothing* was going to stop it."

Anatolia kept to her bed for the next two days. She was rarely without the company of two or three of her twenty-four followers in the town, though she asked them to please leave her in peace to rest. Even Euphemia's attentions seemed to be more than needed to Anatolia, but her nurse was never more than a few minutes from her side. Many times, as she recovered, she thought of how trapped she often felt in the life she was now living. Set's intentions for spreading the word about her visions were good, she knew. He wanted nothing from her notoriety and felt that she should want nothing other than to help people in spiritual need. She felt herself greatly flawed to often resent his assumptions of her selflessness and the needs of those drawn to her.

The community that had grown up around Anatolia in New Phrygia depended upon the patronage and trust of Mrs. Heugyens. In return, the elderly dowager grew to trust Set, Anatolia's husband, with her business affairs in Rochester, Palmyra, and New York City. Sometimes, as now, he was away for months at a time, dealing with lawyers and stockbrokers and bankers on the old woman's behalf.

When Anatolia, Set, and their handful of hangers-on arrived in New Phrygia two years before, it was common knowledge that Mrs. Heugyens regarded them with open suspicion and contempt. Here was a young white man living as a husband with a girl who was half-negro and half-red Indian—a girl who was revered, almost worshiped, by her followers, both black and white, as a seer and spiritual visionary. There seemed to be much that was blasphemous and anti-Christian about it.

Mrs. Heugyens (*née* Smithson) was old enough to remember the religious fervor and blasphemy that swept across this "burned-over" district of western New York State sixty years before. Her own parents had joined the Calmetarians, a prophetic group formed by Ephraim Calmet in 1829 for the purpose of living communally to await the end of days in 1832, as predicted by the self-styled prophet. Her parents gave all their worldly goods to the commune and committed suicide together in January 1833 when it became apparent that Calmet's prediction and his spiritual guidance were false. At fifteen, the young woman married Mr. Heugyens of Rochester, a wealthy land speculator thirty years her senior, and lived her life as a solid Methodist. After her husband's death, she moved permanently into a large stone house he owned in New Phrygia.

Mrs. Heugyens's suspicion and disapproval of Anatolia's little group of followers slowly turned into curiosity as she began to hear stories of the young woman's prophetic abilities. The old woman believed strongly in the unseen world, and, weighing the evidence from all reports available to her, it became clear that Anatolia Montes was not a confidence trickster out to swindle the gullible. She was an honest, spiritual girl given a gift from on high, which, by all accounts, she was reluctant to use and even somewhat embarrassed by. And there was no indication that the young woman intended to do anything but good with her abilities when pressed to exercise them.

Anatolia had never sought a following. She wanted a quiet life, the creative life of a painter, or perhaps a sculptor like her mentor, Perdita Badon-Reed. But, against Anatolia's wishes, Set spread word of her visionary gifts and revived interest in the events at Ste. Odile of twelve years earlier, and how, as a child, she had inadvertently triggered them. Anatolia angrily objected to this, but Set insisted that her visions were given by God to help people, and to refuse to do so would displease Him.

Anatolia sighed as she thought of how important Set had become to her, and how different her life might have been if her father, Asmiel Montes, had never brought her here. Asmiel returned to Ste. Odile just after the death of Miss Badon-Reed and had taken the girl back with him to New Phrygia where, as an ambitious black man, he had found acceptance and a community where he felt he could raise his daughter in peace.

Asmiel had originally come to New Phrygia looking for work, or perhaps even a business opportunity that would provide a safe and comfortable life for himself and his young daughter, then under the care of the Sisters of Perpetua back in Ste. Odile. Asmiel began at Kyper's Sawmill, sweeping floors, stacking lumber, mule skinning, and unloading and loading the lumber wagons. Within a few months, Joseph Kyper trusted Asmiel with bookkeeping duties and the collection of debts from loggers and other clients. In 1882, less than a year from the day of his hiring, Asmiel entered into an agreement with Kyper to buy the sawmill from the old man over a four-year period. Kyper's cut most of the softwoods coming in from the north and east. Having worked many odd jobs in Rochester, Albany, and New York City, Asmiel knew the new rich were building elegant, ornate mansions wherever commerce paid an adequate dividend. He knew that decorative, architectural hardwoods were the key to tapping into that prosperity.

When his business was well established, Asmiel Montes returned to Ste. Odile and retrieved his young daughter. The child Anatolia was in shock at the death of her mentor, Miss Badon-Reed, though she had seen it coming in a vision. Concerned by the fragile, damaged state in which he found her, Asmiel decided to make the journey he and Anatolia would take back to New York as leisurely and pleasurable as he could.

By the time they made it back to New Phrygia, old Kyper's nephew had filed a lawsuit questioning the mental competence of his aged uncle and the sale of the family business to a black man. After months of litigation, the court found in favor of the nephew, and Asmiel lost his business. He moved his daughter to Palmyra, where he found work as a porter at the Trident Hotel. At Palmyra, Anatolia's reputation as a seer and visionary slowly grew, and she became an object of admiration and devotion for a young Irish immigrant named Set Costigan.

Set had often told Anatolia the story of when he first noticed her sitting alone by the iron fence of the Negro School at recess time as he was walking home for lunch from the tanbark mill. Set had quit school the previous year, and he assumed he was about the same age as this girl, who looked both vulnerable and lost but also somehow attuned to mystery and insights beyond his reach. He thought about her the rest of the day and evening, he said, and when he saw her again the next day, he thought he might find the courage to speak to her. As he passed that day, she was standing at the fence, and she spoke to him.

"I don't know your name, but I know you want to talk to me."

Set could think of nothing to say for a moment. He smiled awkwardly and approached the fence.

"Who says so? Who says I want to talk to you?"

"Me. Anatolia."

"Never heard that name before. I like it, though. I'm Set Costigan."

"I saw you talking to me in my dream. I see you walk by here every day."

"Tanbark mill is thataway. I work there. I gotta walk past here. Ain't because of you."

"Shouldn't you be in school? You can't be but twelve or thirteen."

"Have to work. Like to be in school, but I have to work. I read on my own, though, and I like arithmetic. I got to help my family. I *want* to help. It's the right thing to do, I know. How you like the Negro School?"

"I like it fine. They mostly leave me alone here. I just want to be left alone. I ought to tell you now that in my dream I also saw us being friends. Very close and then *together*, later on. Not married, but together."

Set looked incredulous. "Awww, that can't be. Irish and Negroes don't get on. M'daid... Pop would lay into me good if I..."

For several years, Set's father thought little of the friendship between his son and Anatolia, but when he learned that it had become a romantic connection, he beat his son with a strap and put him out of his house. Set lived at the Ganymede House for Boys for two more years, keeping his job at the tanbark mill.

By the time she was sixteen, Anatolia's reputation as a seer had become well established in Palmyra and the surrounding areas. This was largely because Set defined her gift as a Divine tool to help people. He spread the word that she must be an instrument of God and that she had good work to do on the earth. His enthusiasm often exhausted and even angered Anatolia. She was ashamed to feel any resentment for him because she suspected that his frequently expressed belief was probably right.

Anatolia foresaw the death of Roger Crane under a load of logs, and the birth of twins to Antonia Wills. She predicted that the Methodist church on Erskine Street would burn to the ground and that Stephen G. Lambert, a recent transplant from Georgia, would lose in his bid to become mayor. A growing group of people began to seek Anatolia's advice and ask her opinions on personal and business matters. But it was the Concordance River disaster that brought her to the attention of the entire region.

One spring afternoon after many days of rain, Anatolia was overcome by fever. She lay in bed and a vision came to her of the village of Wilton ten miles to the south. She saw the earthen dam built on the Concordance River giving way and flood water washing over the village, causing a terrible loss of life. Convincing Set of the danger, the two of them borrowed a mare from Asmiel and rode to Wilton, arriving late in the evening. Set ran into the church and rang the steeple bell as Anatolia stood in the street, screaming, "Danger! You are all in danger!" Many people emerged from their houses.

"There is great danger," Anatolia screamed. "The dam is going to fail in this rain. The town will be flooded. Please get to high ground!"

"Believe her and save yourselves!" Set yelled, running out of the church. "She is never wrong about these..."

"There is no time," Anatolia interrupted. "No time! Get to high ground!"

About forty people had quickly assembled in the street. There was a din of grumbling, complaints, and laughter. The children looked confused and curious and clung to their parents. Many adults were angry that a stranger had dared to sound the town emergency alarm.

"How do you know this? How?" an old woman yelled above the confusion.

"She is in touch with God and voices in the ether," Set said. "She saw it in a vision today. She is never wrong!"

Many of the people laughed. Some were angry.

"Haven't we had enough of this sort of nonsense?" a man said.

Both Set and Anatolia could see that most of the people assembled were not dismissing her warning. More than half of the crowd hurried back into their houses. The town marshal, a man in his forties with spectacles, emerged from his office next to the church.

"What are you stirrin' up here?" he said. "This is peace disturbance! Who are you two?"

Before he could reach them, Set had remounted the mare and pulled Anatolia up behind him. "Get to high ground!" he called to the crowd as he lashed the mare and they galloped out of town.

That night, the Concordance dam failed, and twenty-nine people who refused to heed the warning were drowned. The survivors left their ruined town over the next few days and moved north to Palmyra, having been convinced that Anatolia had the light of God in her and that she could guide them to Him.

Anatolia and Set decided to take a small house behind the Trident where her father still worked, and a growing number of these followers began to fill the once sparsely occupied neighborhood around them.

One summer evening when Set was away, Anatolia had an especially vivid and unsettling vision. It involved a company of women and girls, mostly if not entirely residents of Ste. Odile, surrounded by rat or ferret-like demons and overwhelmed by a force or presence so dark it seemed less like a corporal being and more like a tear in reality and perception. The vision so troubled her that she was compelled, as she had done as a child, to depict it—to draw it out as an image. She felt, for the first time in her life, that the vision she was about to depict had to be a public one. In a frenzy over the next two days, she painted the image on the outside west wall of her house. Within a week, the number of her followers had doubled. Many debated whether this was a vision of the Apocalypse itself.

Anatolia had no explanation for the vision or why she was compelled to make it public.

"I don't want their attentions," she told Set. "They are giving me power over them, and I don't want it. I can't account for the image. It's some Ste. Odile nightmare... I don't know what it means!"

"You have helped so many of them," Set said. "Think of what you can do. God has given you this gift for a reason, and it's what brings them to you. This picture you've painted... it's only added to your mystery and their commitment to you!"

Two days after losing the mayoral election, Lambert accused Anatolia of causing his loss. Making a speech on the front steps of the Trident before a small gathering of his disappointed followers, he accused Anatolia of using "Negro witchcraft" to defeat him, or at least of planting the idea of his defeat in the minds of voters. Asmiel, working at the front desk of the hotel at the time, came out on the hotel portico to defend his daughter and calm the increasingly unsettled crowd.

"My friends, please calm yourselves," Asmiel said. "My daughter has a gift given her from on high. She has no evil intention or truck with witchcraft."

At that moment, Lambert suddenly moved up from behind Asmiel and punched him forcefully on the left side of his face. Asmiel fell to the ground and three of Lambert's supporters were quickly upon him. The three beat him until they were exhausted and their fists and forearms bloody. None of the remaining onlookers, all Lambert supporters, tried to intervene.

Asmiel had been dead for many minutes by the time they stopped. When Constables Healy and Marquard arrived on the scene, the small crowd had dispersed, and no witnesses to the violence could be found.

The next day Anatolia, Set, and a small contingent of Anatolia's followers resolved to return to New Phrygia.

Anatolia had reminisced enough. She needed more rest, and on the third day, Anatolia felt much restored though still awash in pain.

That evening, the entire congregation of New Phrygians, as they had begun calling themselves, gathered in front of Anatolia's house to pray for her. William Barth led an impromptu service, including readings of the Psalms and from the Book of Acts. Anatolia sat in her rocker on the front porch, buoyed by their love but apprehensive, as always, about the group's growing exaltation of her.

"Did you foresee the attack of the Evil One, Miss Anatolia?" Barth asked.

"I knew something was amiss days before."

The group nodded at the affirmation of their assumption.

"I did have a foreboding, yes," Anatolia went on. "I admit it, but I can't say if that was evidence of my 'gift,' as you all call it. I don't know that. I can't say why, but... I just don't feel as sure about this..."

"But what else could it be, Miss?" Margaret Collins said. Her husband Joseph nodded in agreement. Their eight-year-old daughter India wiped tears from her eyes.

"Your concern and love for me, each of you, has sustained and saved me. I love you all, as you know. Our little community is my family, and I would not wish to lose any one of you from my life. The Greeks had a word, *apotheosis*, that has much significance to me these days. It is the act of deification, of making someone into a god. You have all made me the focus of your lives, I fear. I do not want you to elevate me in this way. I would not lose any one of you from our community, but you must not regard me as leader, or seer..."

"You have helped every one of us, Miss Anatolia," Edmontia Lewis said. "God has given you a gift for a reason! You were attacked by the Devil for a reason. It only proves you are doing God's work!"

"We know how you feel, Miss," Euphemia said. "You have said these things before. You have helped us all, and for my part, even if you never have another vision, I would not want to live a life apart from you!"

Many in the group nodded and agreed. Anatolia *had* said these things before, and to the same response. Looking from face to face, Anatolia could see that devotion and faith had built walls between each of her devotees and their reason.

The next night Set arrived home on the late train from Rochester. His distress on seeing Anatolia's condition and hearing her story was extreme. Euphemia calmed him. She assured him Anatolia was out of danger and should fully recover. She said that Dr. Caton had examined Anatolia and concluded that she would suffer no permanent injury. Set thanked Euphemia for her care and assured her that she could return to her own home now.

When Euphemia left, Set closed the front door and bolted it, something he had never done before. He sat on the floor at Anatolia's feet in the front room.

"We almost lost you," he said. "*I* almost lost you! I should have been here. What in the world *happened*?"

"No, you would have died if you had been here. I know it. This... this has been waiting for me for years. I have always felt it."

"What do you mean? Did anyone inform the police?"

"My protector, my Miss Perdita Badon-Reed, suffered this same fate. The police would be useless. You remember Miss Badon-Reed's good friend, Miss Moira Keane Parnell?"

"I remember the name, yes."

"Miss Badon-Reed came to Ste. Odile to the aid of her friend, only to arrive just too late. She took a position at the school and took me under her wing at St. Perpetua's until my father came for me. As you know, I have corresponded with Miss Keane Parnell ever since."

"Yes."

"She has always been worried about my safety. She has never been completely satisfied that Bastide, Orien Bastide, is dead."

"I remember Bastide, who was stalking Miss Badon-Reed. But surely..."

"The collapsed mineshaft was never excavated. There were, of course, other connected shafts. There is no proof of his death."

"After all this time? Why has there been no sign of this... creature... all these years?"

"Bastide is a being who has existed for ages. Of that I am certain. As a child, he fixed his attentions on me. He sent me a gold coin as a gift. Accepting it from him opened a portal. I didn't know it then. My visions gave me no warning. I am no longer sure he is dead, or that I am lost to him. Miss Parnell fears the same."

Set stood and embraced Anatolia in her chair.

"What do you want to do about all of this?" he said. "What do you want to do?"

"Miss Parnell became interested in the life and works of an old wildcrafter in Ste. Odile named Euphrosine—the Mother of Centuries, as she was known. She saved Miss Badon-Reed after Bastide's first attack and told of her lifelong struggle against the demon incubus. Miss Parnell wrote me last week to tell me she has come into the possession of a journal written by old Euphrosine. A journal *centuries* old. Miss Parnell wants me to have it. She thinks the knowledge it contains may save my life."

"Will she send it?"

"She wants to place it directly into my hands. She trusts no other way."

"Can you make such a trip? Would you want to?"

"I swore to myself I would never return to that baleful place, yet I think of it every day. It is always on my mind. It is, oddly and improbably, the only place I have ever felt connected to. I have been escaping fears and nightmares, but they will not let me be. To face them and expunge them, I feel I need to go back. I hope you will come with me, but I must go if you will or won't. I won't have any peace otherwise. Yes. I am up to it. I do feel different, somehow different, since the attack. I feel I am not the same person I was a few days ago. But I feel I can and must speak to Miss Parnell. I must travel back to Ste. Odile."

# CHAPTER THREE

Susan Henry had served Mrs. Heugyens faithfully for twenty-two years. If circumstances had been different, she would have never left her adopted home in Apalachicola, Florida, suffering as she knew she would in the cold weather of the North. But one night a group of white men, veterans from the war, they said, burned out her father's cabin and the two other negro cabins in her neighborhood. Susan's parents refused to be driven out of town, but Susan left the next week, feeling certain she would find work, safety, and acceptance in New York or New England. She thought of returning to her birthplace in the Sea Islands, but there was nothing for her there but an isolated life of harvesting rice and indigo. Surely, she would be better off in the North.

"Would you like a bit o' cake with your tea, Miss 'Tolia? Maybe you belly pinch'um a bit?" Susan sat her silver tray on the marble-topped low table near the sofa where Anatolia and Set were sitting. Mrs. Heugyens, wrapped in her shawl, sat in her usual overstuffed chair near the fireplace.

Anatolia smiled. "Am I hungry, Susan? Yes, I am, a little. My appetite is coming back."

"I have told you about that home-talk, Susan," Mrs. Heugyens scolded. "This is the North. I want you to talk like you're in the North! And 'belly' is a vulgar word."

Susan had enthusiastically joined her employer as a disciple of Anatolia after a prediction she made about bad news from Florida came true, and she changed her mind about returning to her original home on Monfort Island, South Carolina. She knew her home was with the New Phrygians. When Susan asked Anatolia if she should travel south to search for her mother, she was told, "No, it's too late for that." Susan had always felt a profound admiration for Anatolia as a shining example of a woman of color, so pure and beloved of God that she had been given a special gift to help all people, even those with hearts filled with hate towards the negro race. White and Black followed this young woman without question. Susan had never seen anything like it. And Susan's feelings of kinship grew even stronger when Anatolia's father was also killed by a mob. Susan filled Anatolia's teacup.

"Sit with us, Susan," Mrs. Heugyens said. "This conversation concerns you too."

Susan sat in a chair opposite the sofa. She smiled at Anatolia.

"I think it goes without saying," Mrs. Heugyens smiled, "that the community will want to accompany you on your journey. I have come to depend upon both of you. I feel I am spiritually complete since you have been in my life, Anatolia... and Set, you have made yourself indispensable in managing my affairs. You are the New Phrygians, and where you go, I will go. And I have no doubt the community will follow."

"I don't want to disrupt people's lives like this." Anatolia sighed. "For myself, I must go, but the responsibility of the rest of you..."

Set touched her hand. "They are all free to do as they like," he said. "We are a community, and I think it's best we stay together."

"How do we proceed?" Mrs. Heugyens asked.

"I have been looking at routes," Set continued. "Train travel would be cramped and arduous, but safer. I have business—personal business— to attend to far to the north in Michigan. I must travel the lakes. The rest of you will be better served on the train."

Mrs. Heugyens frowned. "All that way on the lakes? Is that safe this time of year?"

"We have a few more weeks until winter, until it gets really cold." Set said. "I think if I act quickly, I can make the trip ahead of the dangerous weather."

"My own opinion is we should travel together," Mrs. Heugyens said. "Everyone will have their say, of course, but I would choose that the whole group travel with you. We are a unit, a group. I would want us to stay together."

Set smiled at her. "If we disembark at Buffalo, we bypass the falls and we can get to Chicago in eight days or so. From there we can take a train down to Ste. Odile. A few more days."

Mrs. Heugyens wrapped her shawl more tightly around herself. "How do you feel about traveling on open water in cold weather, Susan? Is that a trip you want to make with me?"

"Berry much, Madame. Yes... yes."

"Very much, Susan. The word is very, not berry."

"One way or t'other, the same thin' gits said."

Mrs. Heugyens gave a slight smile that her community knew well. Susan stood and removed the silver tray to the kitchen.

"We'd better call a meeting," Mrs. Heugyens said. "If you make the arrangements, Set, I will pay for everything. However, many of us want to go."

The next evening all twenty-four of the New Phrygians gathered in Mrs. Heugyens's parlor and dining room. All agreed that they would make the trip to Ste. Odile with Anatolia and Set. Joseph and Margaret Collins volunteered to help everyone in the community gather their possessions, pack them in crates to be built by William Barth, Increase Mather Browne, and several other men, and ship them to Ste. Odile.

"My friend in Ste. Odile," Anatolia said, "Miss Moira Keane Parnell, has informed me that a great complex of buildings has become available in the town. It is the old Academy of Perpetua, my home and school as a child. The school is closing and the archdiocese wants to dispose of it. It is more than large enough to house us all communally. If we act quickly, we can secure the property by telegram. It is listing, she says, for nine thousand dollars."

"You think it will suit our needs?" Mrs. Heugyens asked.

"Very well," Anatolia nodded. "There are classrooms, dormitories, many communal rooms, a chapel, a gymnasium, and expansive grounds. There is an old convent building that could house many of us and a rectory down the street which could be your home, Mrs. Heugyens. Much more than a community our size needs."

"We could grow into it," Increase Mather Browne said.

"I should not live better than anyone else," Mrs. Heugyens frowned.

"But you are paying for all of this," Set said.

"Yes, you should have a separate house," Edmontia Lewis said.

"It's more like the life you are accustomed to," Violet Siddons added.

"You're giving the community this gift," Reuben Siddons agreed with his wife. "If there is a grander residence, you should have it."

"It isn't 'grand'..." Anatolia said.

Mrs. Heugyens smiled. "You had better contact the property agent by telegram, Set," she said. "And we will need a bank draft for nine thousand dollars."

# CHAPTER FOUR

Every fall for the last twelve years, Moira Keane Parnell had swept the fallen leaves away from the base of the monument. The maintenance of the grounds of The Academy of St. Perpetua had diminished over the years as the school and convent crept slowly toward extinction. As funds from the diocese dried up and enrollment shrunk, there was little money to pay groundskeepers, custodians, and support staff. Moira herself had paid for the construction of the monument on the edge of the old graveyard of the Sisters of Perpetua. It was a simple obelisk in marble placed atop a pedestal, carved with the inscription:

IN MEMORY OF PERDITA BADON-REED
1843-1882
NO GREATER LOVE

A breeze blew through the cypresses lining the long drive that led from Constantinople Street to the old brick and stone buildings of the Academy. Yellow maple leaves blew onto the stone base Moira had just swept. She swept it again. It was a simple responsibility Moira had set for herself, a small act of respect and affection that she hoped would resonate with her beloved, departed friend watching her from on high.

The familiar sound of wood clicking on paving stones slowly emerged from the sounds of the breeze in the leaves. Moira turned to see Sister Clotilde, Mother Superior of the convent, approaching her from the chapel. The elderly nun walked tentatively and slowly, cane in hand. She had fallen on the stones before. Just last month, Moira found her on the ground beneath the great statue of St. Perpetua she was passing just now. Fortunately, the old woman had only sprained her foot and recovered from the mishap within a week.

"Good morning, Mother Superior," Moira called.

Sister Clotilde waved. "You are fulfilling your daily office, I see, Miss Parnell!"

Moira started to walk toward the aged nun. She didn't want her to try to walk among the weathered headstones and sunken graves of the sisters' graveyard. "Yes, Mother Superior. I gladly do it."

When Sister Clotilde saw that Moira was approaching her, she stopped at the base of the statue.

"What a beautiful autumn day God has given us!" she said. "At my age, you appreciate such things more than you did as a younger person. I try to, at least."

"A good approach to life, I would say, Mother Superior."

"I wanted to ask you about our young friend Anatolia."

"Yes, Mother Superior. Our lawyer, Mr. Purviance, notified me this morning that the sale has gone through. Anatolia's patroness has paid the full asking price, and her group will take possession of the property the week after next. I have another letter from her just this morning, but I haven't had the time to read it yet. I was just going to..."

"And she is coming with a group of people? Some twenty-five or thirty souls?"

"Yes."

"When the realtor told me of this group and that it involved our little Anatolia... well, I haven't been able to sort out who these people are, nor Anatolia's connection to them."

"You look tired, Mother Superior," Moira said. She motioned for the aged nun to sit on the stone bench under the statue. Moira sat next to her. "You recall the kind of child Anatolia was. Unusual. Even visionary."

"Yes, I remember her well. A tough nut to crack. In a world of her own. Odd and *ethereal*, for want of a better word. The other girls bullied her mercilessly. We often found her hiding in the chapel up in the loft, making drawings of the angels in the stained glass. The visions and dreams she had. As I look back on it, it was a gift from God, not just mischief and oddness."

"Her oddness," Moira smiled, "or her gift, if you will, has stayed with her and attracted a following."

"What sort of following?"

"A group of people who believe she has some special vision or insight, perhaps as a conduit to God. You remember her prophetic drawings and verses, as you said. Some time ago, she had a vision of disaster, some sort of terrible catastrophic event which she herself could not explain. She felt compelled to depict this calamity on an outside wall of her house in New Phrygia, New York."

"The 'burned-over' territory."

"Yes. Just so. Prophetic mania seems to thrive in the area. Her mural, as well as some predictions she made which came true, have attracted a following. The whole community will be coming."

"Ah. I see." A sad expression clouded Sister Clotilde's face.

"They will be taking the main buildings as well as the convent and rectory. Workmen will start clearing everything out in the morning."

"Yes. That's quick work. There has been more than a century of holy purpose attended to within these walls. And it all ends tomorrow."

Moira laid her hand upon Clotilde's and smiled at her.

"The last of the girls leaves today," Sister Clotilde continued, "and I will be on a packet Friday for St. Louis. Living out the rest of my days and vocation at the *Domus Requiem*, the last safe harbor for useless old nuns!"

"Your life has been well spent. Your vocation, well served. Think of the countless girls you have provided such a sterling example for—think of it!"

Sister Clotilde seemed exhausted. She always became oppressively sleepy late in the mornings.

"I hope so," she said. "I did my novitiate at Kellismore, County Cork, you may remember."

"Yes. I have heard the story."

"My *first* novitiate. My duties were to help at the Magdalene Laundry there. An asylum for 'fallen girls.' We were contracted to do laundry for the navy. The girls were unwanted and lost. Forgotten and defenseless. Nothing more than slaves. I was appalled to see how my Sisters in Christ, good and pious women, could separate the spirit of God and knowledge of His love for those girls from the station in life they were thrown into. They were Children of God in spite of everything, yet pious and chaste women—my sisters—brutalized them." Sister Clotilde dabbed her handkerchief at the corners of her eyes. "*Brutalized...* I ran away. I slipped out the evening of Epiphany. I nearly died that night; it was so terribly cold. I prayed for God's forgiveness, but I wanted to do good in the world and see the fruits of it around me, not... darkness and suffering with no end to it. My brother hid me and paid my passage to Dublin, where I eventually found my way into a new novitiate, with the Sisters of Perpetua."

The aged nun stood gingerly and stretched.

"I came to this country at twenty-two," she continued. "By God's grace I was sent here, to the Academy of Perpetua. By God's grace I became Mother Superior. Here I was given the opportunity again to work with young women and girls—but with kindness and understanding. I have always tried to execute my mission here with those two qualities. I thank the Lord for the opportunity."

"You have done wonderful work, Mother Superior," Moira stood. "There are no longer red Indians or young children of slaves anymore. Not in these parts. This academy has served and outlived its mission, as I guess we all have. The great constant in life is change."

"You sound like one of those New England philosophers, Miss Parnell—or some half-naked Oriental fakir." Sister Clotilde turned and started to walk toward the convent. "Very tired. Time for my rest."

Moira re-seated herself on the bench. The grounds of St. Perpetua's were quieter now than she had ever known them to be in the twelve years she had been in Ste. Odile. The energy and excitement of the students, the countless girls who had come and gone over the years, was a life force, an essence that she missed terribly. Moira had thought for a couple of weeks about what she would do with herself now that her short career as a teacher was over.

Her father had died back in Boston seven years ago. Her mother still lived in their large old house. Moira had kept a room at Mrs. Zell's rebuilt Tranquille House since coming to Ste. Odile. There was really no reason for her to stay there.

The gravel leading to the rear of the dining hall crunched with footsteps. Moira turned to see Father Vannier approaching, wrapping his scarf tightly around his neck.

"I was looking for you," he said.

"I have been talking with Sister Clotilde. She is leaving Friday."

"Yes, she told me." Vannier sat next to her. He removed a small, leather-bound book from his overcoat pocket. "I am trying to decide what to make of this."

"It is a mystery, isn't it? Must surely be a hoax or a fantasy. Written by a woman who died twelve years ago, but claims to have been begun as a retrospective journal in 1757."

"Yes," Vannier agreed. "A work of fiction, yet it aligns so completely with the tragic events surrounding the deaths of old Euphrosine, Sister Solana, and Miss Badon-Reed. Come to the rectory this evening. We'll have some dinner, build a fire, and discuss it."

Moira noticed that Vannier had gained a little weight in the last few years. The oblique autumn sunlight accentuated how the flesh of his cheeks and neck had lost their firmness over time. She knew her appearance must have changed too, though she was never one for the vanity of mirrors.

"Certainly. I will be there at seven."

Vannier touched her hand, gently, warmly.

"Have you decided whether you will stay or go?" he asked.

"Not quite decided," she smiled.

Vannier smiled back and stood. "I will see you this evening," he nodded. He walked away through the yellow leaves toward the rectory.

Moira remembered the letter in her pocket. She removed it and flattened it out on the stone bench.

*10 October, 1894*

*My dear Miss Parnell,*

*We should arrive five weeks from the above date. All is in readiness. Set has arranged our passage from Buffalo, New York via the Great Lakes to Chicago. From there we will take trains down to St. Louis and on to Ste. Odile. Crates of our possessions will arrive soon thereafter. Thank you for your help in implementing this process. I am so very anxious to see the journal of old Euphrosine you have found, and yet I find I am compelled to return to that odd little village by inducements I can scarcely define myself. The whole time I was painting the great mural I described to you, I could not rid my mind of thoughts of Ste. Odile. It is so irreconcilable to me that only that dark little town has ever felt like my home. Yet it is true. I will never face my fears and thus find peace unless I come back. All must be resolved there.*

*And there is something else that I have hesitated to mention to you which serves a further motivation. Last week while Set was away, I was attacked in the night. Attacked as Miss Badon-Reed was, as Sister Solana was, according to the stories I later heard. Attacked in a brutal, sexual way, almost a lethal way, as those women were. I am recovering now, but I know an old horror has been resurrected and its resolution, its destruction, also calls me back to Ste. Odile.*

*Yours,*

*Anatolia Montes*

Moira folded the letter and returned it to her pocket. The yellow leaves had blown across the base of the monument again. She stood, retrieved her broom, and began to walk toward the stone obelisk.

"The conflict is reborn," she whispered to herself. "I suppose I will not, *should* not, leave this place. I... am not going anywhere."

# CHAPTER FIVE

*22 September, 1757*

Eustace delivered mutton and milk this morning and asked me again to record the rest, the remainder, of my story. So herein, I am doing it. The first effort was lost in the fire at Montsegur ages ago. After untold years of delay, I am doing it. Starting again.

He knows my story. Eustace knows who I am. It was he who started calling me again *Meres des Sicles*, the Mother of Centuries, as in days past, and now the whole village of Ste. Odile does also, but only because I am old. They have no notion of just *how* old. I have been known as Scribonia, then Euphrosine, but to many a mother and child from the time of my arrival here, stretching who can tell how far into the future, I will be the Mother of Centuries. This record is for them.

As I have written before, I was a follower of Circe; I was the witch of Aeaea. I was called Scribonia then. I was born in Thrace during the time of Diocletian. My father retired from the Roman army, having achieved the rank of centurion at the garrison of Lyon in Gaul. He brought us there—my mother, my brother Titus, and myself. There we lived until the destruction of my family at the hands of the minor general in command of the garrison, Quintus Tacitus Gabro.

Gabro had known my father for twenty years and thought well of him. Politics and religion, however, were soon to turn them into the gravest of enemies. Before my father removed us from Thrace, my mother and brother had come under the influence of a small Christian community. When the family was reunited, my father readily converted to the new faith. I did not. I saw little value in a theology that forestalled freedom, happiness, and pleasures to an afterlife. There seemed to be a timidity and a sort of contempt for oneself in this— almost a shame at being born. The immediate power, strength, and fulfillment of Circe and an alignment with nature more greatly appealed to me.

Gabro and his wife Vipsania were childless, but after he quelled an uprising among the Gauls, they adopted an infant orphan, a child reputed to be descended from the great Vercingetorix himself.

They named the boy Medullinus, and he was the pride of his adoptive parents. He had a deep and abiding interest in all things from the natural world, from the arts and culture to the mysteries of human nature. He was an eager conversationalist and seemed to wish to consume all possible knowledge within his realm of experience and beyond.

Medullinus was promised in marriage to Xanthippe, the daughter of Cleander, a Macedonian and retired tribune who had also brought his family to Lyon after his days of service. About the time of their betrothal, Diocletian issued an imperial order to seek out and persecute all Christians across the empire who refused to sacrifice to him as a god. My father, mother, and brother did not make a public expression of their new faith, but some informer apparently got word of it to Gabro.

When the soldiers came for my family, I was away, under the tutelage of Livilla, the oracle and witch of Lyon. Gabro felt my father's conversion to be a personal betrayal and affront to him and an embarrassment in the eyes of the emperor. Gabro ordered that Titus and my mother be torn to pieces by starved bears as a public spectacle. My father was bound in a pool at Gabro's villa and eaten alive by eels as after-dinner entertainment for guests.

Livilla helped me plan my revenge. Gabro's death was hideous. I caused, on the instruction of my mentor, a vile, infected, lesion to open at the deepest part of the fundament. This became suppurated, filled with pus. He became fetid and rank, abiding in a miasma of his own decay. He was a figure of disgust to his family and all those who served him. After a time, when his suffering had grown beyond all bearing, I caused wasps to invade his fissure, to lay their eggs. The larvae that emerged from these fed on his flesh from within, until he was mad with pain. After two weeks, he fell on his sword.

And Livilla said that even this torture was not equal to Gabro's savagery. She advised me that it would discredit my martyred family and all the descendants of Titus, who would now never come into being, if I only destroyed Gabro alone. She said she heard the wailing and lamentations of hundreds of generations who now had no ingress into being. It would therefore be fitting, she said, to curse Gabro's line forever.

So I directed my vengeance upon Gabro's son. I have mourned this decision ever since. Medullinus was, as I have said, a young man of great promise, and of course, completely without culpability in his stepfather's crimes. Still, I was insane with rage at the destruction of my family and the end of our line, and I considered only my need for revenge. For him I planned another parasite, but one whose infestation would be eternal.

A slave in the household of his sweetheart, Xanthippe, was bribed to steal a lock of the young man's hair and a brooch he had given the girl as keepsakes. With these cut to bits and mixed with the fat of a goose that had never flown, the oil of a fish caught in darkness, and the hearts and heads of three asps, I ignited the beckoning flame—a flame which must burn for three nights and two days. With very much effort and the aid of my mentor, three midnight conjurings, prayers and incantations, and the recitation of the *Invocabo*, I caused the demon of old, the great spirit known in the East as Balphoroth, to claim Medullinus as his host.

I drove the demon into the young man. The demon was made to visit the victim as he slept, first entering his open mouth as an insubstantial, formless mass, accreting to more glutinous flesh at the first moment of infestation. The terrified young man struggled and tore at the metamorphizing assailant, and resisted its defilement, unable to scream or breathe for a time, or seize in any way the substance of the vile thing. Medullinus became the host, the carrier of the parasite. By this act, the demon and the host were bound together for all time, for the demon, once immortal, becomes subject to the lifespan of the host, so the parasite must keep the host alive to continue to be. Together they are immortal, but not indestructible. The fate of one is tied to the other. The demon *must* keep its host alive.

At least that is what Livilla taught me. I learned much later that this is not entirely true. I found there were limits even in the great insights of my wise teacher and it was a revelation that promised to make my purpose even more difficult. The final secret has always been just out of my reach. So, in hope, I must watch and wait.

And the nature of the demon Balphoroth was not known to me at his invocation. Not his true nature. This Livilla *did* know. She knew what the cost and implications of our actions would be across the years, but she still thought those actions appropriate and kept that knowledge from me.

Balphoroth was a bringer of nightmares. An incubus. The demon of lust, of monstrous appetites, and sometimes, death. And it happened that the evil spirit, though often deadly on its own, when bound to the increasingly anguished person of Medullinus, became even more deadly.

The being thus created then would attack scores of women yet to be born. Any woman who would accept a simple gift from him would open herself, unknowing, to his assault. And often, if not always, there would be born briefly into the world a spawn of this attack—a creature known as *Le Vorace,* the Ravenous. The creatures were a physical manifestation of the baser nature of the demon, misbegotten and of another plane. They are an accidental effect of the demon, and they reflect his will and consciousness. If they are seen by any woman, then she has come under the notice of the one eventually called Bastide, the parasite and its host. The Ravenous are nearly insensate and beneath commanding. They attack and devour even another like themselves until their vile energy is quickly spent, and they die.

And of course, less frequently, and hopefully never again, thanks be to God, a more terrible and permanent creature is born—the cambion. Cursed and miserable is the woman who bears this demon. I pray it is not needed to speak of it again.

When I understood all this, I asked Livilla how I might stop it. She told me it was too late for that. The combination of the demon and this man's spirit had formed an entity too powerful to be undone. When I understood the suffering of innocents to come that my vengeance had authored, I was in despair. After many days' contemplation and regret, I asked Livilla if she had it in her craft to give me long life—a life stretching into the dim future in which I would do what I could to frustrate the will of the monster or to aid and counsel its victims. She said she did have such a craft, though to administer it would come at enormous cost.

"My dedications and service to Circe have given me a sort of immortality," she said. "I can choose to transfer this state to another, but by so doing, I give up my own life. And I do not give it a moment's thought. Your intention is great, and I must defer to you. But be warned: you must never actively thwart the will of Balphoroth, whomever his victim might be, even if she is well known to you. To do so will cost you *your* life."

The next night, the first night of Saturnalia, a blood sacrifice and oath of transferal was made, and the task was done. Livilla died the next morning.

This was the beginning of this centuries-old battle for my own redemption. I am relieved to have recounted it here and save this history for my successor, should I ever have one. Much remains to be told of the centuries that followed, from the rise of the Church to the fall of Rome and the darkness that came after. For now, though, I am compelled to attend to the years of horror and death that enshrouded Europe and the world much later. It came from the east and swept over the west and has come to be known in the popular imagination as The Black Death.

# CHAPTER SIX

"It's a steam barge, the *Seneca Princess*," Set said. "Steam and sail, 194 feet, crew of sixteen. Shallow draft so we don't have to stay in the dredged channels in the St. Clair River as we pass up into Lake Huron. The bigger ships can logjam there, I am told, but we will be unaffected. The *Princess* will be carrying machine parts, mail, hurricane lamps, corn, and other things unloading at Toledo and Detroit, and carrying us passengers. The only passengers at first. At an average speed of ten and a half knots, or about twelve miles per hour, we should be in Chicago in eight and a half days."

"As always you have arranged everything," Mrs. Heugyens said. She sometimes congratulated herself when she saw the excitement Set took in executing his responsibilities to her. Anatolia had noticed this too, and both women were glad that he had stumbled upon duties at which he excelled and seemed to take such pride in fulfilling.

Mrs. Heugyens tightened the scarf around her head against the cold, sleety wind gusting off Lake Erie's gray expanse. Ten stevedores were moving all the trunks and crates of the New Phrygians up the gangplanks from Dock 17 on the Buffalo waterfront and into the ship's hold. The entire company of New Phrygians stood around her in groups of two or three, rigid in the cold wind, anxious to be finally allowed to board the ship and find their cabins. Rebecca Wallace and several other children played near the water's edge. Susan Henry was standing a few feet from Mrs. Heugyens, shivering from the cold.

"Are you alright Susan?" Mrs. Heugyens asked. "We will be on board soon."

Susan managed a labored smile and nodded. She had been complaining of pain in her joints and fatigue in the last few weeks and had been unable to perform many of her duties to Mrs. Heugyens. Susan had asked Anatolia if she could divine the nature of her malady. Anatolia had been unable to conceive of an answer for her.

Anatolia and Euphemia Wallace stepped out of the shipping office at the end of the dock and approached Set and Mrs. Heugyens.

"We are cleared to board now," Anatolia said. A fresh sense of loss and dread suddenly swept over her. She was surprised by the depth of these feelings and could not account for their origin, coming on as quickly as they did. She glanced over her shoulder back toward the shipping office and noticed a tall figure on horseback in the shadows between two warehouses. The tall man seemed to be watching the activities of the New Phrygians.

"The cabins are midships below deck," Euphemia said. "You get Number One, Mrs. Heugyens, and the rest of us are assigned on this manifest." She unfolded a paper she had been carrying and glanced at it. She handed the paper to Set. He moved among the New Phrygians and told each of them which cabin they had been assigned to. He then returned to Anatolia's side.

"Then let's get on board," he said.

The small groups of the community began to slowly make their way up the gangplank. All the men allowed all the women and the few children to precede them, and the family groups waited, once on the deck, for their husbands and fathers to rejoin them. Mrs. Heugyens and Susan walked arm in arm up the gangplank. Increase followed them with an expression that looked like concern on his face. Everyone had noticed that he had become attentive to Susan in recent weeks.

Anatolia embraced Set. She glanced back toward the warehouses at the end of the wharf. The figure on horseback was no longer there.

"I hope this is the right thing to do," she said as they walked last up the gangplank. "I wish just you and I could have made this trip... alone."

"None of them wanted to be apart from you. It was their free choice to make."

"But I don't feel *I* had a free choice. I asked them early on to stay behind, but they wouldn't have it."

"We are a community, Ana. We live our lives as a community."

Anatolia stopped on the gangplank.

"Something is happening to me. I don't think you have heard me when I have said it before. Things have changed. I feel it. My dreams and visions, if I have them at all, vanish like smoke before I can see them. I don't feel as I did before the attack. These people expect vision from me, but now something seems missing. *I don't know what's going to happen.*"

Set smiled at her.

"Having doubt must be natural for someone with so much responsibility."

"Don't pretend you understand, Set! Don't insult me that way. Don't tell me this is exhaustion or fear. Don't pretend to believe me about Bastide or any of this if you don't. Don't tell me, after all this time, I don't know what I am talking about. Something has *changed*!"

Set was startled by her vehemence. After a moment he nodded and smiled slightly at her. "I try to understand, but how can I?" he said. "I expected to live and die as nothing, as *M'daid* always said I would. No, I don't really know how you feel or what your fears are. I try to, but I...

none of us are capable of that. When I first met you as a boy, I knew right off that the best I could hope for, the best I *should* hope for, was to be some part of the life you were going to live. That's all I am, and all I want to be, when I think of the good we can do."
He took her arm gently and guided her up the gangplank.

# CHAPTER SEVEN

"Do you want any more of this wine?" Father Vannier asked, the wine bottle poised above Moira's glass.

"I think I do. Thank you," she said.

"We'll finish it off then." He emptied the bottle into her glass. "So, to answer your question, no, I had no objection to selling the rectory along with the school and convent. An unnecessary expense for the diocese since I am only here two days a week. Attendance at mass has fallen off so drastically. Why maintain the cost of keeping up this big old house? The apartment in the church cellar is perfectly suitable. The removal men are coming tomorrow. This will be our last evening here."

"Ste. Odile has been slowly dying since Bastide's death and the demise of his business enterprise," Moira said.

"Quickly dying, I would say." Vannier sat next to her on the sofa. "All of this has happened in twelve years or so. The lead ore is played out, and aside from winemaking and the lime works, there isn't much left." He held his wineglass up to the firelight. "I am glad we could have an evening like this again. It's been a little while."

"Always enjoyable," Moira said,

Vannier seemed to be making a point of not looking at her. "It's a great friendship we have, Moira. It means very much to me. I have felt it becoming... a little awkward in the last year or so. I guess awkward is the right word."

Moira shrugged.

"Holy orders is a lonely life. For priests, certainly. Nuns too, I imagine. I would argue it's an unnatural life. I am not sure Jesus cared much or actually stipulated that his followers have no families."

"Didn't he say somewhere to abandon all and follow me?"

"Yes, more or less... in Matthew, he said it would *guarantee* salvation, but not that it was *required* for it. And the Church allowed married priests until medieval times, and then changed its view on the subject because of property ownership in marriages, not for morality or chastity, as I understand it."

"Interesting," Moira smiled, pretending not to grasp the point he was making. Vannier grinned at her a little. He recognized the look on her face and knew she had no intention of granting him rapport.

"I can verify that you have practiced morality and chastity! I'll be sunk if anyone could fault you on those grounds!" she added.

Vannier looked pleasantly surprised. "I haven't heard you use that expression for a while. Years I would say. It made me think of how you were when you first came here. You have changed a bit, in my opinion. I think Ste. Odile has changed you."

"Mellowed a little. Softened to some things and toughened to others."

"Yes, I think that's accurate," Vannier agreed. "Adapted. Evolved, if I may use that word. Like your friend Perdita before you, you have made this a better place. I think that is the cause for my... feelings for you. One of the causes, at least."

Moira smiled. This was as straightforward as Vannier had ever been about their relationship. The taboo of his vocation had bothered her years ago, when she had first sensed his true feelings, but that concern had faded over time.

Vannier's face reddened. "I overdid it with the lamb a bit, don't you think?" he said.

"A little dry, "Moira shrugged. "and I absolutely prefer beef, as you know. Tasty, though."

"Too bad. I hoped to do better for our last meal in this house," Vannier said.

"Well, as it turns out, you will be afforded the opportunity to redeem yourself in the future."

"Oh?"

Moira removed Anatolia's letter from her handbag and handed it to Vannier. He read.

"If you look at the records," Moira said, "this young woman's experiences perfectly mirror those of Marie Delaporte Chardin, Sister Solana, and my dear Perdita twelve years ago."

"I have seen those reports. Very good that you collected the accounts and kept a record of it all. I didn't think at the time that the information would ever be needed again. I never expected..."

"If Bastide survived," Moira said, "he must have gone into hiding with help, perhaps at his chateau at Montsegur, France. I would think he could hardly move around in the world alone."

"Morisot... that was his name, wasn't it? Mr. Morisot ran his businesses," Vannier said. "He disappeared just after Bastide did. He could have done it."

"Possibly. He would've acted quickly. Morisot left Ste. Odile a few days after the cave-in. His wife died in the fire at Tranquille House. Presumably, he headed back to Martinique, his home. He was said to be on a train to New Orleans when a derailment killed him and twenty other people at Baton Rouge. I have never had that account verified, however."

"What about that servant of Bastide's, the Haitian fellow... Tertius?"

"Tertius was shot in the chest by Mrs. Morisot. He was near death at

Tranquille House as it burned, when he was saved from the flames and taken away by one of Mrs. Morisot's servants, LuHelen Dufor. She disappeared, and no one knows what became of him. Perdita mentioned to me in a letter that Tertius was filled with remorse for having served Bastide for so many years and to have not done more to stop his predations."

"I would like to know if Tertius is dead or alive," Vannier said.

"We may soon know the truth of that." Moira stood and approached the fireplace. "I am almost certain I saw LuHelen Dufor on Endymion Street yesterday. Much changed with time, heavier and grayer, but it must have been her."

"Her father lived in the old slave quarters at the rear of the Rennie house," Vannier remembered. "He was freed by the family after the war and stayed on the rest of his days."

"Yes," Moira agreed. "He died a year after LuHelen and Tertius disappeared. His few personal possessions were left there, untouched for many years. She must have come back to find them."

"I am due back at Kaskaskia tomorrow..." Vannier noted.

"I will look into this," Moira said. "I will go back to the Rennie house and watch for LuHelen. If she is not still harboring Tertius, she may know what he knew, and it may be of importance."

"Worth investigating. Which brings me back to the journal of old Euphrosine."

"It has a new value now I would not have predicted if indeed, Bastide survived." Moira finished her wine and placed her glass on the discolored marble mantelpiece. "It is the perfect key to understanding the nature and weaknesses of the incubus Balphoroth and his mortal host, Orien Bastide. There are visions and accounts in it I don't understand. I think... I believe these things may be knowable to Anatolia, with her special gifts and insights. We must place it in her hands."

# CHAPTER EIGHT

*Anno Domini 1348, November, at Riquewihr*

They have done it. Spenger the vintner, Kramer the coppersmith, and Canon Lamark have had their way, and the Jews, Belshom and Milhaud, were burned at the stake at the North Gate last night. Spenger's case was that the two accused had poisoned his well and brought the plague to town when he reneged on a loan to them. And yet I think the case against the two might have faded away if not for the pressure exerted by Yvain of Andlau, the rich man, on his friend the magistrate. The condemned had disapproved of Yvain sequestering his young daughter in the convent of Perpetua a few years ago and railed against him publicly for walling the girl up in an immurement cell soon after. Now their judgments and disapproval have been quieted.

My rooms are less than a single *arpent* from the North Gate, down the dark Lane of St. Enguerrand, and so, as shuttered away from the sight and sounds of the immolation as I could be, I could still smell the odious scent of the burning ones. Yet this barbarous public spectacle was not to be missed by most of the townspeople. Though I could hear the muffled sound of the charges being read, followed by the initial gasp that arises from the crowds when the fire is lighted and takes hold, I heard no cries of the condemned and no cheers and applause of the onlookers, as so often accompany these vile proceedings. Perhaps the world has seen enough death as the pestilence has raged over the land. The old frenzy of a public execution has been benumbed by this morbid desolation that has touched every soul. What is the exhilaration of two more public deaths when Death is within and without our walls every day now?

In an hour or less, the monstrous public pageant was done. As the crowds dissipated and I could hear them filing back to their homes below my window, I knew there was at least one other townsman who had shunned this horror: Orien Bastide.

Bastide has seen enough of human savagery, as have I. A theologian or natural philosopher might assume that, by his nature, Bastide would think nothing of these acts of human abomination, but it is not true. I have followed him through the ages. A thousand years ago my act of vengeance brought him into being, and I resolved to follow him across the centuries in atonement, to aid and attend to his victims and even prevent victimhood whenever I could do so. Despite these dark compulsions in him, and his fascination with human investigation, knowledge, and achievement, he has, by necessity, seen much of the worst of humanity. As have I.

A century ago at Montsegur, he was sent out, with three others from the mountaintop citadel of the Cathars, to preserve their teachings and legacy, as the armies of the seneschal of Carcassonne and the Archbishop of Narbonne besieged the fortress and burned two hundred *perfecti* at the stake in the field below, the *Prats del Cremats*.

Before this, there was the sack of Constantinople in 1204; before that, Tours and the last stand against the invading Moors, and earlier still, Diocletian's final persecutions. All this he saw. *We* saw, because I was always nearby, if he knew it or not, watching him.

Though his mind and thoughts seem to be drawn back to the Albi and his old comrades at Montsegur—he returns there every few years—he settled in this village, or near it, a year ago. As so many have done during this pestilence as landowners and lords have died off, he occupied an abandoned house midway between Riquwihr and Zellenberg. I lost track of him at Toulouse two years before and arrived at Montsegur just after he'd gone. I found him here when I heard stories of the girl Seraphica Roquetaillade, native to this town, who had come under his influence in the previous months but returned home suddenly.

Seraphica had gone into service in the house of Caron, the mayor of Montsegur. She was a literate girl of great curiosity. Caron told me as I made inquiries that she made the acquaintance of a strange man, who, for a period of weeks, seem to fascinate and challenge her. Caron reported that the girl's temperament began to change and her work suffered soon after the connection was made, and she suddenly announced that she was not well and had to resign her post and return home to Riquwihr. I soon followed, hoping I was in time to save the girl.

Back in her father's house, her decline continued. She would not speak to him of the strange man she had been seen meeting at Montsegur, near the abandoned chateau of Raymond VI on the mountainside above the town. Caron had sent a message to Roquetaillade, warning him of his daughter's meetings with the stranger, but when questioned, Seraphica refused to speak of it.

The family's narrow, half-timbered house is to the south side of the Merchant's Guild Hall. I waited and watched for Roquetaillade to emerge from the hall after a meeting. As I approached him, he must have thought me a beggar or one of the diseased. I am always veiled when I go out and will continue so as long as contagion is abroad. And my dress and shawl may be considered shabby. I no longer concern myself with such things.

A look of distress froze the merchant's face. He seemed to calm a bit when I stopped a good distance from him.

"I mean you no harm, Monsieur," I said. "I am not one of the diseased. I am a friend who has followed your daughter from Montsegur out of concern. I want to help her if you will allow it."

"You know her?" Roquetaillade frowned.

"I know something of her story. And I have known many, many young women like her over the years who have shared these circumstances. I help them when I can... "

The merchant's scowl became more severe, and he began to walk away, covering his face with his cloak.

"Some of these girls survive this nightmare, Monsieur," I continued. "But many do not. I must try to help her."

"Who are you, then? What is your interest in these family matters?"

"I am known in these lands as Euphrosine."

"Euphrosine the Wise Woman? The witch? The Mother of Centuries, so-called?"

"The same."

"I have heard the old women in my service mention your name."

A plague doctor in his black mask approached us. "The death cart is fast behind me," he said. "The miasma of contagion envelopes it. You know better! Get indoors, you two!"

Roquetaillade motioned for me to follow him back into the guildhall. Down the street the cart bell could be heard, and the muffled call, "Bring out your dead."

In the darkness of the guild entry hall, Roquetaillade removed his cloak.

"What can you do to save my family?" he asked.

# CHAPTER NINE

"Commerce on the Great Lakes slows in the winter, as you would expect," Set said, sipping his coffee. "We must pray for good weather when we get to Huron and Lake Michigan. Lakes Superior and Michigan are known as graveyards of ships in the winter."

"It looks like we are approaching land." Anatolia looked ill, as she had since the second day of the voyage. She leaned against the wooden taffrail, looking out over the cold, gray water. She had hardly been able to eat anything for days.

Set knew better than to persist in asking her how she felt or show too much concern. She seemed to have no patience with his empathy lately. "It's the Detroit River. We will be in Detroit this afternoon or tonight, depending on the river traffic. Then on to Lake St. Clare, the St. Clare River, and Lake Huron."

Anatolia pulled her shawl more tightly around herself. A light rain had begun to fall.

"Maybe you should get in out of the weather," Set said. "Got colder overnight. Water's a little rough today."

"Tell me why we are making this trip on the water as winter approaches, rather than by rail? What is this secret business of yours up north?"

Set was a little surprised by the question. "It was Mrs. Heugyens's preference, as you know, though she didn't want to impose that choice on the group."

"And it was your preference, too."

"Well, yes, it was. Do you object? You didn't say anything..."

"You seemed determined. But I find this is exhausting me. And the dangers of the weather..."

Set brushed away some strands of hair from Anatolia's eyes. She had lost so much of her vigor over the past few weeks.

"Because... because it is necessary that our route take us past Mackinac Island."

"Whatever for?

Set pulled Anatolia's shawl more tightly around her.

"In Rochester, the last time I was there for Mrs. Heugyens, something happened I didn't tell you about."

"Oh?"

"I always stay at the same hotel in Rochester, the Northrup. As I was checking in, the desk clerk told me there was a message waiting for me, which had been there some weeks. He said the message had been delivered by a small woman whom he believed to be a Negro, though he could not tell for sure because her face and skin were covered almost completely by shawls, gloves, and bandages. In my room, I opened the envelope and read. Here is the note." Set removed a folded paper from his waistcoat and handed it to Anatolia. It read:

*My dear Sir:*

*My name is Tertius. For many years I was in the service of a personage surely known to you, at least by name: Orien Bastide. I hereby urgently inform you that in opposition to popular belief, Bastide still lives.*

*For those years of service I provided him, despite knowing what I knew about Bastide, I feel I must apologize to everyone directly or indirectly harmed by him. Your Anatolia will be one of these persons if she is not already. The danger to this young woman is profound and intensified by the fact that Bastide has been fixed on her for twelve years.*

*Over the centuries, Bastide has survived many calamities. Much injured after the mine collapse, he found his way out through an old ventilation shaft. He eventually found me at Mingo Swamp, where my friend LuHelen Dufor brought me to heal from my wounds. I would not see him. LuHelen told him I died from infection, and he disappeared. I knew his next act would be to find Anatolia Montes, however long it took. I knew I must find her too, and warn her.*

*As you should know, the Bastide who was one of the founders of Ste. Odile is the same Bastide of whom we speak. In 1689, Bastide, de Castres, Moussaut, and their party of voyageurs left Quebec to find the Mississippi and the region so rich in ores and minerals that they were to claim. Unknown to most of the party, Bastide and de Castres also sought refuge from religious persecution, being secret adherents to the nearly annihilated blasphemy of Catharism. As the contingent of canoes passed into Lake Michigan, they stopped at Mackinac Island and spent some days at the Jesuit mission there. The brother of de Castres, Michel, decided to remain at the mission, and Bastide resolved to entrust to his keeping a large chest he always carried with him. He said he would return for the chest when the settlement had been established downriver.*

*Bastide never retrieved the chest. He attempted to, but as awareness of his true nature became known to those entrusted with its safekeeping, it was hidden away from him. To this day, I have found, after much investigation, it is in the keeping of Lucien de Castres, a descendant of Michel, on Mackinac Island.*

*Bastide spoke of the chest often to me. I do not know its exact contents, but I suspect it contains something of great value. This is my suspicion. He repeated many times that he had to find and recover the chest, that his preservation depended upon it. At first, I thought by this he meant his fortune, but now I suspect he meant his very being. You must make your way to the island. You must find Lucien de Castres. I have written to him on your behalf. There is another element that must be applied, of which I will inform you once I know you have the chest.*

*T.*

Anatolia refolded the letter.

"Do you believe this?" she said.

"Why would this man fabricate such a story? To what end?" Set returned the letter to his waistcoat. "More importantly, do *you* believe it?"

"I am afraid... I do. My visions have become weaker, as I have told you, but the day before we left Buffalo, I had a sense that something of great value would come to us on the water. It made no sense until now."

"I didn't want to distress you with this during your recovery. I thought it would be too much for you. When I came home and saw what had happened to you, the last thing I wanted was to help fix your mind on Orien Bastide. But when the necessity of going back to Ste. Odile presented itself, it seemed like a godsend. I meant to tell you in a day or so."

Anatolia's lips were cracked and shivering. Set began to guide her back toward the companionway and their cabin below.

"Yes, we must investigate this, in case there is anything to it," Anatolia said.

"We will be at Mackinac in two days."

# CHAPTER TEN

When Vannier finished his midmorning prayer, he mounted his horse and headed toward the ferry down at Belgique and on to Kaskaskia Island, where he spent two days of every week. Moira had kissed him on the cheek, a modest, sisterly kiss as she always did on the mornings he left. Some evenings they spent in Moira's room at her boarding house. Mrs. Zell had voiced some disapproval of this arrangement at first on the few nights they spent together in her establishment rather than at the rectory. But if the old woman still held any objection to this in the last few years, she gave no sign of it. Theirs was a platonic relationship, Moira said. Mrs. Zell seemed to choose to believe this declaration and never mentioned it again.

Last night they had stayed at the rectory because men were coming early to remove furniture and fixtures from the large house. Moira had known the McReady brothers for many years and trusted them. She felt comfortable leaving them unsupervised to move everything into storage in the church basement.

Moira poured herself a cup of coffee and sat in the rattan chair on the front verandah. She looked out over Constantinople Street and thought about how the town had changed in her time there. The street was nearly empty. River traffic had declined severely in those years, and commerce had shriveled. The Levee Road and Bosphorous Street were once teeming with activity, while the lead mines, the lime works, and the vineyards were profitable. More than these, though, she felt the loss of energy and life as the Academy of Perpetua had faded away.

As every term began over the years, and the dormitories started to fill up with returning girls and new students, the town seemed to be reborn. The noise and confusion were invigorating as the girls got reacquainted with each other, learned their new routines, and adjusted to new teachers. But that time had passed. It was all over now.

Moira sat for more than an hour watching the McReady brothers carting furniture across the drive next door to the church basement. They were twins who had supported themselves by doing odd jobs around town since their father died. Lester was the better-looking one. Vern, his brother, was much homelier but still had a resemblance to his twin. He looked like an unkind, ironic parody of his brother.

When Moira finished her coffee, she stood and stretched her legs. Vannier wouldn't be back for five days. She had no more lesson plans to prepare. She would need to find a way to occupy her time.

She thought about the years back in Boston when she and Perdita were attending concerts and lectures and theatre on a weekly basis. It was a heady time when they wanted to experience everything and be open to aesthetics and every cultural contrivance devised by mankind. It all seemed a little pretentious to her now.

To both Moira and Perdita in those days, from the comfort of their parents' houses, there seemed to be nothing more urgent than these cultural issues, these pursuits. The years since brought struggle and loss, death, and responsibility. Now Moira could think of nothing of greater value than the love and high opinion of other human beings.

Moira rinsed her coffee cup under the hand pump in the yard. She then returned to the kitchen and placed it in a packed crate near the back door just as Lester entered. "I think I'm going to take a little walk Lester," she said. "To stay out of your way."

"That's fine, miss. I found this in one of the sisters' rooms. Looks valuable." He pulled out a gold coin from his vest pocket and handed it to her. She looked at it briefly and dropped it in the crate. Lester nodded and removed the crate.

"Just lock up when you are finished. There won't be anyone here tonight."

Moira removed her shawl and light jacket from the hook near the front door. She had put on her most comfortable pair of shoes that morning, so she felt she could have a long walk around the town and perhaps stop for a light lunch at Herve's later in the afternoon. The courthouse clock struck one as she stepped out onto the verandah. She was surprised it was already so late in the day.

She walked north on Constantinople Street and turned east on Bucephalus toward the river. She walked past the jailhouse where Marie Delaporte Chardin had spent the last few months of her life before being hanged for murdering her young daughter. Perdita had befriended the deranged woman and stood as her only friend as she was executed. Marie had killed her child, Perdita told Moira, to save her from Bastide. A corner of the jailhouse roof had rotted away, allowing rainwater to saturate an inner wall. It had been that way for a year. The town no longer had the resources, or perhaps the will, Moira thought, to repair it.

In a few minutes' time she had reached the Levee Road and turned north toward the landing. There was a bench there where she could sit and watch the river. She wished she had thought to bring a flask of wine with her.

At the landing, a single small packet was docked and unloading mail and crates of farm implements. She sat on the single wood and iron bench to watch. The sun was no longer in the eastern sky, but slightly to the west in an afternoon position. Moira wished she had come earlier because she enjoyed watching the sunlight glittering across the river. In another month or so, ice would start to choke the river channels and river traffic would all but stop. Even at that time of year, she enjoyed sitting on the bench. The river seemed more sullen and secretive then, and the calls of waterfowl, birds of prey, and an occasional coyote were the only sounds to be heard.

A drayman in an old wooden wagon pulled by a two-mule team passed behind Moira on the Levee Road. The man was one of the younger sons of old Aristide, a drayman from Perdita's time, but Moira couldn't remember his name. He backed the wagon onto the landing, and he and three stevedores loaded four wooden crates of farm implements into it and secured the gate. In fifteen minutes, the wagon was back on the road, retracing its way south. One of the stevedores, named Raymond, Moira believed, waved to her and she nodded in response.

Several white egrets flew overhead, across the channel, and perched in a dead cottonwood tree at the north end of de Castres Island. Moira watched them for a few moments until they began dropping, one by one, down to the riverbank to wade the shallows hunting for food. Moira glanced back over her left shoulder. High on its bluff to the northwest, she could see some of the towers and battlements of Bastide's abandoned estate, Jardin Noir.

The deteriorating hermitage had always been a mystery to Moira. With Bastide's disappearance coinciding with her arrival in town and with the house being shuttered and locked up soon after, she had never seen it up close and had never seen the mysteries and wonders inside which Perdita had described in her letters. Moira stood. There were still many hours of daylight, and she needed a constitutional. The forbidding old house on the hill had been all but forgotten by the townspeople. Moira thought there was no real reason why she couldn't finally satisfy her curiosity about the place. She resolved to walk there.

The sun was fully in her face now as it arced to the west. Moira crossed Bosphorus Street onto Mal Ardents and continued up the gradual hill past the blacksmith shop. She passed old French colonial *poteaux-en-terre* houses and newer brick and stone ones, crossing Constantinople Street. In another block, she reached Thermopylae Street at the northwestern edge of town. She turned to the north, where the street slowly devolved into a country road and seemed to lose its way up a craggy, wooded hillside.

Although the day was cool and a chilly breeze was blowing from the west, Moira quickly felt warmed by her exertion. The incline of the road was more severe than it appeared to be from the bottom of the hill. The leaves of the maple trees were starting to turn yellow and red, and the oaks, sumacs, and hickory trees were changing in the advancing autumn. Winter was just weeks away, Moira's favorite season.

Crows were calling off to the west, toward Obli and LaMotte, beyond the hardwood forest and the valley. Crows much nearer to Moira answered these calls, and she saw that there were many of the birds in the branches above her. As she rounded a bend in the road, she saw several of them on the ground ahead of her, feeding on a bloody carcass. She could see that the others above were waiting for their opportunity to tear at the tattered flesh.

As she approached the carcass, the crows were slow to abandon it. When she was within twenty feet, they did, and she could see it more clearly. There was too little of the animal left to identify. The head, neck, upper thorax, and most of the forelimbs were gone, devoured by whatever killed it, Moira thought, not by the crows. In life, the creature must have been over two feet long with its tail, though part of that was missing, too.

Standing over the carcass, she could not identify it as a raccoon, otter, opossum, cat, or any creature she knew. As the crows around her grew more restless, she moved away from it and continued up the dusty road.

By this time, the sun had arced well into the western sky. As Moira climbed another quarter mile up the rugged road, she was beginning to feel exhaustion setting in. The sunlight stabbed through the foliage, which, as autumn progressed, was starting to turn shades of yellow and orange.

At the summit of the hill, as what was left of Thermopylae Street gave way to a wide gravel drive, the foliage opened to a vast, long-abandoned lawn and dreary gardens. All was beginning to be cast in the penumbra of the fading day.

Dominating the lawn to the right was a huge, fantastically gnarled oak tree. Many of its branches drooped to the ground, then turned upward again like the massive necks of an unmoving Hydra. Beyond the oak tree were more dark gardens and a maze of hedges radiating from a barely visible, ornate, wooden observation tower topped by a copper onion dome. And between the expanses of dark garden and the trees on either side of the drive, arose the fantastic and imposing hermitage known for over two hundred years as Jardin Noir.

The gravel drive formed a circle around a lichen and moss-covered centerpiece—a dry stone fountain in which carved demons, griffins, and other mythic creatures battled to dominate a fanciful escarpment. As she made her way around this structure, Moira could see the house more clearly. It was a massive, rambling structure, built almost entirely of dressed limestone, embellished here and there, as were two oriel windows visible on the front side of the building, in Gothic-arched cast iron. It was an odd mixture of styles: buttresses flanked Romanesque towers and round arches; clerestory windows and rosettes topped lintels and columns that were almost Classical or even Egyptian in places. Moira perceived that the enormous house had all the appearances of generations of owners with imagination and refinement, who followed the ebb and flow of two centuries of changing taste and many tangents of intellectual and aesthetic obsessions. As she studied it at length, it was almost inconceivable to her to know that all of this, though not in one lifetime, was actually sprung from the fancies of one man.

Moira made her way to the iron-hinged double front door of the great house. From that vantage point, looking to her right, she could see a long conservatory built of brick in a Gothic or Jacobean style at the northwestern edge of the lawn, in front of yet another maze of gardens. The roof of this building was entirely glazed in glass panes set in iron and bronze frameworks and panels.

The massive front doors, situated under a limestone canopy, were iron-clad oak and covered with mosses, lichens, and spider webs. Moira immediately noticed that the doors did not align perfectly, and she was surprised to find that the left-hand side was slightly ajar. She tugged on the great iron ring that hung from the middle panel and, with some effort, dragged it open enough to fit her body through.

She found herself in a dark vestibule and facing two more ornate doors, the right one of which had partially fallen from its hinges and stood at an angle to the doorframe. She sidled through the fallen door and into the large entryway of the house. As she stepped across the threshold, Moira had an odd sensation of loss and dread, as if she were about to give up some sacred and private part of herself that could never be recovered. She tried to put these thoughts out of her mind.

Moira's first impression of the great room in which she stood was that incredibly, after twelve years of abandonment, everything seemed to be undisturbed. The entry hall was a wide, pentagonal space lined with dark wainscotting, off which radiated several rooms and hallways. A large, round table made of rich woods of various hues dominated the space and was piled with books, papers, pieces of bone, and rocks, all surrounding a silver vase at the table's center, which held many varieties of long-wilted flowers and plants.

Beyond the table was a large, oak staircase that rose to a landing featuring a window that must have been twenty feet high. The fading daylight illuminated medieval scenes of battle, siege, and immolation of prisoners of war, depicted in stained and painted glass across the expanse of the window.

Several dark niches in the entry hall on either side of the staircase were populated by life-sized stone statues from antiquity. A pharaonic figure and ibis-headed god represented Egypt, marble figures of Eros and Psyche bespoke of the Classical world, and bearded, winged bulls of basalt recalled Nineveh and the court of Ashurnasirpal. To the right of this was a large pocket door.

Moira pulled the door open with some effort. This revealed a vast, paneled room—a library rivaling any she had seen in Boston or New York. Bookshelves, in two tiers in some places, covered most of the high walls, except at an oversized limestone fireplace and a ceiling-high oriel window that overlooked the front lawn and the gnarled oak tree Moira had seen as she approached the house.

"All this," Moira murmured, "undisturbed all this time. Fear overwhelmed curiosity. And greed."

The room was scattered with desks and worktables, all of which were buried under books, charts, fossils, and bones of creatures of all sizes and descriptions. Ornate glass display cases formed a barrier between the main expanse of the floor and the bookshelves; these contained specimens of mounted birds and fish, seashells, and small antiquities. One walnut-trimmed case contained the fearsome, enormous skull of a crocodile, and another, a selection of heavy-browed prognathous skulls of anthropoid apes. Moira walked spellbound toward the shadowy fireplace at the opposite end of the room. She stopped at a table she passed to glance over some volumes, dog-eared and smudged, stacked together in front of a brass and wooden orrery that illustrated the movements of the planets around the sun under a painted bronze of Mephistopheles. The smallest volume was *The City of God* by St. Augustine, a larger one was Francis Barrett's *Magus*, and the largest was Collin de Plancy's *Dictionnaire Infernal.* Moira pulled this book from under the other two and opened it. The page revealed held an engraving of the bat-winged, three-headed demon Asmodeus, the personification of rage and lust. She closed the book and replaced the other two upon it as she had found them.

A large painting above the fireplace attracted her attention. She approached it slowly. It depicted a scene in which a dark and brooding sky hung like a shroud over a desolate beach. Ruins of ancient buildings, blasted remnants of a long-dead civilization, were scattered along the low horizon line and ran into the subdued, fatigued surf. Human bones could be seen here and there, being slowly buried by sand and waves. At the center of it all, his giant form dramatically lighted by an unseen setting sun, sat the hideous yet somehow pitiable figure of a Cyclops. A brass plaque affixed to the bottom of the picture's massive frame read *Polyphemus in Solitude by Elihu Vedder.*

Moira suddenly became aware of a sound behind her—a metallic sound that she realized she had been hearing for a few moments before it caught her attention. She recognized that the sound was the large front door, which she had found ajar, being pushed closed.

# CHAPTER ELEVEN

*Anno Domini 1348, November*

Having secured the permission of her father to intervene in this affair, I set about to gain the trust and friendship of Seraphica Roquetaillade in an attempt to save her life. From an alcove across the street, I watched her house for two days. At last, on the third morning she emerged, veiled and carrying a covered basket. I followed her at some distance as she walked east and into a narrow passageway that led to the town square. I could smell the mutton in the basket she carried and knew she must be headed to the Hospital of Perpetua with sustenance for the sisters caring for the plague victims.

The passageway was dank and dark even though the morning sun was rising above the battlements of the town's eastern wall. At the doorsteps of a few households lay a corpse, wrapped in a shroud or homespun. Hanging over each was the familiar stink of the burst pustules and foul blood of the afflicted. Those who had died in the night had not yet been collected by the morning death cart. Rats skittered around some of the bodies, and flies, hidden in the bodies while indoors, had become briefly active on them in the cold, as well as on the scraps of food and garbage not yet swept away by the street keepers.

The passageway ended at the town square, a large, open space bordered by deserted inns, shops, and houses, and the short colonnade of the Hospital of Perpetua. Formerly the Benedictine Hospice for Lepers, the building was given over to the nursing Sisters of Perpetua at the outbreak of the pestilence. The Benedictines moved to an old rebuilt barn they owned on the road to Andlau.

The Hospital is one main chamber within the colonnade. Twelve beds, each one representing and named for one of the Disciples, stand against the far wall and in most cases, each contains two patients. These afflicted have no home in which to die or were sent out of their homes by a family as yet unstricken. And death is the only business of the refuge. No treatment or medicine is administered. The Sisters of Perpetua only care for the dying to make their suffering as slight as is in their power to do.

I stood behind one of the columns in the colonnade and watched the girl carry her basket into the hospital. The distinct odor of the dying wafted out and enveloped me. I knew the nuns normally gave their patients no food, so I guessed the mutton Seraphica brought was intended to sustain the nuns themselves. She placed her basket on a small alms table just inside the main door. A nun greeted her and embraced her.

"I wish I could give more than this food, Sister," I heard Seraphica say. "My father forbids me to help you here, and though I often disobey him, to do this could infect the rest of the household."

"Bless you, Seraphica," the nun said. "Your help is needed now, though you must obey your father. We have seen many more cases this week. The pestilence is getting worse in Riquwihr!" The nun removed the basket from the table and disappeared with it into the shadows at the rear of the room. Seraphica then turned and faced me.

"You have been following me, old woman," she said.

"I have. I am Euphrosine." I raised the veil covering my face.

"The Mother of Centuries. I have heard of you." She approached me. "You are not one of the afflicted."

"No. I do not believe I am destined to die in this pestilence. My purpose will not allow it."

"Yes, I have heard of your purpose also. You are an herbalist, a doctor, a midwife, and a seer, some have said. A protector of women."

"I am rather tired. May we sit?" I took her arm and guided her toward a collection of dressed stones intended to rebuild a damaged corner of St-Cyr's but abandoned there since the onset of the plague. We sat. "Yes, I am a protector of women. Particularly women in a certain type of danger."

The square was empty, but in the distance I could hear the death cart approaching. In a few moments, we would be ordered off the streets.

"A certain type of danger?" Seraphica repeated.

"Those few, those curious, those searching for knowledge and affirmation, who have come under the influence of Orien Bastide."

Seraphica's face went blank.

"Bastide?" she said. "You know of Bastide?"

"I have followed him for longer than you can imagine. I alone know his true nature, for it was I who created it."

"True nature?" Seraphica frowned. "He is a man of great learning and deference. A friend. Someone who regards my opinions and ideas as he would those of any respected man."

I think I must have smiled a little at these words, but compassionately. I had heard them, or similar ones, so many times before.

"Yes, he is all those things," I said, "and truly so. He is artless in his interest in the workings of your mind. That is one part of his nature. But there is another part. And it is a part you must fear."

She turned from me as though she intended to walk back to her home.

"He is odd," she said, "but hardly dangerous. His appearance is frightening, his head wrapped in bandages as it is, but who has not become familiar with horrific sights in this time of death and rot and... pestilence?"

"No one has been left untouched, child. But nothing you have seen in this town has readied you for the horrors I foresee, the things I know are threatening you."

"Thank you, Mother," her tone was curt. "I know you from your reputation. I thank you for your concerns, but I wish to choose my own path. That is something Monsieur Bastide understands about me. My father will miss me. I must return home."

She began to walk away quickly. I followed close behind her.

"I understand the confusion in your heart," I said.

Seraphica stopped and faced me.

"Mother, forgive me," she said. "I am not ungrateful for your attentions, but I think they are misplaced. I believe in the equality and value of all, as Our Lord said: to raise the lowly and humble the mighty. That is why I bring food to the hospital. But it is undeniably true that not all have the same opportunities in life nor the same responsibilities. The serfs are but extensions of the land, tools in the hands of their lords. In these days, as families die out and abandon their estates, many of these lowly are claiming those properties and elevating their lot in life. Still, they are what they are raised to be, as their parents were before them.

"A poor soul of your station, Mother, especially a woman, will never be literate. It is not meant for them to be. Someone must work the land and tend the animals, and there is dignity in that, but what good would reading ever be to such people? To what use would they ever put the theorems of Euclid or the apologetics of Aquinas? It is rare in the merchant class, but my father educated me. I am literate. Although I have read Ptolemy and Boethius and Aristotle, I am still less respected than a butcher or stonemason because I am a woman." She dabbed at a tear welling at the corner of her left eye. "I have ideas, insights, great flights of fancy, but no one to hear them or share them with. My mind exists in an immurement cell, cut off from all thoughtful intercourse..."

"And then came Bastide," I said.

"Yes. Then came Bastide. At the moment I thought my heart would explode, then came Bastide. At Montsegur, he found me and immediately saw more in me than anyone else had ever seen. More even than I knew was within me. It was a validation I have never felt before, and I swear by Cecilia and Aurelia and all women who have died for their faith that it saved my life."

Protestation was futile, as it usually is with these young women. I smiled and longed to touch her cheek or embrace her, but felt neither act of affection would have been understood or well-received.

"Let me ask you one last thing," I said. "Has there been a time recently when you were alone, perhaps walking or just sitting in a room, when you have seen an odd, dark, voracious animal? Something you have never seen before?"

"There has... yes. Two nights ago, as I was leaving the square on my way home. And I caught a glimpse of something back at Montsegur. Two odd, agitated creatures I could not make out in the dark. Badgers, I assumed."

She looked at me for another moment as if she expected some response to this. I made none, as I considered how short her time was and how urgently I must now attend to her. She turned and disappeared down the dark street.

# CHAPTER TWELVE

Manitou Point pier below the old Jesuit mission lay in a natural harbor deep enough to allow the *Seneca Princess* to dock alongside. It was nearly seven p.m. when the ship arrived, and the captain and pilot decided to lay at anchor overnight. Haldimand Bay below Fort Mackinac was full of craft that evening, busy ferrying the last visiting stragglers of the season across the straight to St. Ignace and their homes in the south and east. Captain Traynor told Set he was relieved to avoid the busy port for an all but abandoned one. Early the following morning, he told Set that he and Anatolia had four hours to conclude whatever business they had on the island before the ship continued north into Lake Michigan.

The day was clear and cold. Set helped Anatolia down the gangplank to the pier. She had been unwell that morning. Other members of the New Phrygians were stirring out of their cabins as Set guided the unsteady Anatolia across the Lake Shore Road toward an old stone stairway that wound up a steep hill, disappearing into a forest.

"Pretty steep climb," Set said. "Are you up to it?"

Anatolia nodded. "Slowly... slowly."

Beech, sugar maple, and white pine trees surrounded lichen-covered boulders and glades through which the stone stairway meandered. The maple leaves still left on the trees were flaming red and yellow in the autumn sunshine. After a few hundred-foot climb, the ground leveled considerably, and the stone stairway became a path of flagstones. In a clearing a few yards ahead of them, the remnants of an old stone mission and chapel were still visible in a mass of undergrowth. Just beyond was a brick and stone cottage, which still appeared to be inhabited.

"That must be it," Set said.

What had once been an apparently well-maintained garden was now overgrown with weeds and dying wildflowers. As Set and Anatolia approached a rotting, oaken front door, it opened. An emaciated man of indeterminate age stood in the doorway. He smiled briefly, revealing diseased gums and darkened teeth. He was nearly bald, and his arms bore the marks of numerous injections of a hypodermic syringe.

"My guests, at last," the man said. "I was hoping you would arrive today. We are on the edge here, the very edge, and I wish to be absolved of this responsibility before I go."

Set and Anatolia looked at each other briefly.

"I am Anatolia Montes..."

"Yes," the man interrupted. "You have been long-awaited, miss. I have reached the end without ever having understood my inherited duty. I hope you will be enlightened, and the cost to you will be nothing more than experience and insight. I am Lucien de Castres."

"I am Set Costigan." Set extended his hand reluctantly. Lucian did not take it. He turned and passed through a front room toward the rear of the cottage. Set and Anatolia followed. Lying on the floor of the front room on a filthy mattress in the shadows was another emaciated man with a vacant expression and a glassiness in his eyes that Set recognized as an opium-induced lethargy, which he had seen once through a window on a business trip to New York City. Lucien exited the cottage through a small rear door into an unkempt garden.

"Miss, please sit on this bench," he indicated a stone bench at the edge of an extinct flower bed. Anatolia sat. "I will need your help." He motioned for Set to follow him to a brick-and-stone shed at the far edge of the property.

Leaning against the door of the shed was a two-wheeled hand cart. Lucien removed this and unlocked the door with a large key hanging from his waist. He pushed the door open and pushed the hand cart inside. Set followed him.

There were no windows in the shed. It was dark and musty and cobwebbed. Sitting in the middle of the floor, which was no more than eight feet square, sat a large box that appeared to be made of oak and walnut. Lucien indicated for Set to take the hand cart. "Bring it outside," he said.

With some difficulty, Set pushed the platform of the cart under the box and backed it out of the shed. Lucien preceded him back to where Anatolia was sitting. Set placed the box on the flagstones in front of her. The lid was covered in dust. Lucien produced a small whisk broom and brushed the dust away. The top of the box was carved in odd symbols and robed figures who seemed to be engaged in some sort of ritual. Iron bands reinforced it around its sides and across the lid. Inlaid in ivory on a carved panel below the figures were the words *Legatòri Sagrat*. Below this, across the edge of the lid, were more words of inlaid ivory: *Es pas qu'un*. Just under these words was a row of small rectangular openings or slots of a shallow depth.

"What is this language?" Anatolia said.

"I don't know," Lucien answered. "This box came with Bastide and de Castres from France more than two centuries ago."

Set knelt next to the box and tried to open it. It was locked. "Do you have a key?" he said.

"No."

"We'll have to smash it open, then."

"No!" Lucien scowled. "It may not be forced open. When Bastide and de Castres left it in the care of Michel, my ancestor, they insisted that bad fortune would follow anyone who destroyed this box, or sacred vessel, as they called it. It has been unmolested for two centuries. It was blessed and sanctified. To make sure, a device was included which will destroy the contents herein unless the proper method is used."

"Yes, I sense that. I feel it. The box must not be destroyed," Anatolia said.

"Then I don't know how we will ever open it," Set shrugged.

"My father came to understand that there was evil agency at work here," Lucien continued. "When he realized that the Bastide alive then in your town of Ste. Odile was in fact the same one who escaped France with de Castres and joined the *voyageurs* to explore and look for refuge—as it turns out, in the French diocese of Quebec, down the Mississippi River—he knew there was profanity and sacrilege at work. When he received a letter from Bastide's manservant, the fellow Tertius, his suspicions were verified.

"Now you are here. I will leave no children to continue this duty of my family line. You must take this box away and absolve the de Castres of this once and for all."

"Yes... yes, we will," Anatolia said.

"Load it on the hand cart, young man, and take it to the pier. Leave the cart there. It will be returned to me. Now is the time of day my sickness overtakes me, and I must rest. Go now. I must rest."

# CHAPTER THIRTEEN

At first Moira thought the movement at the front door must be an animal, a raccoon or opossum which had wandered in looking for shelter or food. But she became less convinced of this the longer she listened. She heard what could have been a footstep, then another, and then the sound of a chair or table being pushed aside. Moira slipped off her shoes. She was grateful that the library floor was still covered in enormous Persian rugs. At the far end of the chamber, nearly invisible in the gloom, she could see a door ajar that appeared to lead to a small servant's staircase. She crept across the floor, wincing at every creak the old floorboards made.

Moira stopped at the foot of the small staircase. She wondered if it would be wise to go up the stairs. She knew of no other means of leaving the house other than the front door, and she could tell by the continuing small sounds she heard that the person or persons who had entered the house were still in the front entryway, blocking her escape. Surely soon they would decide to explore the library and find her.

She took a few tentative steps, and the stairs made no sound. She was certain she had not yet been heard by the intruders. In a few more steps she was at the landing. She heard several footsteps below that seemed to be going in the direction of the library door. She quickly climbed the next flight of stairs and found herself in a long, wide hallway. Near the top of the stairs was a small bedroom. She slipped into it and closed the door. She saw to her relief that the door could be locked by a latch from the inside.

Little of the remaining daylight entered the small room. There was a small iron bed, a wardrobe, a dresser with a Bible on it, a washstand, and a single chair. Moira listened at the door. She heard some movement in the library below, which then seemed to return to the entryway and then toward the rear of the house. Moira thought she would wait a while and then try to make her way back down the stairs and out the front door.

The bedroom in which she found herself was modest and neat, even though it was blanketed under twelve years' worth of settling dust. She reached for the Bible on the dresser and opened it. It was inscribed: *Dearest Tertius, from your friend LuHelen.*

"This was Tertius's room," Moira whispered.

She moved to the door of the room and put her ear against it. She could hear movement downstairs that seemed to be coming from two rooms at once. She heard cabinets and drawers being opened and rifled, then footsteps moving elsewhere and more rifling sounds.

"They are looking for something," Moira murmured to herself. She unlocked the door and stepped out into the dark hallway.

She could hear the movement downstairs better now.

"Where are the cellars?" a man's voice said. "I know much is stored below ground."

Moira knew the voice. It sounded like Jean-Joseph, the youngest of the many sons of the old drayman Aristide. Moira heard a mumbled response to Jean-Joseph's question, a voice she did not recognize.

Jean-Joseph was the only layabout Aristide had produced among his offspring. Trespassing on the property was strictly forbidden, and Moira did not want to be found out by the likes of Jean-Joseph or any of the criminal types with whom he associated. If they would harm her there, it might be years before she was found. She thought the men must have come to pillage anything of value that they could sell. But why, Moira wondered, had they waited so many years to do this?

She heard footsteps fading away into the distance and the creak of a door being opened. She stepped further out into the hallway. Her foot caught on the edge of the hallway runner, and she felt herself falling forward. She fell against the stairway newel post and caught herself on the banister before she made any sound. In catching herself, her hand had displaced the cap on the newel post, and it teetered precariously on the back of her hand. She righted herself and carefully stood. She was grateful the cap had not fallen and clattered to the floor. She grasped the cap and as she stood to position it back in its place, she noticed the newel post was hollow. Peering into the dark opening she could just make out that something was hidden inside it. She removed the object.

It was made mostly of wood, but also had bronze, silver, and ivory within it. It was about ten inches long and slender. The top of it was taken up with ivory tiles with grooves cut in their edges. There were three rows of these, and one of the tiles was missing. It appeared to be some sort of puzzle or child's game. But why was it hidden? Moira was surprised to realize that compulsion was overtaking her. She slipped the object into her jacket pocket.

Moira could hear the footsteps again. She could not quite tell if they were in the cellar or on the main floor. The main stairway was down the hallway, about seventy feet from where she stood. She decided to take her chances there and slip out the front door. As she crept quickly toward the stairway, she could hear movement in the shadows. There was a chittering sound, and something like hissing. Suddenly something appeared at the top of the stair. It was a black, slithering creature, moving in an odd, liquid way. It looked directly at Moira and chittered. She gasped and stopped in the shadow of a doorway. It could have been the same type of animal she had seen dead on the road earlier. She knew she had to go back down the servant stairs. There was no other way down.

Still in her stocking feet, Moira crept quickly but quietly down the stairs. There was still no sign that the intruders knew she was in the house. At the foot of the stairs, in the enormous entryway, she could hear voices coming from below, then footfalls on the cellar stairs. Moira slipped silently across the great room and out the front door. She ran across the damp, overgrown lawn and out the front gate into the gathering darkness.

# CHAPTER FOURTEEN

*Anno Domini 1348, December*

Those few nuns who chose to remain in the cloister of Perpetua north of the town are no more. A novice, a girl named Marthe LePelletier, native to Guémar and perhaps fourteen years of age, appeared at the North Gate this morning intending to request from the sheriff and mayor that a death cart be sent to the cloister to collect the bodies of the nuns, seven in number, now all dead.

Marthe appeared at the postern at daybreak. I had been keeping watch overnight outside Roquetaillade's house to see if Seraphica ventured out. I was walking home when I saw the postern, which had been carelessly left unlatched overnight, swing open and the dazed young woman step through. She seemed almost insensible, unsure of where she was or what she was about.

I approached her, but it was not before I was within arm's length that she looked at me.

"What is it, girl?" I asked. "Are you sick? In distress?"

"I must tell the sheriff... or the mayor... All the sisters at Perpetua's are dead. Plague victims. All dead now."

"You're freezing, child. My rooms are just down St. Engurrand's here. Let me feed you and warm you. No one is about yet. I will take you to the sheriff after you have eaten and warmed yourself."

"I don't think I have eaten in three or four days..."

"Come on, then." I put my arm around her. She pulled away.

"I have been tending the sick. I may have the contagion."

"I have greater fears in this world than that." I put my arm around her again and led her down the dark lane.

I had bread and boiled vegetables to give her. She warmed herself at my fire. She ate slowly and over the course of the next hour or so, told me her story.

"There are three other daughters in my family besides me. I am the youngest. My father had nothing more for a dowry after my sisters married, and since the pestilence, there were, at any rate, very few prospective husbands left alive in our town to match me with. So, my father decided to send me to the cloister. I had only been at Perpetua's two months when the Holy Father sent many of our sisters out into the world to comfort the sick. Eight of us were allowed to remain behind and honor our vows of silence and prayer.

"It was my duty at Perpetua's to help with the preparation of meals and to scrub the kitchen afterwards. These labors took most of every day. I felt unhappy and lost at first, but after a few weeks, I came to find some comfort in my duties and in the company of my sisters in Christ.

"We subsisted mostly on grains, vegetables, coarse bread, and water. Rarely did we have fish or meat. Early one morning after prayers a week and a half ago, there was a knock at the kitchen door. Sister Veronica is my superior. She opened the door to find a gamekeeper named Armand Pique, who was known to her, standing outside. He had caught three eels in the river overnight and wanted to give them to us so we would not feel forgotten by the town. He handed her his creel basket.

"Sister thanked him and brought the creel inside. She placed the fish on the preparation table, then returned Pique's creel to him. It was always Sister's task to do the main planning and devising of meals—the main course, I mean—so I swept the larder as she busied herself cleaning and gutting the eels.

"Our supper that evening was unusual. One may even call it elegant. But as the sisters left the table and went to Vespers, Sister Veronica stayed behind. She looked pale and was beginning to sweat. I approached her, but she waved me away, so I left her on her own.

"After prayers, I returned to the kitchen. Sister Veronica was collapsed on the floor under the great table. She was coughing and sweating in a profuse manner. I knelt at her side. There were spatters of blood on the front of her habit and a horrible odor enveloping her. At that moment, I knew the pestilence had entered the cloister of Perpetua.

"In moments of need and distress, our vow of silence may be broken. I ran back toward the dormitory calling to my sisters for help. Sister Lucy and Sister Claire ran to my aid, and the three of us helped Sister Veronica back to her cell. I sat with Sister for the next few hours.

"She seemed to be suffering greatly. She coughed and spat blood as she mumbled prayers on her cot, and the odor that proceeded from her body filled her small chamber and caused a great revulsion and sickness of stomach to come over me. Still, I sat with her. I brought her water, which she could not drink, and washed her brow every few minutes. All the other sisters, over the course of the night, came to the cell to pray over Veronica.

"'Her symptoms show the pestilence of the lungs,' Sister Heloise said, 'not the other, the slower-type plague... of bursting pustules and black blotches. This one is faster. Only prayer will save her now, Sisters!'

"After a few hours, I rose to wash Veronica's face and saw that she was not breathing. She was gone. I prayed over her and told the others. I covered her with a shroud. As I left Veronica's cell, I heard coughing next door. It was Claire. She was showing the symptoms now.

"Over the course of the next few days, each of my sisters in Christ, one by one, became ill. We saw no purpose in calling for a physician. The few physicians in the town are occupied beyond their ability to administer. And each of us knew the symptoms were but a prelude to death. Remaining unafflicted, I cared for my sisters as best I could. I washed their faces, sat with them, prayed with them, waiting for the signs to appear in me. But the signs did not appear."

Tears welled in Marthe's eyes. I put a blanket over her shoulders.

"I took little time for myself," she continued. "When I did, I asked God why I alone remained well. I considered that His intent was to have me comfort the others. I asked, in my prayers, if this was true. No answer came. No sign. I prayed that if the end came for me that God allay my suffering. I wept in terror, thinking how I would endure what I had seen my sisters suffer through. If I were to be taken at such a young age, I asked that it be quick and painless. But when I composed myself, I knew these requests were prideful and presumptuous. God would do with me what He will, and I must accept it. Whatever happened, I must accept that it was with purpose and according to His plan.

"The great quiet of our cloister, which had been such a comfort and blessing to all of us before the pestilence, transformed, it seemed, into a barrier, an adversarial wall of isolation, a curse, a monstrous blockade rather than a blessing, a borderland of death immuring us from life. The peaceful silence of our former hermitage was now somehow denser, deadly, and absolute.

"Sister Heloise died two evenings ago. Sister Monica died yesterday afternoon. I sat at her side, weeping and praying over her. I was truly alone now. All were dead but me, each body covered and silent on their cots. I sat in Monica's cell as the day faded away and evening came. I thought of Vespers, but I did not pray. I felt I was drowning in the silence, and I could not make myself move.

"As she died, Monica mumbled that her charge, the young nun Sister Clytie, imprisoned in her immurement cell against the hillside behind our cloister, was silent and possibly dead. She asked that I check on her and care for her as best I could if I heard signs of life. I had never asked about the immurement cell, and none of my sisters spoke of it. It was a forbidden subject. It had been Monica's duty to tend to the occupant, to bring her food and push it through the narrow oilette in the far wall, a duty she had not executed for two days, as her illness overtook her.

"As I covered Monica with a shroud, I realized how exhausted I was. I walked to the chapel and collapsed onto a pew. I was too distracted and weary to pray.

"I sat suddenly upright and realized I had been asleep. The moon was up and shining through the rosette above the altar. I stood. I knew it was time for me to leave Perpetua's. I walked slowly through the rooms toward the door at the rear of the kitchen. I doubted I would see these rooms again. At that moment, the strangest sensation came over me. It was a feeling of release and freedom. Disconnection, perhaps, from both life and death. My vows seemed meaningless and nonsensical—gibberish mumbled by rote, signifying no more than a child's rhyme. Why should I swear fealty to a god who could create a world such as this? How could his works denote goodness and therefore inspire devotion? My mind was in a frenzy. I did not know what I would do. Perhaps I would help at the hospital, or try to make my way, dangerous though the roads are these days, back home.

"I walked out into the moonlight toward the immurement cell against the hillside. I had never thought of approaching it before. It was beautiful in the silvery moonlight, belying its dreadful function. I made my way to the far side of the small building and found the oilette in the shadows.

"'Sister Clytie,' I called, 'Clytie! I am Sister Marthe. Are you there?' No answer. 'All are dead inside. Only I am left, and I am leaving here unless you need me...' I leaned into the oilette to peer into the darkness of the interior. A ghastly zephyr of corruption wafted against my face, an odor of undoubted death.

"I then walked into town."

Clearly exhausted, Marthe seemed to nearly collapse at finishing her story. I helped her lie on the floor in front of my fire. I covered her with blankets. She slept for many hours.

As the sun was setting, Marthe began to stir. She sat upright suddenly in fear and confusion.

"It's all right, child," I said, comforting her. "You are safe with me."

She recognized her surroundings and stood. She looked at me and was reassured. "We should go," she said. "The authorities must be notified. The cart must be sent to the convent."

"It will be done. The mayor's house is across the square. We will walk there now."

I wrapped her in several shawls and myself in my cloak and veil. As we made our way out into the lane in the gathering dusk, the sextons could be heard at some distance, calling, "Bring out your dead." The death cart was making its evening rounds.

We walked in silence toward the square. As we passed the North Gate, Marthe suddenly stopped. There was a faraway look in her eyes.

"Mother," she said, "I must go home. I will walk all night. I must go, for it is the end of the world. I must be with my people. Please tell the authorities what they need to know... please." She looked at me with terror and desperation in her eyes.

"Yes, child. Of course. All must do whatever brings the slightest comfort. Go, and may God be with you."

She ran across the flagstones toward the postern at the gate and was gone. I whispered a prayer for her. As I crossed the square toward the mayor's house and disappeared into the shadows, I saw another figure I had not noticed before also making for the postern. After a moment, I realized it was Seraphica. In a second, she was through the small gate and had closed it behind her.

# CHAPTER FIFTEEN

With the help of two crewmen, Set stowed the great box in the cabin he and Anatolia shared toward the stern of the *Seneca Princess*. Anatolia was exhausted by the morning's excursion, and as the ship pulled away from the dock to continue west and south into Lake Michigan, she lay down to rest.

Over the next few days, the *Seneca Princess* stopped at Manitowoc and Milwaukee to offload cargo and take on a few more passengers. On the evening of the ninth day of the voyage, it made port at Chicago.

Set made his way to a telegraph office near the pier and verified that the crates containing the furniture and other possessions of the New Phrygians had arrived in St. Louis by train three days earlier and should arrive at Ste. Odile later that day or the next.

The New Phrygians made their way wearily down the gangplank and off the ship. They followed Set to the head of the pier and gathered around him for their next instructions. The enormity of the city seemed to overwhelm them. Many stared awestruck at the towering gray buildings arising from the lakeshore, and many seemed oppressed and unsettled by the din of noise and activity all around them. Longshoremen removed larger items of luggage from below deck and loaded them onto a dray wagon to accompany the group to their lodgings for the night.

Set led the group across the quay toward the street and a waiting cable car. As they started to board at the front of the coach, the conductor said, "Watch your step. Colored section at the rear of the coach. Please move toward the rear."

Set stopped and held out his arms so no one else could step into the coach.

"Our group travels together..."

Anatolia recognized the anger in his voice. She gently lowered his arm.

"Think nothing of it," she said. "Expected. We are tired. We want no further delays in getting settled tonight." Set nodded reluctantly, moving into the coach; Anatolia and the rest of the group followed. When all were seated, the coach moved west on Grand Avenue, then north a few blocks on LaSalle Street. It stopped in front of a towering, grimy edifice called The Demarest Hotel.

Mrs. Heugyens with Susan, and Set and Anatolia, had private rooms. All the rest of the company shared six more rooms on the hotel's second floor.

At seven the next morning, the New Phrygians gathered in the hotel lobby. Once all were assembled and accounted for, they boarded another coach to take them to Canal Street station to board the PRR Line train to St. Louis.

Set and Anatolia sat near the front of the coach. Mrs. Heugyens and Susan sat halfway back, among the other congregants. Anatolia smiled to think that was one of the affectations the great lady employed to demonstrate—she did not elevate herself above the others. Or perhaps it wasn't an affectation. She knew Mrs. Heugyens well enough now to realize she truly had an artless, humble nature, and felt blessed to have the resources to animate and sustain the community of New Phrygians.

The train departed the station nearly on time and made its way past a crush of cold, gritty, early morning activity as the city and its sprawling array of commerce came to life.

In forty minutes or so, the train was clear of the city limits and soon after that, into open countryside.

"Eight or ten hours to St. Louis," Set smiled at Anatolia, "Then on south to Ste. Odile. We should be there by early tomorrow. We catch the St. Louis and Iron Mountain train at six tonight. Hopefully, there won't be any..."

"Not much longer. Not much longer," Anatolia interrupted.

"I know you are exhausted. You only must hold on a little longer."

"Yes. I can do it. I am almost frightened to return there. Back to that dark little town. I never thought I would. I have spent twelve years trying to wipe it from my memory. I don't know what to make of it all. I don't know how I feel."

"Try to rest. Best thing for you. Once we are there and settled..."

Anatolia closed her eyes and rested her head against the back of her seat.

"Rest," Set continued. "I need to speak to Mrs. Heugyens for a moment. He stood and moved toward the rear of the coach. In a few seconds, Anatolia felt someone sit in the seat next to her. It was Susan. She smiled at Anatolia and touched her hand.

"We switch de place, Set an' me."

"Yes. He said he had business to discuss."

"I'm wantin' talk to oonah anyways, Miss 'Tolia."

Anatolia opened her eyes fully and sat up. She was accustomed to the congregants coming to her for dream interpretations or predictions. "I will help in any way I can. These days though, I don't think..."

"Miss 'Tolia, 'ere oonah well?"

"I've seen better days," she smiled slightly.

"In my islan' back home, Monford Islan',' 'cross from Hilton Head, it was a wise woman who read de signs. She teach me a little. I learn a little." Susan leaned toward Anatolia and inhaled a deep breath through her nose. "She teach me to know de look and smell. De look and smell oonah has."

"What look and smell, Susan?"

"Of de woman carries de chile. Of de woman is pregnant."

# CHAPTER SIXTEEN

The rectory appeared empty as Moira walked past it in the dark. Perhaps the workmen had finished removing all the contents that day. She would check on it in the morning as she had promised Vannier. She was exhausted now and needed to rest.

When she arrived back at Tranquille House, Moira found Mrs. Zell wrapped in a shawl waiting for her on the porch. Mrs. Zell showed a small smile of relief when she saw her lodger approaching. She placed her teacup on a nearby table and stood.

"Miss Parnell, I was *worried* about you. It's so *late*!"

"I am sorry, Mrs. Zell. I... took a long walk today. Longer than I intended in time, if not distance."

"Would you like a cup of *tea*, my dear? And there is cake if you are *hungry*."

"It sounds wonderful." Moira sat on one of the wicker chairs on the porch, and Mrs. Zell disappeared into the house. Moira was flushed and warm from her long walk, but the longer she sat, the more she felt it was almost too chilly to sit outside without her mittens and cold weather coat. In a few minutes, Mrs. Zell returned with a steaming cup of tea and a slice of yellow cake with white icing. "A bit cold to be sitting out here this evening," Moira said.

"I was *concerned*," Mrs. Zell replied. "Not like you to be out this late *alone*. I knew Father Vannier was leaving this morning."

"Yes, he left. I occupied my day with a long walk."

"Oh?"

"Yes. I walked up to Jardin Noir today."

"You *didn't*! Oh, my dear, you didn't go up there *alone*?"

"Yes. I have wanted to see it for years. My curiosity finally got the best of me."

Mrs. Zell was speechless for a moment.

"It's a cursed place," she said. "Morisot filed *papers* before he left. It remains restricted. *Trespassing* is strictly forbidden. And... horrible things happened there. It's surely haunted. I shudder to *think* you went up there alone."

"It looks the part. I have never seen such a place before."

"You didn't go inside?"

"I did. I expected it to be locked up, but the front door was ajar."

The sound of horse hooves on pavement gradually arose above the other night sounds. Moira glanced toward the street as a maroon Rockaway carriage drove slowly by. In the darkness, she could not clearly see the driver. Mrs. Zell looked disapprovingly at Moira.

"Curiosity *killed* the cat, Miss Moira!" she said. "Where is your common *sense*?"

"I was not the only curious one. Someone else was there. Two men, I think. I got away before they saw me. I didn't see them, but I heard their voices. One sounded like Jean-Joseph, Aristide's son."

"Worthless layabout!" Mrs. Zell scoffed.

"But the other voice I did not recognize."

"We know the *company* Jean-Joseph keeps."

Moira pulled her jacket more tightly around herself and sipped her tea. "The front door must have been ajar for a while. Wild animals have gotten in the house. I saw something in the hallway. Vicious thing. I couldn't tell what it was."

Mrs. Zell shuddered.

"All the loss and *death* we have had in Ste. Odile, all coming from that old *place*!" she said. "Please promise me you will stay *away* from there! The town has all but *forgotten* about Jardin Noir, and that's for the best."

"The place is... incredible. I have seen nothing like it outside of a great museum. I can't believe it sat unmolested all these years. It's a treasure-trove..."

"No one knows what's there, nor *wants* to know!" Mrs. Zell scolded.

Moira's excitement grew as Mrs. Zell's agitation intensified. "It's a great collection. It must be preserved and protected, not left to molder in that decaying old house!"

Mrs. Zell sighed in exasperation. "If you could only have *seen* what it was like when Miss Perdita came," she said. "Perdita, Solana, Marie Chardin, and so many others... all drawn into him, *irresistibly*. His nature, his possessions, his *allure* to those hungry to be heard and respected. They say he is dead..."

"I am so grateful for your concerns, Mrs. Zell. No one since Perdita has cared for my wellbeing as much as you have." As she leaned forward to touch the old woman's arm, the object she had found at Jardin Noir fell out of her jacket pocket and onto the porch floor. Moira picked it up. "I found this in the great house," she said. "What do you make of it?"

"It's a child's toy. I have seen similar things in the German-settled *villages* north of here. Teaches children their *alphabet* and numbers. Just something made by *Germans*."

"Yes, that's what I thought, too. Odd to find such a thing at Jardin Noir."

"Tertius had nieces and nephews back on his home *island*. Haiti."

"I am exhausted." Moira stood. "I must check over the rectory and school grounds tomorrow. Anatolia and her entourage will be here in a few days, and all must be ready for them."

"Yes. I heard the crates of their furniture and belongings started *arriving* today."

"Good night, Mrs. Zell."

# CHAPTER SEVENTEEN

*Anno Domini 1348, December*

I gave Seraphica enough time to make her way through the gate and onto the road before I followed her. Since the roads are so empty and deserted now, I wanted to be far enough behind her that I would not draw her attention. The moon was rising and bright enough that I cast a shadow on the ground. When I saw that she was headed for the south road, I held back even further and kept to the hedgerows and dormant grape vineyards, letting her precede me by a full arpent or more.

The evening was beautiful. The winter stars were scattered across a clear, cold sky and the moon bathed the quiet and mystical countryside in silvery light. All was still and perfect. How little the travails and horrors of human life impress or affect Nature. Beauty, rebirth, balance—all continue in forest, stream, field, or vast ocean, no matter the suffering and evil humans bring upon themselves. And so it will be, long after the final judgment, when we are wiped away from the face of the earth to despoil this Eden no more.

Just then I heard the snort of an ox and the creak of cart wheels ahead of me. I could just make out the death cart passing Seraphica, returning from the burial pit. I remembered I had not yet conveyed Marthe's message to the authorities about the deaths at Ste. Perpetua's. I stopped in the road and waited for the cart to approach me.

"Antoine... Antoine d'Estang!" I said in a high whisper.

"Yes, who is it? Keep your distance... Ah, it's you, Mother."

"Yes. I have more sorry news for you."

"Nothing else these days."

"A young nun left Riquewihr not a half hour ago. From Perpetua's. They are all dead who stayed behind at the cloister."

"How many?"

"Seven or eight."

"That will fit. One trip. I will collect them in the morning then..."

He continued past me, never slowing, moving away toward the town. Soon I heard him whistling "The Mordant Trollop" as he walked, and I thought how one must accustom oneself to any grim duty, no matter how onerous, or go mad.

When I looked ahead again, I saw Seraphica had stopped on the road and turned toward me. She must have heard Antoine's voice. I was confident it was too dark for her to tell who I was. In a moment, she continued on her way.

As I feared, she turned onto the Zellenberg road. In another arpent, she had reached the stone house now occupied by Orien Bastide. A great sense of dread passed through my body. I sat on the ground behind a low-growing chestnut tree to watch the house. I thought how great must be the emptiness and need for acknowledgment in the souls of these young women, stretched across the centuries, to ignore my warnings and the evidence of their own experience, and put themselves under the influence of the demon Bastide. It has always been so. My greatest hope is that it will change in the future or that I will discover a way to destroy him.

I watched the house for an hour or more. After a time, I heard the sound of another oxcart coming from the direction of Zellenberg. In the gloom, I could see the cart coming down the hill. Two men sat atop it. They stopped the cart in front of Bastide's home.

A tall, gaunt figure opened the door. It was Bastide. I heard him greet the men. The phrase he spoke sounded something like *Te`n esperavi*. I did not recognize the words. A few seconds later, Seraphica emerged from the house. She said something to Bastide, wrapped her shawl around herself, and walked to the road, back in the direction of the town. The visitors stood before the open door, watching Seraphica depart. I felt she was walking away from danger, so I did not follow her. I continued to watch the men at the door.

When Seraphica was out of sight, the two men moved to the cart and dragged out of it a large wooden box. With much difficulty, they carried it into Bastide's house. The door closed. After a few minutes, I walked across the road to the north wall of the house. There was a single window just above eye level. Standing on a few faggots of kindling, I could just see inside.

The interior of the house was a confusion of beakers and jars, clumps of dried herbs hanging from the ceiling, animal bones, books, papers, and writing instruments. The two visitors were standing in my field of vision, blocking my view of Bastide. I could see that he was kneeling on the floor before the great box.

*"Vòli saber ço qu'es dins."* He said. Then he continued, "I must know what is inside. The box was made and blessed by *perfecti* and may not be destroyed under penalty of eternal separation from the light. There must be a key to opening it, a trick. *I must know.*"

In that instant, I understood. It was a mystery I did not learn from my own teacher, which has caused me to pursue this evil across the centuries. Some key to the secret of the destruction of Balphoroth, and Bastide himself, must lay hidden in that box.

# CHAPTER EIGHTEEN

Four draymen and their wagons were waiting under the gas lamps in the dark at the train station at Belgique. The New Phrygians stepped down onto the platform, haggard and exhausted but joyous at having nearly ended their journey.

Moira had sat on a horse rented from the livery, waiting for the train's arrival for more than an hour. When she recognized Anatolia stepping onto the platform, she slid off the saddle and ran to her.

"Anatolia, it's you! My God, look at you! What a young woman you have become!" The two embraced. There were tears in Anatolia's eyes.

"Oh, Miss Moira, it is so good to see you again!" she said. "Seeing you reminds me of Perdita and the sisters, and... so many memories!"

The New Phrygians gathered around the two women and Anatolia introduced each of them to Moira in turn, starting with Set and Mrs. Heugyens.

The draymen loaded two of the wagons with the luggage and possessions of the New Phrygians. The community climbed into the other two wagons as their transport to Ste. Odile. Moira remounted her mare and led the way north on the Belgique Road. After a half mile, she dropped back to ride alongside the first wagon, carrying Anatolia, Set, and Mrs. Heugyens.

"The large crates arrived a few days ago," Moira said. "They were stored in the old dining hall at the school. Everything is out of the rectory and convent. Plenty of room for all of you."

"It's so exciting to begin this new life!" Mrs. Heugyens said. "All of us together communally! Together!" She shivered as a cold gust blew in from the river, and she seemed out of breath.

"It isn't too much farther," Moira said. "You will soon be situated in your new homes."

"I'm going to have pets... at last," Mrs. Heugyens continued. "I have always wanted pets but never had them... for some reason. This is my new home, and I will have cats and a big dog, I think! Yes! An enormous dog!"

"I'm sure I can help you with that," Moira said.

The wagons carrying the luggage drove to the old school building and unloaded. The wagons carrying the New Phrygians drove to Tranquille House. Mrs. Zell had offered to house the group in her many vacant rooms and in the apartment above her carriage house until they were ready to move into their new homes.

Mrs. Zell greeted Anatolia as warmly as Moira had. Anatolia was surprised at the strength of the elderly woman's embrace.

"What a *beauty* you have become!" Mrs. Zell said.

"It is so wonderful to see you, Mrs. Zell. I never thought I would set foot in Ste. Odile again!"

"I hope it isn't a *mistake* that you have done so, child."

"I want to see Miss Perdita's grave. Maybe tomorrow. I want to see it and pay my respects."

Moira embraced the two of them.

"Are you well, Anatolia? You look very tired," she said.

"I am. Very tired. If I could rest..."

Moira showed Anatolia and Set to a room just at the top of the stairs. They were joined by Mrs. Heugyens and Susan, and Edmontia Lewis, who were to share the room with them. Set and Anatolia prepared for bed once in the room. Their three room companions left their bags on their beds and went back downstairs for tea.

Once in her nightgown, Anatolia collapsed into the brass bed she was to share with Set. He pulled the blanket up to her shoulders and noted how pale she looked. He regretted that he had brought her with him on the Great Lakes route on their journey. It had taken so much out of her. He should have insisted that she and all the New Phrygians come by rail, and he make the trip north alone.

As he took off his collar and shirt, he heard Anatolia groan.

"Set, I am sick. Very sick!" she whispered.

He ran to her side. There was blood at the corner of her mouth and her eyes were glassy. Her face was warm, and she seemed paler than before. Set ran to the top of the stairs outside the room.

"Mrs. Zell! Miss Parnell! We need a doctor. Anatolia is ill!"

The two women hurried up the stairs, followed by the entire company of New Phrygians. Anatolia was writhing in pain, holding her lower stomach. Mrs. Zell and Moira rushed to the bedside. The New Phrygians waited at the doorway, watching their seer with concern and terror.

"Oh dear," Mrs. Zell said. "I don't like the look of *this*."

"I'll get Dr. Treves," Moira said.

"Bah! He's a quack, a *vivisectionist!*" Mrs. Zell scoffed.

"But only two houses away!" Moira hurried out of the room.

Set sat at Anatolia's bedside and dabbed at her face with a damp cloth. After a few minutes, her pain seemed to subside, and she fell asleep.

"She rest some," Susan Henry said from the doorway. There was a concerned look on Susan's face as she moved through the crowd back into the hallway. The front door was heard to open and close. Moira and Dr. Treves were hurrying up the stairs.

Treves placed his leather bag on the floor near the bed and sat next to Anatolia.

"Thank you for coming so quickly, Doctor," Set said. "I am so worried about her."

"Let's see what we're about here," Treves said. His gray hair was disheveled and his face red from the cold. He touched Anatolia's face and took her pulse.

"Tell me Treves," Mrs. Zell said, "do you *remember* how to treat women's complaints? Since you have spent *so* much time cutting up *helpless* animals?"

"It hasn't been that long ago I was in practice," Treves said, never looking at her. He glanced at Set reassuringly. "I am more of a theoretician now, but I still know my business here."

Treves pressed on Anatolia's stomach. She stirred a little. Treves stood.

"If you please, everyone out of the room," he said. "I need to examine her thoroughly."

The New Phrygians filed slowly back down the stairs to the front parlor. Set closed the bedroom door as he stepped out into the hallway. Moira and Mrs. Heugyens waited with him outside the door.

"What do you think is happening to her?" Set asked.

"It could be nothing more than exhaustion or female hysteria," Mrs. Heugyens said.

"Shouldn't jump to conclusions," Moira said. "Could be something very simple. No sense speculating and worrying ourselves to death. We'll see what the doctor says."

Set paced the hallway for another ten minutes. Dr. Treves opened the bedroom door, drying his hands on a towel.

"I gave her a sedative," Treves said. "She is exhausted and needs the rest." He turned to Set. "She is pregnant, young man. You are her... husband, I assume? Or her...?"

"Yes, I am." Set's face was a mix of emotions and confusion. "I am. Will she be all right?"

"It's like nothing I have seen. Not for many years. She will have a hard time of it, I'm afraid."

"Thank you for coming, Doctor," Moira said. A dark expression had come over her face. She turned suddenly and ran down the stairs and out the front door, past the puzzled New Phrygians who were waiting for news.

Moira hurried toward Mal Ardents Street and turned east toward the river. She ran to the levee and out onto the narrow pier where most steamboats that still stopped at Ste. Odile unloaded. At the end, some sixty feet out on the dark river, she turned and looked toward the northwest. From that vantage point, she could clearly see the spectral prominence dominating the north end of town and the black pile of Jardin Noir sitting atop it. The silhouette of towers and spires pierced the indigo of the night sky. And high on what must have been an upper floor, dim lights shown through three large windows.

# CHAPTER NINETEEN

*Anno Domini 1348, December*

I had to discover what was in that large box. I crept back to my hiding place across the road and hid myself in the shrubbery, pondering what to do. I heard movement and voices coming from Bastide's house. I looked toward the sound and saw the two visitors, the men from the oxcart, running in my direction. I had no chance of escaping them, but I stood and ran as best I could down to the road and toward Riquewihr.

They were upon me in a moment and began raining punches and blows upon my face and head. I felt the bones of my cheek and jaw breaking as I fell insensible to the ground, and all was darkness.

I awoke to a mixture of sensations. I could tell my feet were elevated and my head was in some sort of depression in the ground. My face hurt, and my left eye was swollen nearly shut. I could see a dim light and thought it must be dawn. All was damp and cold, but I noticed that two spots on my arms exposed to the air felt like they were burning. I struggled to sit up. I braced my right hand against something that seemed somewhat rigid. As I braced against it, the surface of the object immediately cracked and collapsed, and my hand pushed through to a damp and glutinous interior as a miasma of putrescence billowed out from the opening. I looked to my right and strained to focus my eyes. My hand had pushed through the ribcage of a corpse partially wrapped in a winding sheet.

I sat up in horror. Pain enveloped nearly my entire body. I gasped short, desperate breaths as I struggled to regain my faculties and get to my feet. I found myself at the bottom of an escarpment of corpses all cascaded down from the lip of a deep pit. Bastide's men had taken me for dead and thrown me into the mass grave of the victims of the pestilence.

My short breaths made me feel I would faint. I closed my eyes and tried to calm myself. I looked at the burning spots on my arms and saw it was quicklime, thrown into the pit to absorb the smell of death. The stench was still within the pit, though—burst pustules and rot. I felt my gorge rise, and lightheadedness again swept over me.

The edge of the pit was about as high as the highest level I could reach with my arms extended. The only means of egress was to climb over the bodies.

I slowly began my climb. At each step, I looked for spots where I could secure my foot between the bodies. In most places, the corpses were two and three deep, and I had no choice but to step on them. Again and again, I would step down onto an arm or a leg, and my foot would slide off as it tore away rotting skin from the gray, odious flesh underneath. The odor was nearly more than I could endure.

My face and body throbbed in pain, and my vision was, from moment to moment, either very blurred or clear enough to find my way. An unwrapping corpse sat atop the other dead against the pit wall. I braced myself to step on his shoulder, which I felt would provide enough elevation for me to climb out. I could see a beech sapling just above the rim of the pit. It seemed close enough for me to reach if I could just climb up.

I put my right foot unsteadily on the left shoulder of the carcass. I threw myself upward and reached for the sapling. The clavicle and shoulder of the body gave way, and my foot penetrated the thorax. I had managed to grab the sapling and hold on. I pulled myself painfully out of the pit.

I lay on the ground next to the road for many minutes, weeping uncontrollably. The dawn sky was clear and clean, and a stork flew over me in the direction of Zellenberg. There was frost on the ground, and I knew Antoine would appear soon with his cart.

Eventually I calmed myself and managed to get to my feet. I began to walk slowly back toward Riquewihr.

Luckily, I encountered no one on the road. I made my way through the gate and back to my rooms without being seen. The odor of the dead was upon me, and I wanted to clean myself. I stoked up my fire and, item by item, stripped off my clothes and burned everything. I had clean water in my basin. I scrubbed my skin carefully and dried it.

As I stood naked in the firelight, I thought of the rituals of Circe that had brought me to the life I have lived for these centuries. I did not know, nor could I divine from evidence, whether Bastide knows if I, whom he knew as Scribonia of old, still exist. His men could have heard me and considered me nothing more than a peasant spying on them. It is by no means certain that Bastide knows of me or of my mission against him. Yet though I cannot prove it, I think he *must* know.

I made a poultice of mallow leaves steeped in hot water to reduce the swelling on my face. I could tell my jaw was fractured if not completely broken, as was my left cheekbone. After applying the poultice, I wrapped a long strip of linen under my jaw and around the top and back of my head and tied it firmly to provide protection and support.

I was exhausted. I lay in my bed, and after some time of seeing images of corrupted, bloated carcasses in my mind, I fell into a deep and thankfully dreamless sleep.

The sun was high when I slowly ascended from my deep sleep to the sound of frantic pounding on my door.

"Mother! Mother, are you here? It is I... Seraphica!"

I wrapped myself in a sheet and hurried down the stairs. Seraphica was shocked by my appearance.

"Come in, girl... come in. What is it?" I said the words as best I could through the linen.

She stepped inside. She was speechless for a moment.

"My father," she said. "You know him. I know you spoke to him... about me."

"Yes, yes, I did."

"I must know... you must be involved in this somehow, or did you see it coming? He is dead! My father was murdered in our house last night!"

# CHAPTER TWENTY

The morning after their arrival was one of activity and confusion for the New Phrygians. The men first moved Mrs. Heugyens's furniture into the rectory, which took half the day. The convent had ten larger bedrooms that were assigned to families, and the smaller rooms in the old dormitory were given to couples with no children and to single people.

Set looked pale and distracted. He had sat with Anatolia all night, and when she fell asleep late in the morning, he came to the dormitory to see if he could help. Moira had been watching for him to appear on Constantinople Street. She intercepted him near the front gate.

"Come with me a moment," she said, taking his arm. "There are things we must discuss immediately." She guided him along the avenue of cypresses and into the old chapel where they could speak privately.

"I'm not myself today," he said as he sat in the rear pew. Moira stood facing him.

"I am sure you are confused and exhausted," she said.

"Yes... yes. I don't understand what is happening to Anatolia."

"I think perhaps you don't *believe* what is happening to her. She has told you of all that went on here twelve years ago. I am afraid it is happening again. You understand it."

"So, it must be true. Bastide is still alive. I have always tried to believe her, but I hoped she was under some sort of delusion about the night she was attacked, that it was an intruder, a maniac. I have done my best to believe her because she has such a gift of divination. But I thought— I *hoped*—this was one thing she was wrong about. Or at least that she would eventually let it go. How could anyone live for centuries? M'daid... my father used to frighten us with talk of demons and devils. I didn't want any of that to be true. I refused to believe it because *he* believed it. To me it was the superstition of a stupid man." He sat with his head in his hands for a few moments. "I had to go up to Mackinac because I had a letter from that fellow Tertius. He wanted me to see a man named de Castres. Tertius also said Bastide is alive. I just thought it was some delusion the whole town shared, like witch mania... but it isn't."

"You have supported Anatolia through everything."

"Yes, and I never betrayed any doubt about anything she said, even if I felt it."

Moira sat in the pew in front of Set and turned to face him.

"You said Tertius sent you to see a man named de Castres?"

"Yes."

"A de Castres helped found this town. Why did you have to see him?"

"He had an old box or chest he wanted us to take away. Something under the care of his family for centuries."

Moira looked at him with an expression of both excitement and terror.

"The chest? Do you have it?"

"Yes. We have it in our room at the convent."

"We have to see what is inside."

"It's impossible to open. Anatolia refuses to destroy it. She says great calamity will happen if we do."

Moira stood and put her hand on Set's shoulder. "I realized last night that someone is living in Jardin Noir again."

Set frowned at Moira for a moment.

"Could be squatters," he said. "It could be anyone."

"Yes, it could be. Few people in town will dare go near it. In fact, *no one*, according to Mrs. Zell. It's supposed to be locked up and secure, yet I got inside a few days ago, and I wasn't alone. Two men came in after me, but I got out before they saw me. With all that has happened to Anatolia and with the New Phrygians coming here, I am certain Bastide is back. Anatolia is in the gravest danger. And Bastide will want that chest."

"I'll go up there and see," Set stood. His face hardened. "He won't hurt her again. If he's there, I'll end all this. I'll kill him!"

"We must plan what to do. We mustn't act too hastily." Moira's face went blank. She sat on the pew again.

"What is it, Miss Moira?" Set asked. "Are you all right?"

"I am not sure." She had the look of someone who has just understood some truth and is shattered by the revelation. "When Lester McReady was clearing out the rectory and convent, he found a gold coin, which he gave to me. When I went to Jardin Noir, I saw a creature, a vile, fluid thing. I refused to recognize it at the time. Refused to consider the possibility. But it must have been *Le Vorace*. They are the spawn of the incubus. They are seen by those women who have come into Bastide's awareness. He has found me, too. I am also in danger."

"All the more reason to end him!" Set said.

"Not yet. There is a woman, LuHelen Dufor. I must find her first. She is in touch with Tertius. And Tertius has the key to all of this."

# CHAPTER TWENTY-ONE

*Anno Domini, 1348, December*

I quickly dressed and veiled myself, then hurried with Seraphica back to her house. By chance, the Royal Coroner had spent the night in Riquewihr, having come to the district to certify a murder and a suicide. The torrent of plague deaths had benumbed royal officials, but in violent or illicit death, the crown may still profit.

Seraphica led me up a narrow stairway into her bedchamber. Roquetaillade lay dead before the hearth, his throat ripped away. Blood was spread across the floor and splattered on the stonework of the fireplace. The Sheriff was there, as was a small, prim man, well-fed and fastidious, whom I recognized as Armand the Coroner. An older woman I took to be Seraphica's mother wept uncontrollably nearby, and two servant women moved in and out of the room, seeming unsure of how to occupy themselves in the presence of such tragedy.

Armand nodded sympathetically to Seraphica. "My deepest sympathies, young woman," he said, smiling slightly.

"Why are you still here?" Seraphica said. "Why is my father still here? We can't continue to see him like this. Why haven't you taken him away yet?"

"Miss," Armand said. His tone was practiced and artful. "Miss, I have a very serious determination to make. The Crown has interests in these cases. If this death be the result of suicide, then this estate is forfeit to the crown in that the king has lost a taxpayer. If this death be done by murder, then arrangements must be made to find the culprit, bring him to justice, and *his* estate be forfeit for having taken from the king a taxpayer."

"Suicide?" Seraphica buried her face in her hands in exasperation. "How may a suicide rip out his own throat?"

"Yes," Armand nodded. "That is the conclusion I have reached."

"I would agree," the Sheriff added. "Suicide is unlikely here."

"But I would ask you, miss," Armand continued, "how your father came to be in your bedchamber last night."

I feared that the question would stoke Seraphica's rage, but she answered calmly.

"I was having a nightmare. A terrifying nightmare. I dreamt a demon or spirit had pinioned me in my bed and that it meant to crush and suffocate me. I cried out. I remember my father opening my door, and then I lost consciousness. When I awoke, I found him as he is now."

"A spirit?" Armand repeated. "A spirit or demon did murder, you say. You give me a supernatural explanation when a plainer and simpler one is at hand. You could have done this."

Seraphica was speechless for a moment.

"*I* could have done it?"

"Your father entered your room," Armand continued. "Perhaps he was in the habit of entering your room? Perhaps you could take no more..."

"It's a hideous suggestion!" Seraphica screamed. "And not true."

"I care less about what family secrets you have to keep than I do about the king being denied his fair levies from his subjects. That is my true concern. I must determine who it is that owes the crown for this great crime."

"What of the bruises on my wrists and arms?" Seraphica protested.

"You could have caused those."

"Seen it before," the Sheriff agreed.

"Or your father could have caused them," Armand continued.

"No," I interrupted. "This girl has done no such thing. She was attacked by an individual known to me, and her father was killed when he came to her aid."

"Who are you, old woman?" Armand asked.

"Euphrosine the wise woman," the Sheriff said. 'The Mother of Centuries,' so called."

I removed my veil. "His name is Orien Bastide. He has taken possession of the home of Theophraste Sophier, lately killed by the pestilence. It sits at the juncture of the Zellenberg road."

"Bastide?" Armand repeated.

"I have followed him over many years," I said. "It is my belief he has committed many such crimes in France and across Europe."

"For some time, Euphrosine has been warning me against Bastide," Seraphica interrupted. "I reject her accusations. I do not know Bastide to be such a man as she describes."

"Have you not reported your suspicions to authority?" Armand looked at me.

"Many times. I am either not taken seriously, or..."

"Certainly, this man bears meeting and talking to," Armand interrupted. He looked at the sheriff. "Bring two armed men and meet me in the square immediately. We will find this person. Miss Seraphica, you must stay within the town walls until I contact you again. I will arrange to have the body removed within the hour."

Armand and the sheriff left quickly. I had meant to question the girl's mother and servants about anything they might have seen or heard of this crime but realized nothing would be gained from this, and the household was too distraught.

"I only want to protect you." I tried to embrace Seraphica, but she moved away from me.

Still in much pain from my assault, I walked home and tried to rest after applying another poultice to my face. I was awakened again by pounding on my door some hours later. It was Celeste, one of Seraphica's servants.

"Miss Seraphica sent me to tell you, Mother," she said, "that the officials could not find Bastide. His house is empty. He is gone."

# CHAPTER TWENTY-TWO

Mrs. Zell was slow getting to the door. She was surprised to see a familiar face when she opened it, though one she could not immediately identify. It was a portly, short black woman bundled up in a red winter coat and scarf.

"Mrs. Zell, do you remember me?" the woman said. "I am LuHelen... Dufor. It's been so many years!"

Mrs. Zell's face brightened, and she embraced LuHelen.

"Oh, *goodness*, LuHelen, of course, it's *you*! All bundled up like that, I didn't *recognize* you."

"I am stouter now than I was then. All those years ago."

"Miss Parnell mentioned she *thought* she saw you recently at your father's old cottage, but she couldn't be *sure*."

"Yes, it was me." LuHelen stepped inside and closed the door. She removed her coat, and Mrs. Zell hung it on the pier mirror. "I had been reclaiming Papa's old things."

Mrs. Zell led LuHelen into the parlor.

"I'll call Miss Parnell *down*," Mrs. Zell said. "She wants to see you. I'll make *tea*!"

LuHelen sat in a large chair near the fire. She heard Mrs. Zell calling up the stairs, and in another minute, Moira hurried into the parlor. LuHelen stood.

"LuHelen, Miss Dufor!" Moira extended her hand. "I didn't know you well when I first came here. Just by sight."

"No. I worked for Mrs. Morisot. I left town when she died."

"Well, I am glad to see you again. I wanted to talk to you... about Tertius."

"Yes. I've come here on his behalf."

The two women sat as Mrs. Zell entered the room with a tray of cakes, cups, and a steaming teapot.

"Luckily the *kettle* was on when you came to the *door*, LuHelen," Mrs. Zell said.

"Yes, Tertius sent me," LuHelen continued. "It's sad I am to report, though, that Tertius has died."

"Oh... I am so sorry to hear it," Moira said.

"Yes. Three days ago. I was raised in the Mingo Swamp. That's where I have been caring for him."

"Oh *dear*," Mrs. Zell said.

"That terrible night," LuHelen went on, "I followed Mrs. Morisot here. When I saw that the house was afire, I ran into the back to see if anyone was left inside. I got upstairs and saw that Mrs. Morisot was dead. I saw Tertius through the flames. I thought he was dead, too. Then I heard him groan, and I saw his arm move. I managed to get to him and drag him out the back. A few of the crowd watching the blaze helped me get him to Dr. Treves.

"He nearly died that night. I had always admired him from a distance, though I knew he had never noticed me. His injury was grave. Dr. Treves kept him in his clinic, secretly, at my request, for two days. By then, I had found a governess cart to rent. It was all I could afford. Aristide sent his youngest son with us to return the cart. I made Tertius as comfortable as I could on the floor, in such a small space, and headed south toward Mingo."

"Oh goodness, that must have been an *ordeal*!" Mrs. Zell said.

"Yes," LuHelen continued. "But I thought it was necessary to get him away from Ste. Odile and the life he had with Bastide. I felt he could no longer be a part of it. I wanted the town to forget about him. My aunt was still alive then and living in my family's old cabin. I took him there, to our old home at the swamp's edge.

'Tertius was never really well again. He had much damage to his liver and kidneys. He lost the ability to walk three years ago and has been an invalid ever since. He died early this month, a year and a day since my aunt passed."

"Oh no..." Moira said.

"Yes," LuHelen said. "He was always filled with regret about standing by while Bastide committed his crimes. He made what he came to consider small efforts to warn or dissuade young women who came under the influence. His family was desperately poor back in Haiti and dependent on him. He did not want to risk his position, for the cost was great. He was especially worried about the child, Anatolia. I got word she was coming here."

"Yes," Moira said. "She and a group of followers have just recently arrived."

"But she is very *ill* just now." Mrs. Zell refilled LuHelen's teacup.

"Yes," Moira continued. "It may be too late for Anatolia."

"Oh Lord, I hope not!" LuHelen said. "I traveled to New York with messages for Set, the young man. Messages from Tertius with secret information."

"What secret information, LuHelen?" Moira asked.

"Did Anatolia and her group bring with them a large chest or box?"

"Yes."

"Tertius told me if the box was in their possession, to give them this." LuHelen reached into her small handbag and produced a wide gold bracelet. She gave it to Moira.

The bracelet was made for a small wrist, though it was substantial in its width and weight. On one side, it carried an image of a dove taking flight. On the opposite side was the image of a robed figure with arms extended. From the right hand arose another dove, and in the left, the figure held a long object of some sort that appeared to have an irregular bottom edge and a segmented top edge. To the left of this figure was a flame that was consuming a large book. The sides of the bracelet were banded in a line of indecipherable words that seemed to form one continuous phrase. On the inside of the band was engraved the French phrase: *Il n'est que la progeniture d'un monde maléfique.*

Moira studied the wording for a few moments.

"My French is lacking these days," she said. "I think it says, 'He is but the issue... or offspring... of an evil world.'"

"'He is but the *offspring* of an evil world,'" Mrs. Zell repeated.

"I don't recognize the language on the outer band," Moira said. "The engraving on the inner band looks much newer."

"Yes, I believe it is," LuHelen said. "Another thing Tertius told me: the box that Anatolia brought with her must be opened only by the method originally intended to do so. To guard its secrets. If it is forced open or opened incorrectly, there is a device within by which the contents will be destroyed."

"What device?" Moira asked.

"I don't know," LuHelen said. "When old Euphrosine the wildcrafter died, she left a protégé trained to replace her, Genevieve Gothard. Maybe she can help you with this?"

"Oh, Genevieve died some *time* ago. Only Mesmin her *husband* lives out at Euphrosine's cabin now," Mrs. Zell said.

"How do we learn by what method must it be opened?" Moira pressed.

"I am sorry to say I don't know that either," LuHelen stood. "It has been wonderful to see you both again. I have fulfilled my promise to Tertius, and a burden has been lifted from me. Although I wish you all the best in the duties facing you and pray for your health and long life, I hope to never see the likes of Ste. Odile again."

# CHAPTER TWENTY-THREE

*Anno Domini 1348, December*

After much talk, I convinced Seraphica that to stay in her father's house would put the lives of her mother and servants at risk. She would not be persuaded that Bastide had any part in her father's death, but the murderer, whoever it was, had apparently come for her and may do so again. She did not want to be the cause of any more collateral deaths.

I brought her to my house. She resolved to stay with me until, to my satisfaction, it was safe for her to return home. I was surprised to learn she had some knowledge of herbal medicines. The injuries to my face had become more swollen and painful. She prepared my mallow poultice and one of her own, which I found to be more effective than mine. Very soon after its application, the poultice had greatly reduced my swelling.

The first night I watched over her as she slept. The death cart came and went under my window, and she remained undisturbed. When I knew the dawn was an hour or less away, I lay down next to her and tried to sleep as best I could.

When I awakened late in the morning, Seraphica had stoked up the fire. She warmed the lentils and had set my place at my small table with bread and spiced wine. When I stood from my bed, the pain in my face returned. I treated it with theriac I kept in my cupboard of medicines, then sat at the table.

"I don't always eat a morning meal," I said.

"It is only *just* still morning," she frowned. "I know you watched over me most of the night."

"I didn't expect you to cook or care for me. Thank you."

"I hate being useless."

If Seraphica had been a dull, illiterate girl, she would, of course, have never attracted the notice of Bastide. Being literate and curious to an extraordinary degree, she was immediately drawn to my few books. She spent much of that afternoon in a corner overlooking the street, reading through the *Consolation of Philosophy* and *Dialogues*.

"Why did you leave your home and move to Montsegur?" I asked after she closed the books.

"I wanted to see more of the world than the Alsatian plain," she said, "More than this small town and these villages scattered hereabout."

I watched over her again that night. The next day her father was buried in the churchyard at St. Cyr's. Aside from Seraphica, myself, and her mother, only the priest and sexton were in attendance. Death is as common as birdsong these days, and it attracts little more notice than that.

After the rite of burial was pronounced, Seraphica's mother embraced her.

"Are you comfortable where you are, girl?" she asked.

"Very comfortable. I was glad to see the sheriff posted an armed man at your door."

"For a few nights, yes."

"She has been most indispensable," I said. "I wish I could tell you I think this displacement will be temporary, but in honesty, they will never find Bastide. I will do my best to keep your daughter safe... for as long as I can."

The two women embraced again, and Seraphica and I walked back toward my house.

As we walked along St. Engeurrand, Seraphica seemed troubled.

"If the authorities will never find Bastide," she said at last, "how is it *you* find him?"

"To discover his victim, she who is the focus of his attentions, is to find him. Such young women tend to be obvious in these villages. If you are still the focus of his attentions, he will find you."

"You still haven't proven any of this to me," she scoffed. "It's too fantastic."

"I think, in the main, that is his greatest protection. Disbelief."

"I miss our conversations, our debates."

"Yes, I know you do. I am sorry."

Seraphica was quiet for the rest of the afternoon. She sat in her corner by the window, alternately reading and dozing, hardly stirring from the chaise. After a few hours, she stood and closed her book.

"I overheard women talking about the Flagellants being seen on the Bergheim Road yesterday. They are coming this way."

"Yes, I heard that, too. They are usually in this area at this time of year. I thought they were overdue."

"I would like to take some food to the sisters at the hospital tomorrow."

"Certainly. If you want to help me here, we can bake some bread. I don't have any meat or fish in the house, though."

For the next hour, we prepared the dough and stoked the fire. After we had baked six loaves, Seraphica washed her hands and collapsed on the bed. She fell asleep almost immediately. I scraped and cleaned the table, washed myself, and lay down beside her.

The street seemed unusually dark that night, and the stillness was almost like a veil smothering the whole town. These impressions were in my mind as I dozed off, my body aching with exhaustion.

After a while and from a great distance, I heard a low moan that grew into a muffled wail, and suddenly a hand struck my fractured cheek. I gasped in pain and opened my eyes to see Seraphica staring down at me, her eyes vacant and glassy, her expression full of rage. She growled something I could not make out, then closed her hands around my throat.

I struggled to push her away, and we rolled off the bed and onto the floor with a crash. She hit the floor first, and I fell on top of her. She mumbled in a husky, gruff voice:

"Evil came with you. Death. You brought it on us..."

I shook her roughly and slapped her face. In the gloom, I could see her senses coming back to her. She seemed out of breath and confused.

"What has happened?" she said.

"I'm not sure. You were... in a somnambulist's nightmare, or... it was Bastide's doing. I have seen something like it once before. Long ago." I stood and helped her up.

"A nightmare, I'm sure," she said.

I knew the injury to my cheek would need another poultice, and so I began to prepare one. Seraphica walked to the window and sat on the chaise. She stayed there for the rest of the night.

I awoke late in the morning to the sound of commotion in the street. There were footsteps shuffling along the cobblestones, a lashing sound, and a jumbled phrase that I recognized as "God forgive us."

The Flagellants had returned. There were perhaps fifty of them, shirtless in the cold, lashing their own backs with rods and whips just below my window. I looked out at them, thinking of the pointlessness and delusion of such self-loathing as is bred in our faith.

Amidst the company of the half-clothed penitents stood one who remained fully clad in dark robes. A cowl partially concealed the dirty bandages that were wrapped around his whole head. And in that moment as I noticed him among that company, he was looking up, directly at me.

# CHAPTER TWENTY-FOUR

Anatolia was sitting on the edge of her bed. She had been on her feet very little in the last few days. She seemed to be a little stronger this morning but still had no appetite. Father Vannier, just back from Kaskaskia Island, prayed with her while Moira and Susan sat in silence. When the prayer was finished, Anatolia seemed revived. She stood.

"You don't know where Set has gone?" Moira asked.

"I didn't hear him leave," Anatolia said. "I was awake before dawn, and he had already left."

The door, which was ajar, opened fully. Mrs. Heugyens stepped in, smiling.

"I wanted to check on our patient," she said. "How does she look to you, Susan?"

"Better," Susan said.

"I feel a little stronger today," Anatolia said.

"Oh, you look better, too," Mrs. Heugyens went on. "We need to get some food in you. I sent young Rebecca to fetch you a glass of cider, if you don't mind."

"Yes, thank you, and I'll eat a little something, or try to," Anatolia smiled weakly. She walked to a chair near the window and sat.

"Did you show Father the bracelet, Miss Parnell?" Mrs. Heugyens asked.

"Yes," Vannier said. "I was in late last night, but I looked at it. It's very old. I have it with me here."

"Is it of any value to us?" Mrs. Heugyens continued.

"Tertius certainly thought so," Moira said.

"It's medieval, obviously," Vannier said. He removed the bracelet from the pocket of his cassock and studied it for a few moments. "The dove was often a symbol of the heretic Cathars. The book in the fire is probably the Bible."

"I thought they were Christians," Mrs. Heugyens said. "from what I have heard of them since this business began."

"They considered themselves Christians," Vannier continued. "But they thought the world too evil to have been created by a loving God. They rejected the Old Testament and most of the New, except for the Gospels. Especially the Gospel of John. The engraving on the inside says, 'He is but the offspring of an evil world,' in French. I am not sure about the words on the outer band. Much of it is worn away, but it may be the same phrase in a language with which I am not familiar."

Mrs. Heugyens positioned her pince-nez on the end of her nose and studied the outer band of the bracelet.

"Looks like the letters E and S at the beginning of it," she said, then *d'un* further on, and the last word is *mau*. Of course, those could be just parts of words and not entire ones. Does the 'he' referred to mean this... creature we are looking for?"

"I don't think so," Vannier said. "I don't know what connection he would have to ancient Cathars. The phrase probably refers to the pope, the king, or the archbishop of the district. Someone in power who persecuted the sect."

Anatolia had stood, unnoticed by her visitors, and walked to the large chest sitting against the far wall. She examined the front of the lid.

"I knew I had seen that word before," she said, touching the lid. "*Es.*"

"What?" Moira said as she moved toward Anatolia.

"It's here," Anatolia ran her fingers over the inset ivory words. "*Es pas qu'un,*" she read.

Moira knelt to study the words more closely. "What language *is* this?" she frowned.

Vannier looked at the words. "The Cathars made their last stand in southern France," he said. "In the region of the Albi, they did not speak modern French. These words could be Old Occitan. There is not much here to go on. I can't say for certain."

"I wonder if these serve any purpose?" Moira said, touching the row of openings below the words. "Could be just decorative..." She suddenly stood. "Mrs. Heugyens, if I may..." She took the Cathar bracelet from the old woman and studied the figure represented on it. She hurried out of the room.

"What's that about?" Mrs. Heugyens said.

Anatolia made her way unsteadily back to her bed. She sat. As Vannier and Mrs. Heugyens studied the chest, Susan sat next to Anatolia on the edge of her bed.

"It's a gal I wants oonah... *you* to know about," Susan said in a low voice. "She taught me things and can he'p if you ever needs to disappear."

"Susan, what are you talking about?"

"If de time come when you needs to disappear, go to Hilton Head islan'. It's a settlement der call Mitchelville. Dey keep dey secrets. Hire a skiff an' go across to Monfort Islan'. You fine my 'ooman Tendetta Estrille. She he'p you. De buckruh... white folks don't go der. Dat where you disappears."

Just then, Moira rushed back into the room.

"I don't know why I didn't think of this before!" Her voice was loud with excitement. "I found this hidden in a newel post at Jardin Noir. It looked like one of those German alphabet toys!" She held up the object with the inlaid ivory tiles and handed it to Vannier. "This is the device the figure is holding on the bracelet!"

Vannier studied the object. "I think you're right." He said. "It appears to be made of the same materials as the chest."

"It could be a key," Anatolia's voice was weak. "The man on Mackinaw Island, de Castres, said there was some sort of key."

Moira took the object from Vannier and studied it. Some of the tiles were blank, but most had a single letter etched into them and painted. Most of the letters were repeated many times. She discovered that the missing tile allowed the others to be slid into an innumerable variety of positions.

"Hmmm!" Mrs. Heugyens scoffed. "It *is* a toy! I've seen such as this before."

The underside of the object had what seemed to be small gears and rods of bronze that were moveable but deeply recessed into the mechanism. The profile of the thing exactly matched the profile of the box lid just below the three strange words affixed there.

"It definitely fits under here somehow," Moira said. She tried to fit the object into the slots under the words, but it would not nest in the spaces. She noticed that only about the upper third of the mechanism was designed to engage with the slots in the lid, and the bottom two-thirds extended below and made no contact with the box. "Only the top line matters. The rest of the space is just to move the letters into and out of position."

She slid letters around and made a space in the upper left corner of the letter grid. She slid the letter T into the position and examined the object. Nothing had changed. She moved more letters and placed an O on the corner position. She pressed the tile to see if it could be moved. Again, nothing changed. She then positioned a D there and pressed the tile. As she did, the tile was pushed into the grid to about twice the depth of its width. Simultaneously, a bronze peg extended from the inside of the object underneath and locked into position. She looked at Vannier.

"We need to translate the phrase on the bracelet," he said. "I remember there is an old phrasebook and dictionary in the Carthesian Library in St. Louis... for Old Occitan. Father Matthew will send it if I ask to borrow it."

"I agree. We must translate the phrase." Moira said.

# CHAPTER TWENTY-FIVE

*Anno Domini 1348, December*

I did see a trace of apprehension in Seraphica's face when I told her of the bandaged man in the street, and she immediately masked the emotion. She seemed adamant to gainsay my warnings about Bastide.

The day after the Flagellants passed through the town, she asked if we could bring bread to the sisters at the hospital. We prepared four loaves and filled her wicker basket. She wrapped herself in her cloak and shawls as I veiled myself, and we walked the empty streets and lanes to the Hospital of Perpetua.

Every few houses had a shrouded corpse lain at the doorstep waiting to be collected. We could hear the death cart approaching from the east.

"I wonder how many have died in the town?" Seraphica said.

"Nearly half, I have heard."

"I wonder if it will ever end or if we are seeing the end of days."

"If God has grown weary of his creation and the human nature that controls it, I would have to say... I understand."

At the hospital, Seraphica placed her basket on the alms table. Two of the nuns came to greet her. I heard them talking of the deaths of the sisters at the convent. The odor hanging across the room was overpowering. All twelve beds in the open area in the great room were occupied with the doomed. Behind these, on the north wall, was a row of curtains, concealing beds reserved for the landed and more noteworthy of the town's victims.

"The pestilence makes all equal before God," a voice said behind me, "but not just yet!" I turned and caught the glance of a young nun passing by who had seen me noticing the wall of curtains. I nodded at her and smiled slightly.

I walked toward the back wall. Three of the afflicted, all very near death, lay on a bed denoted as "St. James," just opposite a curtain. One gurgled in an attempt to make words; another gasped shallow breaths. They all had oozing buboes at the mouth and armpits and were in delirium. Their stench made me lightheaded.

A low growl arose above their sounds. After a moment, I realized none of the afflicted were making the new sound.

"You are my shadow." A deep, tortured voice rasped the words. "You follow me like my own dark image cast on a wall." The voice was wet, viscous, and seemed to be coming to me from every direction at once. But then I understood: it was coming from behind the curtain next to me. I drew back the drapery.

In the penumbra of the dim chamber, standing an arm's length away was the gaunt figure of Bastide. He towered over me in a dark cloak, his entire head wrapped in filthy bandages.

"Bastide!"

"You have hidden yourself well, Scribonia!"

"Yet I have always been near you. Near at hand. I am known as Euphrosine in this time and place."

"Or the Mother of Centuries, as they say. For so many years, how well you hid yourself. I was not certain, not *certain,* until well after the massacre at Montsegur that I was being watched and followed."

"I condemned you to this vile existence," I said, "and when I understood the harm I had done, I condemned myself to follow you to protect those you would consume."

"Yes, you did this terrible thing to me and posterity." I could see his wet lips moving through a gap in the bandages and his glistening, yellow eyes draped in heavy eyelids. "And now this thing you have done is a powerful force which cannot be stopped. You were powerful once..."

"I am still powerful. You dare not harm me."

"Someday, you will not be strong. How much longer can you last? I will be rid of you forever, in time."

"The same is true of you. Livilla told me you cannot keep this dry husk of a host alive forever. If I kill your host, you too, Balphoroth, will die."

The vaguest smile seemed to flutter at the corner of his mouth. "You survived a beating and a night in the death pit," he said. "I didn't know then that it was *you.* My shadow."

"I will never stop."

"Someday, there will be no force of life left in you. You know not to interfere in my..."

"Yes. I was warned."

"Remove your veil. Let me see you!"

I turned quickly and left the chamber.

Seraphica was still talking with the nuns. As I walked past her, I grasped her arm.

"We must get home," I said. "Quickly!"

# CHAPTER TWENTY-SIX

"Set did not return all night." Anatolia's voice was weakened with worry. Euphemia Wallace had hung a curtain around Anatolia's bed so she could examine the progress of her healing and the state of her pregnancy in private since it was rare there were no visitors in the room.

"I will go this morning and tell Sheriff Aubuchon he is missing," Moira said, preoccupied.

"I should know where he is," Anatolia continued. "I can't *see* things like I used to! He wouldn't just leave without telling me."

"Of course not. We will find him."

Later, Moira helped Vannier load the great wooden chest onto a four-wheel cart. They carefully guided it out of the room and across the grounds of the Academy of Perpetua to the church. Increase Mather Browne met them at the rear door of the church and helped get the chest downstairs to Vannier's small apartment.

"I have written to Mathew at the library," Vannier said, "and asked him to rush the volume to me."

"Good," Moira nodded. "I am going to see Sheriff Aubuchon. I am worried about Set. Increase, will you go with me?"

"Surely I will."

Moira and Increase climbed the cellar stairs and walked out onto Constantinople Street toward the sheriff's office.

"You have known Set for years," Moira said, "Is it unusual for him to be gone all night?"

"Very unusual," Increase said. "As dependable as a pocket watch, Set is. No doubt about it. He takes care of Mrs. Heugyens's money and her business affairs. He is gone a lot, but never with no word."

Sheriff Aubuchon was sitting at his desk sipping coffee and reading a week-old newspaper. He looked surprised when Moira and Increase opened the front door.

"Miss Parnell, Increase… it's Increase, isn't it?"

"That's right. Good morning, Sheriff," Increase said.

"I don't get much company these days. Your people settling in?"

"Yes, they are," Increase nodded. "You know, I can fix that roof leak you got back there over the jail. Just provide the materials."

"I'll take you up on that if we can afford it."

"Sheriff," Moira interrupted, "One of the New Phrygians has gone missing. The young man Set. You met him the other day."

"Yes, I remember him. How long has he been gone?"

"Overnight. Not long, but it's very unlike him."

"Very," Increase said. "Nobody steadier than Set. Never known him to…"

"If it's only overnight, a few hours," Aubuchon frowned, "usually we wait a couple of days before searching. My man is out at LaMotte today. Somebody's stealing cows. I'd have to wait until he gets back, at least."

Moira removed her hat and brushed back her hair. She sat on an oak bench against the rear wall of the office.

"Sheriff," she said. "You know what my concerns are."

"Yes. I was talking to Mrs. Zell yesterday, and she told me what has been on your mind."

"There has been activity at Jardin Noir. Somebody is living there."

"Tramps? Squatters?" Aubuchon shrugged. "No trespassing, but you can't keep everyone out. What does that have to do with the young fellow, Set?"

"Anatolia was attacked in the same manner as Perdita and Sister Solana and… Marie Chardin. Bastide is alive. I am certain of it now. Set is convinced also. He will do anything to protect Anatolia. I am afraid he has gone up there."

"I am waiting for a prisoner transfer from Lesterton sometime today. Fellow burned down two barns in Ste. Odile County. Has to be tried here. I must be in the office to receive him. When my deputy is back, late tonight or tomorrow, I will go up to Jardin Noir and look around. That's all I can promise you for now."

Moira knew there was nothing more to be said. She and Increase moved toward the door. "Thank you, Sheriff. Please keep me informed."

Moira and Increase stepped out onto Constantinople Street and walked back toward the convent.

"I'll get one of the other men to go with me," Increase said. "We'll go up and see what we can find up there."

"That's a wonderful idea," Moira nodded. "Tomorrow may be too late."

"I'll get one of the white fellows," Increase continued. "Negro alone don't want to get caught rummaging through an old mansion."

"I suppose not," Moira smiled.

As they walked up the avenue of cypresses toward the dormitory, they found Reuben Siddons occupied with pulling weeds around the statue of Perpetua. Reuben heard them approaching and stood to greet them.

"How is Miss Anatolia today?" he asked Moira.

"Set hasn't returned," Moira said. "She is very worried."

"Wonder if you'd take a little walk with me, Reuben?" Increase said.

"We want to see if he wandered up that hill yonder and maybe got hurt...?"

"Certainly. I was just trying to make things look a little more cheerful here." He brushed the dirt from his hands. "That can wait."

"I'll tell your wife where you've gone," Moira said. The two men walked north toward Mal Ardents Street.

When Moira got back to the convent, Anatolia was dressed and on her feet.

"She's getting her strength back," Euphemia said. "I will check in on you again before supper, miss."

"I won't be eating anything if Set hasn't returned," Anatolia mumbled.

Euphemia looked at Moira and left the room.

"He isn't coming back, Miss Moira!" there were tears in Anatolia's eyes. "That much I know. That much I can still divine. I won't see him again."

"Increase and Reuben have gone looking for him." Moira sat on the settee and reached for Anatolia to join her. "Sheriff Aubuchon will begin an official search later today or tomorrow when his deputy is back."

Anatolia seemed not to hear. "He won't be found. My Set won't be found," she said. "We were wrong to come here. I have put all these people at risk. I should have refused to let them accompany us." She sat next to Moira.

Moira stroked the young woman's hair. "You know, child, it would not have mattered if you stayed where you were or came here. Bastide has his ways, and we must learn how to stop him. You know if he has set his attention on you, somehow, he will find you. There is nowhere to hide."

# CHAPTER TWENTY-SEVEN

*Anno Domini 1348, December*

I sat up keeping watch over Seraphica for two nights. I only slept briefly and fitfully those three days while she was awake and active. I drifted off briefly on the afternoon of the third day. When I awoke, she was sitting on the stool pulled near to my bed, watching over me. She smiled when I opened my eyes.

"You are exhausted," she said. "You are using yourself up to protect me."

I sat on the edge of the bed. "I will do whatever is needed. Whatever I can."

She touched my arm and stood. She poured a small bowl of hot herbal broth and brought it to me. I sipped it and thanked her. She walked back to her corner by the window and retrieved my *Consolation of Philosophy,* which she had left in the windowsill.

"If all your stories are true, you are doing a centuries-long penance," she said.

"Yes. That is what I am doing."

"I haven't seen such concern and care in anyone but my father. However legitimate your fears for my safety are, they are genuine. I should thank you for that."

"All this will be over someday. I only hope my strength outlasts Bastide's. To become vulnerable is to die."

Seraphica opened the book on her lap.

"This volume was copied some time ago," she said.

"More than a century. It was a gift from another father, at Rheims."

"Did you protect his daughter?"

"I did, thankfully."

"If you are truly ageless, as you say..."

"You have grown to trust me," I interrupted, "and have, I think, some regard for me, yet you still imply that I am either deranged or a liar." I smiled a little to soften the tone of my declaration.

"Let me pursue my point," she went on. "You have seen so much, more than any one mind could store and tabulate. If men might be tested by Fortune and thereby grow in grace, how do we find so much evil in the world? Only by the abandonment of Fortune may we know ourselves. Isn't this pestilence such a test? Why has not humanity been transformed by it?"

"Do all seeds cast on the field take root?" I shrugged. "Not all are transformed. Not all are saved. There are those who are. All are free to do so, but many fail. Grace, as you call it, and good works persist even though all the world seems bent on their annihilation. I have seen this. If you finish that book, then throw it into the fire, are its impressions left in your mind destroyed along with the pages? No, they persist and live until you put those principles into action or convey them to someone else."

"They persist even if I do neither."

"They do."

"But what do you know of grace and good works if you do not profess to be Christian?"

"Do you think people knew nothing of kindness and charity before Christ?"

"But you said, 'all are free to do so,' talking of free will, I suspect."

"Yes."

"What sort of free will is it to give one a choice between bliss and torture? Is that a *choice*? If God is truly a god who says follow me and live in joy or reject me and be thrown into the bonfire... that's coercion and threat, not free will."

"I am not a theologian; I am a wildcrafter. These are questions for your priest. As I told you, I never accepted the new religion. Perhaps now you understand why."

Seraphica frowned and settled into her chaise. She read until dark, drifting off to sleep several times. In an hour, she was snoring peacefully.

As I moved my chair nearer to her to watch over her for the night, she began to murmur and mumble in her sleep. She had not done this since the night she attacked me in her somnambulist frenzy. Although I was exhausted, I watched her closely and knew for her safety and mine, I had to stay awake.

She grew more restless and agitated over the next few minutes. Her agitation grew into thrashing and violent movements accompanied by inhuman growls, wails, and guttural gasping. The sounds she was making slowly formed into words.

"You will burn us alive! You will burn us all alive! I will not submit!"

She sprang from the chaise and fell upon me, knocking me from my chair onto the floor. As I fell, I saw a dark form, indistinct and black as a tear in the known world, collected in the beams of the ceiling. It moved out of my sight as I toppled. I slapped Seraphica's face repeatedly and desperately. Suddenly, she came to her senses. She rolled over on the floor, gasping for breath and sweating. It took her a moment to remember where she was.

"What has happened?" she coughed. "What has happened? I was being led to the stake with many others. Led to be burned alive... by you!"

I sat up and tried to catch my breath. "It's him... it's him," I said. "He knows he cannot destroy me. His host cannot yet be empowered to do it. He is influencing you. He communes with women through dreams, a connection of spirit. He will have you do it for him."

"No. I can't. I won't."

"I don't know any more if we can hide from him, from the demon. I am not sure. But we must try. We must leave here immediately."

# CHAPTER TWENTY-EIGHT

Sheriff Aubuchon pulled his chair closer to Anatolia on the settee, facing her. His expression was glum and hopeless, and she already knew what he was going to tell her.

"There was no sign of Set or the other two men who went looking for him at Jardin Noir," he said.

Anatolia sobbed.

"I am sorry to report it," Aubuchon continued. "We have organized searches as far as Obli and LaMotte and as far south as Belgique and beyond. And there was no indication at the mansion that anyone is living there or has even been inside. No one in town wants to go near it."

Moira had been standing at the window. Vannier expected the book Father Matthew was sending him from the Carthesian Library to arrive today, and she was watching the church for any special delivery.

"I suppose you have done all you can do, Sherriff," she said, moving to sit next to Anatolia.

"No... no!" Anatolia protested.

"We will keep searching," Aubuchon reassured her. He stood and walked to the door. "Word is out to all the surrounding counties. We will keep looking, Miss Anatolia."

As Aubuchon left the room, Anatolia wiped the tears from her eyes.

"We won't give up hope," Moira said. "I'll be sunk if I will ever accept defeat."

"I am the center of all this," Anatolia said. "Everyone who protects me is in danger."

Moira stroked Anatolia's hair. "We may have some means to find the end to it," she smiled.

"Putting all our hopes in that old box," Anatolia frowned. "It could all amount to nothing. One fact remains, that anyone near me is in danger." She stood and walked to the window. "Set..." she gasped, and collapsed into sobbing. Moira rose and put her arm around the young woman.

"You are still not strong," she said. "Lie down now and rest. I will leave you. Do you need anything?"

Anatolia dropped weakly onto her bed. "Please ask Susan to come see me." she said.

Moira stopped at the rectory and gave Anatolia's message to Susan. She then walked to the church and made her way down the steps to Vannier's apartment. She found him unwrapping a package.

"This just arrived," he said. "Matthew paid a king's ransom to get it on a mail packet Monday." Vannier cut the strings binding the parcel and tore the wrapping paper away. The large book within was bound in worn and, in some places, scorched blue leather. Embossed onto the front cover was the title: *A Practical and Leisurely Phrasebook and Dictionary of the Ancient Occitan Language. By Q. W. Phyffe. BA, MA, Edinburgh.*

"A very old book," Moira said, touching the cover. "Seen better days."

"Yes," Vannier agreed. "Eighty or ninety years. The usage and phrases may have changed somewhat since then. Very damaged. Many pages are stuck together. Let's see what we have here." He carried the book to a large sideboard against the rear wall upon which he had placed the chest. He examined the ivory words inlaid in the lid. "The two words at the top here are *Legatòri Sagrat.*" He skimmed through the old volume, running his fingers up and down columns of words. "Legacy," he said. "The first word is 'legacy.'" Continuing his search, he leafed backward many pages. "'Sacred' is the other word. If the adjective is first in the phrase, it would be 'sacred legacy.' This could contain the Cathar scriptures."

"Yes," Moira nodded. She opened a drawer in the sideboard and removed the gold bracelet LuHelen had given her. She found a pencil and a scrap of paper. Looking at the French phrase engraved on the inside of the band, she wrote down her translation on the paper. "'He is but the Offspring of an Evil World.'" She handed the paper to Vannier. He began to search for the words in the old book. In a few minutes, after separating several adhered pages, he had transcribed the phrase: *Es pas qu'un Descendent d'un monde Mau.*

Vannier removed the puzzle key from the pocket of his cassock. He began to position and press the letters on the letter grid. When he had finished reproducing the phrase, an irregular line of bronze pegs had emerged from the underside of the key.

Vannier and Moira looked at each other. Vannier positioned the device against the slots on the front of the chest lid. He pushed slightly. There was a muffled clicking sound, and the lid released and rose slightly from its closed position. He carefully opened the lid.

A shallow wooden tray was revealed under the lid, filling the whole space. It held several packets consisting of sheets of parchment sewn together at the top left corner.

The top packet had a title page with the phrase *Es lo rituala destruccion del diable* written across the top. Below that was a packet with the phrase *L'Evangel de Joan l'Evangelista,* followed by a packet of what appeared to be floor plans of a castle or fortress. At the bottom of the tray was a single sheet of parchment containing a list, which Vannier took to be an inventory of the contents of the chest.

*La Questions de Joan*
*La Vision d'Isaïe*
*Lo Rituél*
*Lo Llibre del Dos Principis*

"It looks like a collection of their sacred writing," Moira said.

"Yes," Vannier agreed. "Let's see what is under the tray." As he lifted the tray, a small wooden catch he hadn't noticed before broke off and fell into the tray. Inside the chest could be seen an open wooden rack with four wide compartments and slotted bottom. Each compartment contained more packets of parchments. Below the rack on the floor of the chest, surrounded by gold trinkets, was an odd, flat ceramic object, looking like a large, round oil lamp. A wide copper tube connected this object with a glass orb affixed above it to the inside of the front wall of the chest.

"I hope that wooden catch wasn't important," Vannier said. At that moment, Moira noticed a series of leather cords and pulleys attached to a small but complex mechanism nearly hidden in the chest. A small iron chime hammer suddenly fell forward from a hidden compartment on the back wall behind the document rack and shattered the ceramic object in the bottom of the chest, revealing a light-colored substance inside. A moment later, a second chime hammer fell forward and smashed the glass orb at the front. Liquid splashed out of it across the floor of the chest.

Vannier instinctively pushed Moira away from the box, and they fell backwards on the floor as the chest as it exploded into flames.

"My God, my God," Moira screamed. She scrambled to her feet and grasped Vannier's washbowl, still full of water from early that morning.

"No!" Vannier said, "Water will make it worse!" He pulled the burning chest onto the stone floor. "Blankets! We must smother it!"

Moira pulled all the blankets off Vannier's bed, and together, they threw them over the fire. In a few moments, the fire was extinguished. The chest was severely scorched, and the documents stored inside destroyed. A few gold trinkets, bracelets, medallions, and coins, still intact, spilled out onto the floor. Smoke had partially filled the room but was quickly drawn up the stairs in a draft caused by Moira leaving the cellar door ajar.

"What on earth…" Moira said. "What happened? What is that smell?"

"Naptha, I think," Vannier answered. "It may have been Greek Fire. Ignited by contact with water." He knelt and smelled the remnants of the shattered glass orb. He touched a shard with his finger and lightly touched his tongue. "Sour alcohol smell," he continued. "Very old wine and salt. Added to the water in the orb to keep it from freezing over the years. Water alone would freeze and shatter the orb."

"But why would they devise such a trap to destroy their own scriptures?" Moira said, fanning smoke away from her face.

"I think this may be all there is of the so-called Cathar Treasure," Vannier said. "Their sacred writing, a few baubles, and whatever is in that tray we salvaged. This would have been smuggled out of their mountaintop fortress at Montsegur before they were all killed. The *credents*, the *perfecti*, hoping to preserve their legacy and perhaps re-establish the faith elsewhere, planned this. But this could not fall into the wrong hands. If this chest were discovered by the Church, it would mean torture and death for those in possession and final obliteration of the Cathars. The documents were stored loosely like that so they would burn better."

The wooden tray and its few documents had fallen on the floor. Moira picked them up. "This is all that's left," she said. "Let's get some fresh air until the rest of the smoke clears."

Moira and Vannier climbed the cellar stairs and exited the rear of the church. Rebecca Wallace, Euphemia's young daughter, was running across the drive toward them.

"Miss Moira, what happened?" she called.

"An accident, Rebecca. No harm done."

"I'm glad to hear it, miss. It looks bad. Is Miss Anatolia with you?"

"No. I left her some time ago."

"Nobody knows where she is. We are all looking for her!"

# CHAPTER TWENTY-NINE

*Anno Domini 1348, December*

With the many abandoned estates, manors, and peasant hovels on the plain, I considered where best Seraphica and I could conceal ourselves. Just before dawn, we slipped out the North Gate, each of us carrying as much food, fuel, clothing, and medicine as we could carry in homespun sacks. I wondered if all this was futility since I could not be sure if Bastide knew of our movements, or could be somehow watching us through some demonic agency unknown to me.

The North Road wound up into the foothills and mountains beyond. That way lay forests owned by the king, private hunting grounds and timber reserves, and the abandoned Convent of Perpetua. There being no villages or estates for many arpents in that direction, I resolved that the convent should be our refuge.

"But what of the contagion?" Seraphica asked.

"Whatever spreads it does not seem to linger without hosts to germinate it," I said. "You visit the nuns freely at the hospital surrounded by the dying. I am sure you are in much greater danger there."

"Yes, I suppose so."

It took us nearly until midmorning to reach the convent. Our burdens of provisions slowed and tired us. We passed and saw no one on the road, which was fortunately dry and clear of obstacles. As the grounds of the convent came into sight, I thought of Marthe, the young sister who had attended the dying here and had determined to try and make her way back home. I wondered if she had found her way back and if she had contracted the plague or been one of those who is miraculously spared when so many others die.

The grounds were just starting to show signs of neglect. The paths and walkways were scattered with twigs and branches and dead leaves which, in more settled times, would have been cleared daily by the scrupulous sisters. The immurement cell to the right of the path looked as though it had been abandoned for years rather than months.

"Nobody comes here anymore," Seraphica said as she preceded me up the hill to the kitchen door. The door was slightly ajar, and as she pushed it open, there was a rapid yipping sound and a crash of breaking pottery as a fox darted past her and out the door.

"The building wasn't closed up after the bodies were collected." I said.

"I just hope Antoine removed them all," Seraphica said as she stepped carefully inside.

There was much evidence in the kitchen, hallways, dining hall, chapel, and bedchambers that many animals had found shelter in the buildings since humans had abandoned it. High in the beams of the chapel ceiling, an owl had made a nest, and in the shadows under the altar, a badger watched us intently.

"Nature reclaims everything," I said. "And she is wasting no time across our lands in these dark times."

We returned to the dining hall and began to unpack our provisions. I built a fire in the fireplace there with kindling and firewood the nuns had left.

"We should decide where we will sleep," Serahica said.

"Yes, and we should both be in the same chamber. We will pick one and drag a second cot into it."

"Mother," Seraphica unpacked the two books she had brought with her. "I think it would make great sense if you were to tie me down at night. Tie me to my bed."

"I agree. I was going to suggest it. We will need to find cord or rags or something to do it."

Seraphica searched the kitchen and cupboards and found lengths of hemp cord hanging on pegs in the larder. Then we began to search for a cell large enough to accommodate both of us as a sleeping chamber.

An arched corridor, connected to the dining hall on one corner and the chapel vestibule on another, led to the sleeping cells. The corridor was completely unadorned except for a single black crucifix on the end wall. The rooms were situated only on the right wall of the corridor, as the left wall must have been shared with the chapel.

Each chamber was small and bare, containing a cot, a small table, and a wardrobe and a single window. As we moved deeper into the area, we noticed a familiar odor slowly engulfing us.

"Oh no," Seraphica said.

"There is something dead in here," I said. "It could be an animal..."

The odor was coming from the end of the corridor, from the last small room. The tiny cell was darker than the others, as branches outside still laden with dead leaves, had fallen across the now broken window. In the gloom we heard the rustling of feathers and the *kraaa* call of a raven. There was a violent fluttering and flapping of wings and the large black bird settled on the windowsill. With another *kraaa*, it flew out the broken window.

As our eyes became accustomed to the dark and the odor in the room, we could see a swollen black body lying on the cot. The light and dark of the dead nun's habit gradually distinguished themselves from each other, and the black orbs of eye sockets showed where the departed raven had been feeding.

"Antoine overlooked someone," I said. "His death cart was perhaps overfilled, and he decided one more was not worth returning for, or... he missed this one."

"Lord," Seraphica groaned. "I see so much of this and think I must be accustomed, then I realize I am not. What should we do?"

"Bury her."

We resolved to lift the poor nun on the blanket upon which she lay and carry her out thus to a suitable burial spot. I grasped the corners of the blanket at her head and Seraphica, at her feet. In this manner we moved up the corridor, through the kitchen and out the kitchen door.

The stink was powerful, and Seraphica came near retching more than once. In the sunshine the carcass was splotched gray and black, much bloated, and the wet hollows of the eyes seemed to be watching us. As we exited the kitchen door and moved toward the edge of the forest, Seraphica stumbled on an unseen stone. She dropped a corner of the litter, and the corpse's feet fell to the ground. There was a muffled snapping sound and the nun's left leg below the knee fell off and rolled onto the ground. Seraphica could contain herself no longer. She dropped her burden and vomited violently for many minutes. She seemed very unsteady.

"Go inside, girl," I said. "This is too much for you. Clean yourself. I will do this."

She made her way slowly back into the kitchen. I dragged the carcass across the dormant vegetable garden further up the hillside to the tree line where there were rows of gravestones and sunken old graves. I saw a rusted mattock that had been dropped in the garden before the pestilence came. I retrieved it and selected a spot to bury the unfortunate nun. I hacked and chopped at the cold ground for many minutes, but was unable to dig into the icy sod. I was soon exhausted and knew we would have to cover the sister with stones and branches until a time when she could be properly buried.

I started to make my way back down the hillside toward the convent. As I stumbled down the slick stones, I glanced further down toward the road below. There stood two darkly dressed men, peasants, watching me. They made no greeting or acknowledgement that they were watching my every move. I kept moving down the hill, and when I looked back to the road again, the men were gone.

# CHAPTER THIRTY

Anatolia's greatest fear was blood loss. There had been unpredictable pain, cramping, and bleeding ever since she had found she was pregnant, and it seemed the damage she suffered in the horrific attack had never completely healed. Although the episodes were becoming less frequent, to have one while she was traveling alone with limited means to wash herself would be disastrous. Once she had to move out into a coach seat from her private compartment, anything could happen.

It was her third day on the train. Susan had given her most of her savings and pledged herself to secrecy about Anatolia's plan. If no one knew where Anatolia had gone, the secret could be kept, and she believed her absence would ensure that no one else in the community would be harmed.

Anatolia was allowed to secure a private sleeping compartment at the rear of the car as far as Atlanta, and she kept to her bed most of the time. For the last leg of the train journey, from Atlanta to Bluffton South Carolina, she would only have a coach seat.

By the time the train left the Atlanta station, Anatolia had gathered her few things and moved out of her sleeper compartment and forward to a general seating car. She took a window seat.

Susan told Anatolia that there was a telegraph office at Bluffton which would forward messages across to the islands with the mail. Susan said she would contact Anatolia by telegram if she needed to get a message to her. Susan told her for twenty dollars, she could find a shrimper or some other fisherman to take her to Hilton Head and the village of Mitchelville, where the *buckruh*, the white people, never go. There she would have to engage another boat to Monfort Island, where she would disappear. And at the village of Navillus, she would find Tendetta Estrille.

It was late in the afternoon when the train stopped at Bluffton. Susan had told Anatolia there was a dormitory here for young women across the street from the train station. Exhausted, Anatolia made her way there and rented a bed for the night.

The dormitory room contained six beds, but all were unoccupied. Anatolia placed her satchel on the bed nearest the hall door. She then stepped into the water closet in the hallway and washed herself.

She thought she might be too exhausted to sleep. As she lay in the small bed, she thought about how she had once been able to look into the world unseen by others, to know things unknown by them. But now all was void. There were glimpses and suggestions that stole through her mind in an instant and were gone. Where there were once images and messages, now all was darkness. In the earliest days of her illness, before anyone else knew, she tried to find some path to believing the being inside her was Set's. But she could never convince herself that this was true. Although she felt her powers were fading before she was attacked, the thing growing in her and feeding on her life forces had all but destroyed them for good.

Anatolia slept well. In the morning, the woman at the front desk told her to walk due south on the front street, which ends at the May River. Many shrimpers keep their boats there. She said to ask for Franklin Post. For twenty dollars, Post would certainly take Anatolia to Mitchelville, she said, as that is more money than he makes in half a month.

Anatolia slung her satchel on her back and walked south on the street until it ended at the May River. The riverbank was eroded at that spot. To the east, she could see the expanse of Calibogue Sound and an island beyond she took to be Hilton Head. Several larger boats helmed by white men were heading out to sea. Ahead of her at the end of a short dock, an old black man with an enormous white beard sat in a bateau with a single mast, tending his nets.

"Sir," Anatolia called, "can you tell me where I might find Franklin Post?"

The old man looked up and nodded at her. "Most of days yuh might fin' him anywheres, but todays yuh lookin' right at him," he said.

"Good Morning. Woman at the dormitory said you might take me over to Mitchelville? For twenty dollars?"

"Ain't nothin' at Mitchelville no mo'. It ain't no town these days. Ain't but two, three famblies now. What yuh want to go dere fuh?"

"I need to get a boat out to Monfort Island."

"What yuh gots to go to Mitchelville first fuh?"

"A friend told me I was more likely to find someone at Mitchelville to take me over..."

"Naw, naw, naw," Franklin interrupted. "For twenty dollar, I'd take yuh. I runs errands on de'water. Nobody come or go from Monfort. Yuh know somebody?"

"Yes. A Miss Estrille."

"Lemme see what yuh money look like."

Anatolia withdrew a twenty dollar gold piece from her satchel.

"C'mon, den," Franklin nodded. "Be a cold trip out on de water. Bundle up."

Franklin helped her climb down into the boat. Anatolia sat at the front, and he sat at the back to man the rudder. He pushed the boat away from the dock and drifted out into the channel. The wind was strong and easterly as he unfurled the sail. She wrapped her shawl tightly around herself against the piercing wind. She had never seen the ocean before and wondered what apprehensions she might have had sailing these choppy, wide waters if not for her long journey on the Great Lakes.

Franklin shouted questions and comments at Anatolia, but the distance between them in the boat and the sounds of the circling gulls made it too difficult to converse. Out in the Sound, the winds were stronger and colder. The sun was coming up on the eastern horizon but was not yet affecting the temperature.

Franklin maneuvered the bateau past the northern point of Daufuskie Island and the southern tip of Hilton Head very quickly. Just past the headland of Hilton Head, about a mile to the southeast, another small island appeared.

"Monfort," Franklin shouted.

With the shifting breezes, it took Franklin about forty more minutes to run the bateau up onto a wide, glimmering beach of Monfort Island.

Anatolia stood unsteadily. There was no one in sight. The beach extended great distances both to the east and south and back, perhaps three hundred feet from the shore to coarse sea grass and thickets of pines and palmettos beyond.

"Lemme hep' yuh git out," Franklin said as he stood. Anatolia stepped out into the shallow, cold surf on her own. She dropped her satchel onto the sand. Franklin joined her as she stooped to retrieve the twenty-dollar gold piece from her bag. She gave it to him.

"Ok, den," he said. "Yuh alright, girl? Seasick?"

"No, I'm fine. Thank you for bringing me."

A little girl of four or five years of age appeared out of the thicket of palmettos. She was dressed in a tattered white cotton shift and shawl and her hair was fixed in a top knot bound by a blue ribbon.

"Here come yuh welcome party," Franklin said.

Anatolia waved at the child, who began to walk briskly toward her. As she approached the child started to suck her thumb.

"What's your name?" Anatolia said.

"Oonah pitty 'ooman." the little girl said.

"What did you say, child?" Anatolia frowned.

"She say yuh a pretty woman," Franklin said. "Dey gots dey own talk on dese islan'. Take time to git used to it. Yuh in good hand now. Good luck." He pushed the boat back into the surf and jumped in. Soon he was out past the breakers.

Anatolia knelt next to the child. "Will you tell me your name,dear?" she said.

The little girl shook her head yes and after a few more moments she removed her thumb from her mouth and said, "Eba."

"*Eva?*"

The child nodded her head.

"Eva, do you know a Miss Tendetta Estrille?"

Eva nodded and returned her thumb to her mouth.

"And can you take me to Navillus? The settlement of Navillus?" Anatolia stood. Eva took her by the hand and started to lead her up the beach toward the thicket. Invisible from the beach, a path appeared in the palmettos that widened into a sandy road. Tall pines, palmettos and ferns formed a dense barrier on either side of the road that blocked the chilly sea breeze.

"Where do you live, Eva?" Anatolia asked after a few moments of silence.

"En de billage." Eva's voice was tiny and preoccupied.

"The village. Is it close by?"

Eva nodded yes. She pointed straight ahead down the sandy road.

"Well, thank you for showing me the way. I want to stay a while with Miss Estrille."

"Ma mek de gunjun!" Eva's voice was excited, as if she had just remembered good news.

"I'm sorry, dear," Anatolia frowned. "What did you say?"

"She say she momma make a molasses cake," It was a man's voice, surprisingly close by. Anatolia looked toward the voice. A man in a worn black suit was leading a mule toward the road. Behind him stood a well-kept white clapboard church partially hidden by tall pine trees. Eva waved at the man.

" 'Mawnin' Reb'ren Smif," Eva said.

"Better beat dus' home, chile. Ma gone wear dat buttom' out. Mawnin' Miss," Smith nodded to Anatolia. "I'm Reb'ren Smith. Uriah Smith."

"How do you do Reverend? I am Anatolia Montes. I have come to stay with Miss Estrille."

"Yes, I heerd oonah tell little Eba. Welcome to Monfort. I lib in Sabannah a while. I know de islan' talk hard to follow 'till oonah git used to it!"

"She punkin'-skin!" Eva blurted, giggling.

Anatolia frowned in confusion.

"She say oonah half-white. Dey say... mulatto?" Smith said.

"Tamaroa Indian, actually," Anatolia said.

"Miss Estrille berry 'spectabble 'ooman. She at praise meetin' ebery Sumday. Hope oonah come too!"

"Thank you," Anatolia nodded. Eva grasped her hand again and they continued along the road a few hundred more feet until a clearing in the pines and palmettos appeared. A neatly painted wooden sign nailed to a post beside the road read *Navillus*.

The sandy road widened to a rough square lined with tiny wooden houses and a small dry goods store. Sparse rows of more small houses could be seen behind the square trailing off into the woods, and more were scattered randomly back into the pine trees. A few people milled around the mercantile and around the small houses. Women swept steps or shooed Dominecker chickens or piglets into pens or sties.

Some hung laundry on lines at the sides or rear of their houses, and a group of men with shotguns over their shoulders were walking away toward the south where the sandy road continued toward open fields. A few children played in the sand in front of one of the houses. Some of the women noticed Anatolia and watched her suspiciously. Others took notice then went back to their work.

The door of a small shack to the left, which bore traces of blue paint, opened. An older woman with her head wrapped in a brightly-colored cloth stepped out and walked toward Anatolia.

"Eba!" the old woman called, "Oonah hab brekwus yit?"

"Nuh-uh." The child shook her head.

"Cut-out home, din."

Eva started to walk toward a group of the small houses but only went as far as the children playing on the ground.

"Chile allus wander off of a mornin' and miss her brekwus," the old woman said.

"I just got a boat across the Sound," Anatolia said. "She was wandering on the beach."

"I see oonah comin' in my dream las' night. I'm Tendetta Estrille." Tendetta embraced Anatolia. "Gots a talleygraf fum Susan Henry. She say oonah gots a bush-chile in de belly, an I see in oonah face it's true. She say de Plate-eye is arter dis gal."

"Plate-eye?"

"De debbil. De demon. Oonah be safe here. Mus' be hongry. Fetch up to da house an' I makes some baddle-cake."

# CHAPTER THIRTY-ONE

Moira was exhausted. With the help of young Rebecca Wallace and India Collins, her playmate, she had spent the day cleaning the smoke and fire damage in the church cellar caused by the immolation of the Cathar chest. The cellar still smelled like smoke and burnt wood and Moira hoped that with time, the odor would fade. At least, over the last two days, she and her helpers had managed to clear out the damaged furniture and whitewash the walls.

Mrs. Zell was asleep on her settee in the parlor with a cold cup of tea sitting on the small marble-topped table next to her. Moira often found her this way when she came home late. She awakened the older woman and helped her up the stairs to her bedroom. She then went back downstairs, locked the doors, and put out the lights for the night.

As she went about the house, Moira realized she found herself missing Vannier more as she got older than she had as a younger woman. The change concerned her at first, but in the last few months she had settled into it and accepted it. It gave her a certain variety of comfort with which she had been unfamiliar before.

Vannier had found little time to work on the Cathar documents. Father Valmont, the parish priest at Fort de Chartres, was thrown from his horse crossing a creek on his way to perform last rites for a farmer at Prairie du Rocher. The sheriff later surmised that something frightened the old horse and he reared, throwing Valmont. The priest fell against a boulder in the creek. His neck was broken, and his lungs were full of water. The horse stood next to the dead man for a day and a night until two boys who were ice-fishing found him. The parish was given to Vannier temporarily. Vannier told Moira the parish was in disarray, and he suspected the responsibility for it would be his for years. Vannier had taken all the Cathar documents with him.

Moira always prided herself on her independence. Like Perdita, she had lived with her parents as an adult woman, but that was the wish of her parents, and not done because she was unable to make her own way in the world. She had worked as a teacher, a nurse, a volunteer at orphanages and lunatic asylums, and cared for her aged parents between terms at the Academy of Perpetua. As a woman of thirty-eight, she'd told Perdita she expected to remain a spinster. She said she was certain she would have no patience then or in the future for a "man's nonsense."

A year after coming to Ste. Odile and meeting Vannier, she was surprised to realize the ease and contentment she felt in his company and to accept that she must define those feelings as affection. She thought that perhaps, with the loss of Perdita, Vannier was filling her very limited need for human connection and closeness. She soon realized that her feelings for him were more than that.

But he was a *priest*.

Moira struggled to know the difference between God's will and the biases, hatreds, and proscriptions of men falsely attributed to God. She knew most of the dogmas of the world's monotheistic religions fell into the latter category. Vannier had taken the vow of celibacy at his ordination, though he often argued that the priestly requirement only dated back to medieval times and was meant as a means of preventing the clergy from acquiring property. Still, he had taken the vow. But as she aged and had lived through the loss of friends and loved ones, she comforted herself less with the vagaries and contradictions of religious tradition and more with the tranquility of service, connection to others, and perhaps love. She asked herself often: Is anything more important than these things?

As she mounted the stairs, Moira's thoughts turned to the situation at hand. Susan Henry readily admitted to the other New Phrygians that she had helped Anatolia to disappear, and she knew where she had gone. Susan insisted that for the safety of the group and Anatolia herself, no one else should know what she knew. Even Mrs. Heugyens, who questioned Susan for days, could get no information from her. Moira convinced the group and Mrs. Heugyens that Susan was right.

With both Set and Anatolia missing from the group, the New Phrygians seemed fragmented and disconnected. Mrs. Heugyens recognized this fact and confided it to Moira but said she felt powerless to address it. Moira assured her and others in the group that wherever Anatolia was now, she was safe, and that once Vannier had been able to translate the Cathar texts, surely a solution to the dark curse hanging over them would be found.

When the New Phrygians arrived in town, Moira considered giving up her rooms at Tranquille House to move closer to Anatolia. But her affection for Mrs. Zell had grown considerably over the years, and Moira realized that she felt more at ease keeping a degree of distance between herself and the newcomers. But a terrible fear came over her when Set disappeared. She remembered Perdita's anguished letters after her friend Hypollite Robert disappeared when he and Perdita's Uncle Tancred attempted to purge Bastide from the community. That seemed to be happening again to Anatolia. As a child, Anatolia had been under Perdita's protection. Now Moira felt she had become responsible for the young woman's wellbeing.

She knew, of course, that this was nonsense. Moira had no more capacity to protect Anatolia than the young woman had herself.

Anatolia had already proven herself to be strong and resilient and had survived circumstances since early childhood that Moira could barely imagine. Still, however great the illusion, the compulsion is strong, even in the impotent, to protect a loved one.

In her own room, Moira quickly prepared for bed. Aside from the physical exertion of the last two days, she had also slept poorly, and a deep weariness numbed her mind and body. Her dreams had been odd and foreboding and had left many unsettling images in her mind—images too disturbing to allow her to fall back to sleep.

She remembered receiving a letter from Perdita, written when her friend had a few more days to live, telling of terrible nightmares she was having. Perdita said this repeated a pattern Sister Solana and Marie Delaporte Chardin had experienced. This concerned Moira, though she comforted herself somewhat with the knowledge she had an imaginative and suggestible nature, and that perhaps she was summoning the dreams herself.

Moira settled into bed. She had been reading *The Woman in White* at bedtime for the last few nights, or rather, skimming it. She found herself too distracted lately to tax her concentration with a mystery story. After a few minutes' reading, she was relieved to realize she felt sleepy. She returned the book to her nightstand and put out her light.

The wind was high and rattled her windows. The full moonlight was starting to filter through the bare branches of the large oak tree outside her south window and penetrate her room. A riverboat sounded its whistle, from what seemed like a great distance: probably from the main channel of the Mississippi, east of de Castres Island. Her body ached with exhaustion. She was soon asleep.

The Cathar chest was being prepared for removal from the citadel. It sat on a table in the center of the sparse room. Two robed *perfecti* had finished placing the sacred documents within it and had prepared and carefully installed the incendiary mechanism designed to destroy the contents, should the chest fall into the wrong royal or ecclesiastical hands.

Four men in peasant dress, *credents*, stood behind the *perfecti*. One seemed oddly familiar, though Moira was certain she had never seen such a drawn and gray face before.

"*Lo document es necessary?*" the man said. One of the robed figures turned to the man.

"*Tu es nòstre germá, mas ta natura lo fai imperatiu.*" he said.

The two *perfecti* then closed the chest, and by inserting the key device Moira recognized as the object she had found in Bastide's house, they locked it. The key was then given to the *credent* nearest the chest.

Moira saw herself in a dress made of homespun, watching these proceedings from a corner of the room. A group of children stood around her, transfixed on the scene as she was. As she watched, she thought of the deaths of Perdita and Sister Solana and Marie Delaporte

Chardin, and more recently, Set and Increase Mather Browne, of all the destruction and death caused, apparently, by Bastide.

Moira suddenly understood that the *credent* in front of her, the man with the drawn face, was Orien Bastide.

Now he and the other three peasants were filling pouches slung over their shoulders with gold jewelry and sacred objects being given to them by the *perfecti*. Moira knew the men were preparing to slip out of the citadel that night with the chest and its sacred contents. They were to lower themselves down the mountainside and escape the martyr's death awaiting their compatriots making their last stand in the besieged fortress. They were to escape to salvage some vestige of the beliefs that sustained them and for which the company was willing to die. These four would preserve perhaps the last evidence that the Cathars had existed at all.

As Moira watched the four men making their preparations, she could not account for the sensations that were overtaking her. Some of the children gathered around her were those of new converts. They began touching and stroking her, expecting from her some explanation, apparently, of what was happening to all of them. She could not answer the children's questions or respond to their attentions. She could not take her eyes off Bastide nor think of anything else.

She was distracted in the extreme from the questions and demands assaulting her at that moment. Her limbs were weak, her thighs and stomach flushed with blood and tingling. She felt overheated and excited by a lust that horrified her. But still the children pulled at her skirt, prodded her.

Moira jolted herself awake. She was covered in sweat despite the coldness of the room. She felt drained and weak, too weak even to lift her head. A stab of fear shot through her as she realized the nudging and prodding she'd dreamt of was continuing—was real. It was not the children she had felt. She became rigid as death and dared not to move.

A cold prod at the top of her thigh, a probe against her groin, a paw, a snout, the brush of coarse fur. She screamed a muffled scream. Forms writhed under her blanket, against her, front and back. They chittered, growled, nipped at her flesh. She tried to throw herself over the edge of her bed, but she could not. She could not move. She wanted to kick at the creatures that were swarming furiously over her, scratching and biting her, but her legs would not respond.

Suddenly the creatures burst violently from under the blanket and leapt upon the desk. There were two of them, *Le Vorace* as she realized now—the creature she had seen at Jardin Noir. They were silhouetted against her window. One of the creatures abruptly and savagely attacked the other. There was a squeal of pain, and in an instant, they crashed through the window, onto the snowy ledge outside, and were gone.

Moira, finding she was now able to move, leapt from the bed and looked out the window to watch their escape. She then closed her eyes and tried to catch her breath. What was happening to her? She did not want to see or hear anything else; nothing else that might still be near that was unnatural or horrifying. She wanted a moment to recover before her senses could admit stimuli of any kind. A cold wind from the broken window bore heavily against the back of her neck and head. She would have to block it with something, then spend the rest of the night in some other room.

Moira became abruptly aware of a rank odor that surrounded her, which became stronger with each gust of breeze. She was frozen again; she tried to move her legs, but they would scarcely budge. She moved her heel just enough to feel something against it, behind her in the bed. She closed her eyes and heard herself whimper slightly. An eddy of numb terror washed over her as she sensed a presence in the room. It was a pressure she felt against her back from a form that seemed to extend beyond hers from head to foot. And it was wave after wave of breath she felt against her neck.

Moira could not force herself to open her eyes completely, not so horribly close to the thing she did not want to see. Through barely parted eyelids, she saw an unfocused gray mass—liquid, obscene and monstrous—forcing her onto her back on the bed. A limb with a texture she could not identify as either fur or skin slid up her leg, pushing her gown aside. She felt a sharp, stabbing pressure on the inner surface of each knee as if a barb or thorn were being snagged into them. To her horror, she realized the pressure was forcing her legs apart. She thought she heard a voice, it may have been behind her, or inside her head. It said one word, a guttural spitting of the word, an infernal ululation delirious with craving: "*You.*"

Moira tried to scream for help but could not draw breath deep enough to do so. A great pressure was overwhelming and suffocating her. In another second she felt a stabbing pain at her secret and unbroken core. It was broken and breached now, overgorged, surrendering, with a tearing and searing inside her.

"Bastide!" she gasped.

# CHAPTER THIRTY-TWO

*Anno Domini 1348, December*

I promise I will bury her when the ground thaws. The weather turned much colder and has frozen, I assume, the body of the nun I dragged up the hillside. It has been a day and a night, and I smell nothing of the carcass. I pray for her soul and swear I will get her in the ground as soon as I am able.

Seraphica has busied herself with cleaning and scrubbing the parts of the convent which we most use. She swept out our bedroom and the hallways and kitchen. She broke off large chunks of ice from the eaves and melted them in a cauldron near the fire to have water for washing the walls and for us to use to bathe. When she has finished her self-assigned chores, she prepares or helps to prepare our simple meals. After all is done, she reads.

At the beginning of my service to Circe, I swore I would never bear children of my own. I had resolved to devote my life to practices and investigations that would certainly, at some moment, put anyone near me in danger. And I considered that there would be dark curtains I would peer beyond, monstrous planes I would investigate, opening portals and insights to truths too horrific for anyone unwittingly exposed to them. I had chosen this path for myself. I considered that I had no license to bring anyone into these infernal regions with me.

Yet, I had started to feel what must be parental affection for Seraphica. I felt a sense of appreciation as I watched her in her efforts to make our grim habitation as pleasant and agreeable as she could. In the evenings, as she read her Boethius or Marcus Aurelius, the only name I could give to my feelings was pride.

The morning of the third day after we removed the dead nun, Seraphica was preparing a vegetable broth in the kitchen while I took stock of what was left in our larder. It had snowed the night before, and the oven was doing little to warm the room. As Seraphica removed the pot from the heat, a sound came from outside the kitchen window.

*Roouh... roouh.* The sound was high and soft, like a child's cry, but plaintive.

"What is that?" Seraphica said.

"It sounds like a young lynx," I said, opening the kitchen door. Just under the kitchen window sat the young animal. It was a silvery winter color and not fully grown. There was blood on its left forelimb. "Not old enough to have left its mother," I continued. "Its mother may be dead or abandoned this kit when whatever attacked them..."

"My God!" Seraphica interjected. "Do you think they were feeding on the dead Sister?"

"Probably so." I approached the kit slowly. It hissed a little and mewed, but its protestations seemed halfhearted since it appeared to have come to us for help. I picked it up and brought it into the kitchen. I placed the animal on the table. "A male," I said.

"Beleth!" Seraphica interrupted. "His name must be Beleth!"

I nodded in agreement. "Seven or eight months old," I continued. "Not fully grown. A badger must have done this to him."

"Let me wash off the blood, and I'll make a bandage." Seraphica moved to the kit's side and stroked his head. He began to purr.

"If I can't bury the poor sister, I will have to pile stones on her," I said. "If you want to tend to Beleth, I will do that."

Seraphica filled a bowl with water and placed it in front of the kit and found some dried strips of mutton, which he immediately devoured. I wrapped myself against the cold and walked outside and up the hill to see if I could better cover the nun's body.

There was, fortunately, a glade with many exposed stones just up from the tree line in the forest. In an hour I had dragged and carried enough of them down to the body to completely cover it. I whispered another short prayer and repeated my pledge to her spirit to bury her properly when I could.

By the time I returned to the convent, Seraphica had bandaged Beleth's leg, and he was napping peacefully in a corner of the kitchen.

"I can't believe how quickly he has taken to us," Seraphica said. "I would never expect such from a wild animal."

"It's you he has taken to," I said. "If he were a year older, he would have learned to distrust us."

"As all animals should," Seraphica nodded.

Beleth slept for several hours. Late in the afternoon, he stirred, stretched, and, regardless of a pronounced limp, began to explore his new surroundings. He had been missing from our sight for more than an hour when we heard a slight squeak come from the vicinity of the chapel. Seraphica and I followed the sound and found that, despite his injury, Beleth had captured a rat, which he was now devouring.

"Well, there's a benefit to his affection for us!" Seraphica smiled.

I still felt a chill from my labors on the hillside earlier in the day. I thought I would retire early. Seraphica had made her way to her reading nook in the dining hall and was lost in her book. I bade goodnight to her, but she didn't hear me. As I turned to make my way down the hallway to our room, I noticed two partially eaten rat carcasses lying across the threshold.

"Did you see the offerings Beleth has left you?" I said, turning to

Seraphica. She still did not hear me. I stooped and picked up the still-glistening little bodies and moved toward the kitchen door to throw them outside.

As I opened the door, it crashed against me, and I was thrown against the opposite wall. Two men, peasants, burst into the room. They were the same two I had seen in the road days before.

Both were large men. I again suspected they were the ones who attacked me on the Zellenberg Road. The thinner one wore a felt Lappvattnet hat, and the heavier one, a leather biggin.

"We've been watching you, witch!" the thin one grinned. "and the girl you're hiding."

"Look at the vermin she's holding," the heavy one said. "Eating rats or preparing a spell! Training the girl in witchcraft, too. That's my wager."

Their tone was one of affectation. I suspected; I *knew* they didn't believe the accusations they were making. Beleth had been sleeping under a cupboard. He looked out from his hiding place for only a second, then hid again.

"There," the thin man said, "If proof were lacking, here is her familiar!" The man blocked Beleth into his hiding place and grabbed his injured leg. He pulled the kit out and held him fast by the scruff of his neck. "What do you call this little monster?" he said.

"His name is Beleth," Seraphica said, rushing into the room. "He came to us today, injured. Get out of our home!"

"A demon's name if ever I heard such!" the heavier man said. "And this is hardly your home. I tithe to the church as any man does. It's as much my home as yours!"

Beleth writhed and wriggled in the thin man's grip. He scratched his forearm, and the invader nearly dropped the kit. In a fit of rage, he threw the animal against the kitchen wall. It fell dead to the floor. Seraphica screeched and rushed toward her dead pet. The thin man grabbed her. I got to my feet and moved to aid her, but the heavy man grabbed me and threw me out into the cold. He slammed the kitchen door and barred it.

"I will deal with you... after!" he said.

I was in a panic. Seraphica screamed, and I could hear pans and crockery crashing around the kitchen. The light in the kitchen suddenly went out, and I could hear Seraphica's cries fading away, into the chapel or the bedrooms. We kept the windows locked, so the only way I could get back in was to smash one, but most were above my reach.

The hallway of the bedchambers pushed into the ascending hillside a bit at the far end, so I thought I could better reach a window back there. I remembered that the window of the last room in the hallway, where we had found the dead nun, was broken. I found my garden mattock in case I needed to further clear the opening and ran back to the window.

I heard muffled screams, but not those of Seraphica. The men were screaming! Furniture and other objects crashed against walls and hallways, and then suddenly, all was silent. "Seraphica!" I called, "Are you there, girl?"

I heard a gasp and much sobbing. "Yes... yes," she cried.

"Let me in... back to the kitchen!"

I went back to the kitchen door and, in a moment, she opened it. Her clothes were torn, and welts were arising on her cheeks and forehead.

"What happened? What *happened?*" She shook her head and could not answer. I ran to the back hallway.

Fragments of the men's bodies were scattered across the floor or stuck to the walls with glistening gore. In the second bedroom on the right, their torsos lay ripped and shredded on the cot and table. Both their throats were ripped out. I felt Seraphica press against my back.

"I don't know what happened!" she sobbed. "It was all a blur, a shadow. It happened in an instant. I don't know what happened!"

I embraced her. "He is protecting you," I whispered. "He is saving you for himself."

# CHAPTER THIRTY-THREE

"Navillus ain't but Sullivan backwardy," Tendetta said. "When de slabes come from Afriky or de Caribbean, dey took 'em to Sullivan Islan' first an' drop 'em off. Navillus is de name here because it de opposinte ob slabery."

Anatolia smiled. "That makes sense. Thank you for the batter cakes. I haven't had those since my grandmother made them."

"Oonuh granny a good cook fuh true?"

"A very good cook!" Anatolia smiled.

"She still 'libe?"

"*Alive*? No. She died a long time ago. She raised me. She was a Tamaroa Indian. Had gout. She never could tolerate white man food, though she tried."

"Awww, de gouch! It h'ut! Mary Biggs had it. She gone-cross, t'ank de Lawd. Bury her on de beach under a libe-oak. No... de buckruh cain't cook. Doan mek de Hoppin' John or baddle-cake."

Tendetta's tiny house was built of well-maintained cypress and cedar planks. The roof was metal, and the small front porch had room for a rocking chair and a milking stool. The inside consisted of two rooms: a kitchen with a back door and a front room used for sleeping and sitting. All the interior walls were covered in newspaper. Anatolia sipped the strong coffee Tendetta had made.

"I think you have saved my life, Tendetta," she said, "and maybe other lives, too."

"Uh only sabe oonuh life *so fuh*!" the old woman laughed. "We sees how uh doin' a munt fum now. Uh onduhstan' oonah special gal, and de bush-chile in de belly, too. De Sea Islan' a good place fuh to pruhtek a gal. Nobody in de Newnited State know we hur."

Anatolia laughed a little. She realized she understood most of what Tendetta had said.

"Let's go walk de billage. Uh show oonah aroun' an' meet some folks."

The children who were playing on the sandy road, including Eva, were still there. They had drawn a circle on the ground and were playing marbles.

"Eba! Oonah bin home yit?" Tendetta called. Eva stood, thumb in her mouth and shook her head no. "Mama gone strip onnah nakedy an' whop thet buttum. Fetch on home now!"

The child turned and walked toward one of the small houses while the other children paid no notice to the two women.

"Why aren't these children in school?" Anatolia asked.

"Miz Gray, de teachuh move back to Chaa'stun. Yent no mo' teachuh fo' de chiggen."

"Well... that's too bad," Anatolia said.

"Dat de schoo-house ovah yondah," Tendetta nodded toward a single-room clapboard building back in the pines. "Jes' use it to sto' cotton, an' rice an' indigo in season now."

An old woman wrapped in a shawl emerged from the dry-goods store across the road and began to walk toward them. The woman had a pronounced limp.

"Awww, Goshen, here come Edny Culpepper," Tendetta said. "She a clap-hat-bitch like you nebuh see!"

Anatolia giggled.

"Tendetty!" Edny Culpepper called. "Dis oonah frien' Anatoly?"

"Jus' come in at dayclean..." Tendetta said. She glanced at Anatolia. "Dawn," she clarified. "This Edny Culpepper. Hu' juntlemun name Norman, an' she son name St. Michael..."

"No needs fuh all dat now," Edny interrupted.

"I am pleased to meet you, Mrs. Culpepper," Anatolia said.

"Uh jus' Edny. Jus' calls me Edny. Tendetty, you mix det salbe fuh dis hip like I ax?"

"Uh done tolt oonah it be Jinnywerey Munt."

"It pain me *now*!"

"Come on up t'house. Gots sumpfin' det hold oonah ovah till din. Anatoly, dis take a while..."

The two old women walked together back toward Tendetta's house. Anatolia considered whether she should follow them or not. It seemed Tendetta expected her to wait there.

"Miz punkin-skin!" a small voice called. Eva was being led by the hand by a woman a little older than Anatolia. The child was giggling uncontrollably. Eva broke away from her mother and ran toward Anatolia.

"Eva, that's not polite!" the mother called.

When Eva ran to Anatolia's side, she grasped her hand and started leading her toward her mother.

"Miss Anatolia, I'm sorry Eva's not bein' more polite than that," the mother said. "I know I taught her better!"

"It's all right," Anatolia said. "She is my first friend here."

"I'm Tooney Mason," she extended her hand and Anatolia took it. "Welcome to Monfort!"

"Thank you... Tooney. Seems like the whole island knew I was coming."

"It's big news. Nothin' much happens. Nobody got any secrets here! How you doin' with the island talk?"

"Pretty well, I think. Are you from somewhere else?"

"Georgia. Around Milledgeville. I was born on a little plantation the day the peace was signed. We sharecropped until I met Robert, my husband. He was from here. He was a shrimper. Drowned in a squall two years ago."

"I'm very sorry to hear it. I've lost... my man, too." Anatolia could not suppress a sob. Eva's expression as she watched Anatolia's sudden sorrow changed from puzzlement to distress. She started to cry. Tooney picked up her daughter and hugged her, and put an arm around Anatolia.

"Them two old women ain't gonna be back any time soon," she said. "Let's take a little walk." Tooney took Anatolia's arm, and they started walking toward the sandy road leading south. Eva wriggled to the ground. "They call this 'gone hook-han,'" Tooney said. "It means walking arm in arm."

"Thank you," Anatolia said. Eva grabbed a handful of fabric on her mother's dress and walked alongside. A path crossed the main road ahead of them.

"Docks off thataway," Tooney said, pointing west. "Fishin', oysters in season, shrimpin'. Fields back the other way. Cotton, indigo, rice, beans. We do all right. Never want for much."

"I never knew any of this was here," Anatolia said. "A friend, Susan Henry, grew up here."

"I heard of her," Tooney nodded. "Her people come into many troubles after they left."

"Yes, she told me."

"The buckruhs brung us here to grow cotton and rice. They left us on our own because of the malaria. It killed them but not us. Everybody either forgot about us or never knew we was here in the first place. You're safe here."

"I don't know," Anatolia said. "I'm not sure... not certain I am safe anywhere. I worry that I put those around me in danger."

"The old people said it's the Plate-Eye, the demon that's after you."

"It's... something like that, I guess. Evil from ancient times. It killed a teacher of mine, a protector, and so many other women."

"What they call the incubus? Tendetta said somethin' about that..."

Anatolia looked at Tooney in surprise. "Yes."

The sandy road curved to the southeast. The woods on either side were thick with palmettos, live oaks, and pine trees. Small houses were scattered out in the forest, some surrounded by gardens and some offering a view of fallow, winter fields off in the distance.

Soon the sound of the surf became louder, and the ocean could be seen through the trees ahead. Eva ran ahead to the nearly white beach that opened a hundred yards away, brilliant in the early afternoon sun.

The beach emerged from an almost solid line of live oaks. Under the fantastically gnarled branches were scattered dozens of gravestones and wooden grave markers.

"The cemetery is so far from the village," Anatolia said.

"From the old times, people wanted it that way," Tooney said. "The slaves, all the stolen people, pined away for home. Even if they weren't born across the water, it was still home. They wanted their spirits, their souls, to be able to find their way back over the water to Africa."

Anatolia said nothing. She and Tooney walked among the grave markers for more than an hour. At length, they sat in the shade of a live oak and watched Eva playing in the surf. Neither spoke for a long time.

"Do you ever think you might take Eva and go back home? Leave Monfort Island?" Anatolia asked.

"Never. This is home for us. My husband loved it. I love it. Eva is safer, better off here. So am I."

"You know... when Eva walked me into town, the people we met told her you were going to spank her or punish her somehow for running off. You don't seem like that kind of mother to me."

"Naw. Violence will make a child fearful and angry, and violent theyself someday. That ain't me."

After another hour, Tooney called Eva, and the three of them began the long walk home. As they came to the crossroad from the docks, two small boys approached them from the opposite direction.

"The taller one is Gog Culpepper," Tooney said. "He had a twin, Magog, who died. The shorter one is Len Dyson. I think they're both six or seven. Boys! Where you a-goin'?"

Anatolia noticed that Gog was carrying a tow sack.

"Sammyterry," Gog said. "Uh fin' a daid squinch-owl. We gone bury it."

Eva looked at her mother.

"No!" Tooney shook her head. "You ain't a-goin' with them, Eva!"

Eva frowned and stuck her thumb in her mouth.

"Watch out for that wild hog over thataway," Tooney called after the boys as they continued toward the beach.

Anatolia watched the boys walk away. "I should find a way to make myself useful here," she said. "Maybe I could try my hand at teaching since Miss Gray left...?"

"Well, that's an idea, ain't it?" Tooney smiled. "You obviously a educated woman. We have to talk to Reverend Smith. He decides these things."

"Anatoly!" Tendetta was approaching from the village. The old woman was waving her arms in excitement. "Wes Jones at the dry goods gots a tallygraf fuh oonah in care of me!"

Out of breath, she handed a folded paper to Anatolia. It read:

*Dearest Anatolia: I am writing this for Susan to send, as she insists on keeping your location a secret. I regret to inform you that Miss Moira is dead. Attacked and torn to pieces as you were. We love you and pray for your safety!*

*M. Heugyens*

# CHAPTER THIRTY-FOUR

Vannier felt that the bottom had fallen out of the world. The endemic, terrifying emptiness of life, which his reading, his withering attempts to maintain faith and belief, and his love of Moira kept in abeyance, yawned before him now with nothing to mitigate it.

After reading the first few words of Mrs. Heugyens's letter, he felt a lever engage in his mind like a railroad man switching an oncoming train from one track to another. Knowing the letter contained bad news, he read it numbly, absorbing none of it until he read it a second time.

Moira was dead.

Vannier didn't know if he could have protected her had he been there, or if he would have died too, as many others had done. Choosing one outcome or another was pointless. He should have been there, regardless. The vague ease and comfort, the formless happiness he imagined when he thought of the future, was gone now. The future, as he saw it at that moment, was cold, empty, and frightful.

Mrs. Zell had pronounced herself unable to perform the function of identifying Moira's body. Vannier decided this responsibility must fall to him.

He did the best he could at Fort de Chartres and Prairie du Rocher as quickly as he could. He organized finances, settled disputes, and caught up on a backlog of baptisms. With the terrible news he had received, he felt he must have forgotten some key element, but he couldn't think of what that might be. He was able to place Father Rolfe, just out of the seminary, in charge temporarily until he could make his way back. The congregation at Kaskaskia would just have to wait.

The coroner of Ste. Odile County, Mr. Napier, had his office next door to the jail on Bucephalus Street. A sallow man in his 70s, he greeted Vannier soberly and offered the priest condolences for the loss of someone who, it was no secret in town, was very close to him. Napier filled out a short form regarding Vannier's identity and relationship to the deceased. At the bottom of the form was a line for a signature verifying the identity of the body, which Vannier was to sign after the viewing. Forms detailing the results of the autopsy, authorizing the release of the remains and release of personal property, were also visible on Napier's desk.

The autopsy room was neatly kept but deteriorating. The iron and marble table at the center held Moira's body, covered in a splotched, red-stained sheet. Napier drew back the sheet, and Vannier shuddered in horror and grief.

"Dear Jesus..." he said, tears welling in his eyes.

"Cause of death was traumatic blood loss," Napier said. "I doubt you want all the details, but it's all in my autopsy report."

Moira's flesh had a pallor that ranged from gray to blue. She was bruised badly, and her arms and hands were covered in cuts and scratches.

"There are many defensive wounds," Napier said. "She struggled. The attack was a sexual one. Blood loss was predominantly from internal damage caused by the incredible violence of the attack."

Vannier tried to steady himself to speak.

"You have seen..." he said at length, "you have seen this before, Mr. Napier?"

"I was coroner in Cook County, Illinois," Napier said. "...for eight years. That included the great city of Chicago. Yes, I have seen this before, but only in this small town. There hasn't been a new case for more than a decade, I would say. For all my experience, I never saw anything like this before I came to Ste. Odile."

Napier said he would arrange for the undertaker to remove and prepare the body. Vannier dreaded the fact that he would have to officiate at Moira's funeral. When he left the coroner's office, Vannier decided to walk south to Tranquille House to look in on Mrs. Zell.

Mrs. Zell opened the door for him just as he decided, after minutes of knocking, that she must not be home. Her eyes were red and swollen from crying.

"Oh, Father, it's *so* good to see you," she said. "Please come in."

Vannier found himself becoming overwhelmed by emotion as he entered the parlor and sat near the fire. "I have just come from Mr. Napier. Almost more than I could bear..."

"I *couldn't* go." Mrs. Zell sat on the sofa. "How can this horror be *stopped* once and for all?"

"Has anyone heard from Anatolia?"

"No. And Susan is *right* to keep her whereabouts a secret. The *fewer* of us who know, the better."

"Yes, yes, I agree. There was a journal, an old leather journal, that Moira gave to Anatolia. It was the diary of old Euphrosine. There were things in it that we thought might help us in this."

"If the book had the *answer*, why didn't Euphrosine put it to use and *kill* the demon?"

"Apparently, she didn't have all the information she needed. She could not put together a solution with the incompleteness of what she knew. Now we have the same problem. I must translate the remaining Cathar documents and find the journal. I must reread it and collate it with the new information the documents provide."

"After Anatolia *disappeared,* we went through the *possessions* she left behind, looking for some clue as to what she was *thinking* and where she had gone. We found no journal."

"I must at least finish the translations just in case..." He stood. "I must get to my rooms. I have a letter to write."

"A *letter?*"

"To the archbishop. I am giving up my vocation. Resigning the priesthood. I have but one objective now."

# CHAPTER THIRTY-FIVE

*Anno Domini 1348, December*

Seraphica's face was streaked with tears. I gave her a cup of broth, but she ate none of it.

"If Bastide can find us anywhere, what is the purpose of moving around?" she wept. "We are safe nowhere!"

"If we move, we may be safe for a few days. Here we know we are not," I said. "Since we have been here, you have not been beset by dreams of violence against me as you were in town. I think that is because, for a short while, at least, he did not know you were here."

The sun was coming up as we finished gathering our few possessions

"What about these two?" Seraphica said, glancing at the tattered remains and scattered flesh of her two attackers.

"Let the ravens have them," I said. "It's as well as they deserve. They were in Bastide's service. They are the only reason he found you."

Snow had fallen in the early morning hours, and making our way down the hill toward Riquewihr was difficult. Seraphica seemed to be insensible to what we were doing. She said nothing, and her eyes never lifted from the road before her. She slipped on the icy and rutted road twice, falling with some force, but she righted herself both times and seemed not to notice that either fall had happened. I slowed my pace and walked next to her, arm in arm, to keep her steady.

Half an hour later, we neared the walls of the town. Seraphica was in tears again, and I felt a shudder go through her.

"How are you feeling?" I asked.

She closed her eyes and let me guide her to the south, toward the Zellenberg Road.

"So many terrible things have happened," she sobbed quietly. "What is more terrifying than helplessness, to be at the mercy of whatever fortune has planned for you? There was nothing I could do to stop those men. To think I was so unable to resist the profane force of their intent... their intent to destroy whatever comfort and solace... respect and love for my own being as I may have... for all the rest of my life..."

"Yes, child."

"It isn't what they would have done to my body... it's what they would have done to my *mind,* my spirit. So much worse."

"It is. Yes, it is." She was nervous and near tears as she spoke.

"And this pestilence," she continued, "we are so powerless against it. We are... victims of the capricious will of fortune and God. *Too* harsh, *too* brutal to bear."

Neither of us spoke again until we were well south of Riquewihr. As I wore my veil and Seraphica was in a disheveled state, I hoped we would be unrecognizable to anyone we may pass. I did not want anyone to notice our movements. But the roads were empty.

"Where are we going?" Seraphica asked at length.

"To one place I do not think Bastide would expect to find you."

"No," she said. "That is the Zellenberg Road. We are going to Bastide's farmhouse."

"Yes. I believe he will never return there."

"But we can't *know* that."

"No, not for certain, but the authorities are looking for him. I think he will not wish to be seen here again."

As we crossed the road onto the property, we could see that the door was standing open. Our footsteps crunched on the frozen ground, and as we approached the open door, a red fox ran out of it and across the road. Two ravens quickly followed and pursued the fox into a vineyard.

The interior of the house was smaller than its outside suggested. There was a single bed, a stool, and a small table with dried herbs, animal bones, and a few scraps of parchment on it. Rubbish filled one corner—fabric, crockery, scraps of kindling, and more dried herbs.

Seraphica placed her sack on the table, as did I. "You should sleep on the bed," she said. "I will make myself a place on the floor."

"There was a large chest here," I said, looking around the room. "I wished to find it here, but he has managed to take it with him."

"Anything could be hidden in this pile..." Seraphica moved to the collection of rubbish and began to rummage through it.

"It's too big to be hidden there..."

"But what's this?" Seraphica pulled a large, old book from the pile of rubbish. She placed it on the table and opened it. "It's in Latin, fortunately," she said. "It's the Gospel of St. John. Illuminated. Annotated."

"I doubt Bastide meant to leave that behind," I said. "Perhaps his illiterate helpers thought it worthless."

As Seraphica leafed through the book, a slip of parchment fell out. She picked it up from the floor. "More Latin," she said. She read aloud.

*The world, wizened, old, and so familiar to the powers of darkness and the earthly god, will not see the demon pass away. The world must be made anew and then will come a holy woman, marked on her back, who [indecipherable]. If she doth fail, never will the curse be ended.*

Seraphica frowned and reread the message. "Part of it is

unreadable," she said. "What does it mean?"

"I have no notion," I said. "I suspect this, along with something in the chest, are parts of the same... solution. A mechanism Bastide fears. I wonder if he even knew this message was hidden here. Another gift of the Cathars as he left them."

"The 'holy woman' is surely not either of us?"

"No, I think not. This may become clear with time, but for now, I don't know what to make of it."

# CHAPTER THIRTY-SIX

Reverend Smith questioned Anatolia about her education, her reading, and her ability to communicate new ideas to children. Nearly all of the citizens of Navillus who were parents had remained in the church after Sunday service for the interview. Anatolia was feeling especially sick that morning, but she answered the reverend's questions as completely as she could.

Smith agreed with Toony and most of the other villagers that Anatolia should be the new teacher. Edny Culpepper raised a mild objection about the example an unmarried pregnant woman would set for children, but when she was reminded about the circumstances of Anatolia's condition, she agreed with the Reverend's decision.

It was decided that Anatolia would begin teaching immediately and Smith gave her the few textbooks she would need to look over until then. Word would be spread that all children at fifth-grade level and below must be present at school by eight a.m. the next morning.

When the meeting ended, Anatolia, Toony, Tendetta, and Smith stood outside the church and thanked all the townspeople for attending the meeting and approving of Anatolia's appointment. Tendetta and Toony looked at Anatolia with concern as the last congregant left.

"Oonah still feelin' po'ly?" Tendetta said. "Oonah want to cut-out home?"

"Yes, I need to sit," Anatolia nodded.

"She look bad," Toony said.

"Us give her ginger an' a cool compress." Tendetta said.

"It just comes over me all of a sudden," Anatolia's voice was weak.

"Us doan haf'ta start school tommory," Reverend Smith said. "Not 'till oonah feel better."

"I just need to rest a while," Anatolia said as Toony and Tendetta steadied her. Anatolia had noticed a level of deference toward her from Smith, and Toony's occasional sidelong glances seemed to verify that she had noticed it too.

The women helped Anatolia to the rocking chair on Tendetta's porch. Toony found her a quilt in the front room and placed it over Anatolia's lap. Tendetta went inside to slice ginger and prepare a compress. Toony sat on the milking stool. Eva, who had followed the women from the church and was carrying the few books Smith had given them, stood next to Anatolia and put her head on the sick woman's shoulder.

Tears welled in Anatolia's eyes. "Poor Miss Moira!" she said. "She would have never been killed if I hadn't come to Ste. Odile. Nor Increase, nor..."

"Its nothin' you can do about that now," Toony said. "You just as well shoot you mule 'cause he can't spell as mourn over the past. Don't make no sense."

Eva removed her thumb from her mouth. "Aminals cain't spell, Momma."

Anatolia hugged Eva. "Yes, I know, you're right," she said.

"Mebbe we ought to git you to a real doctor," Toony went on. "Not just a wise-woman or midwife."

"I thought about that," Anatolia said, "but I don't think a doctor could help much in my case. This isn't anything they learn about in medical school. I think I'm going to have to get through this mostly on my own."

Eva placed the books she had been carrying into Anatolia's lap. Anatolia unbuckled the leather strap.

"Let's see what we have here," Anatolia said. "*McGuffey's Eclectic First Reader*, arithmetic, geography, history. I have used several of these before. I taught the children of the New Phrygians for a while."

Tendetta came out of the house with a damp cloth and some thin slices of ginger. She placed the cloth on Anatolia's forehead and gave her the ginger to eat. "Oonah feel betta now," she said. She glanced at Toony.

"Eva, honey," Tooney said, "Go 'head on an' play a while. Gog an' Len ovah yonder."

Eva grinned and ran across the road to where the two boys were playing in the sand.

"So, how you feelin', gal?" Toony asked.

"Still yent gots um appytie?" Tendetta said.

"No. I can't eat anything," Anatolia answered.

"Oonah look piety an' dry-bone," the old woman frowned.

"She means pale and skinny," Toony explained.

"Yuh, fuh true," Tendetta agreed. "Uh worried how this all hittin' oonah."

Anatolia nodded.

"This bush-chile no natchul chile," Tendetta went on.

"No,"

"We sutt'nly hab sumpfin' unholy in de belly. Wan't sho' at firs', but now uh am sho'."

"Mebbe you can conjure somethin' to end it, if she agrees?" Toony said.

"Yes, I would agree to that," Anatolia said.

"Fo'-fibe week ago de time fo' dat. Too late tuh cunjuh now," Tendetta said. "Now it could shet-out-de-light. Kill oonah."

"Then I'll have to face it... somehow" Anatolia said.

"Uh heerd 'bout de spawn ob de debbil oncet," Tendetta continued. "Gal fum Jamaicky tolt um. French-talkin' gal. She say she granny see 'ooman find a chile thet weren't human. Dey called it Rabenous."

"Ravenous?" Toony asked.

"*Le Vorace* in French-talk," Tendetta said, struggling to pronounce it correctly. "It berry, berry oagly to look at. Oagly as a monkrey an' hair all ovah it too."

"Yes," Anatolia sighed. "I know of them."

"Le Vorace," Toony repeated.

"Dey biolent, mean an' hongry," Tendetta said. "Sabage aminals, but dey die quick."

"That's what's inside me, then," Anatolia said. "It's what Susan feared."

"Jus' doan know," Tendetta said. "Uh pray ovah det but de' feelin' doan come. All de notions doan marriage-up. Doan mix. Sumpfin' wrong. Uh mean *mo' wrong* then a monkrey debbil in oonah belly."

Anatolia rested for the remainder of the evening and looked over her textbooks by the light of Tendetta's old lantern. She was familiar with most of the texts and felt she could serve as an effective teacher for as long as she was needed, if her condition permitted.

Tendetta had been letting her guest sleep on the bed. The old woman seemed perfectly comfortable on the floor. When Anatolia woke the next morning, Tendetta was already up. She had made coffee and grits and biscuits. Anatolia politely ate a little, but she had no appetite. All she really wanted was strong coffee.

A little after seven a.m., Anatolia gathered her books and walked down the road to the schoolhouse. The front door was unlocked, as Smith had said it would be. The inside of the schoolhouse was one single room consisting of rows of benches, each with a long, continuous desktop in front of them. There was a small teacher's desk at the front of the room, along with a blackboard and a wood stove. Extra space at the back of the room was filled with cotton bales, sacks of grain, a second wood stove, and firewood.

Anatolia collected some firewood from the back of the room and soon had a good fire going in both stoves. A few minutes before eight o'clock, she heard children's voices outside. Two children, a girl of about eight and a boy of about six, pushed open the front door and walked in.

"No, it yent true!" the boy said. Both children went silent when they saw Anatolia. She smiled at them.

"Good morning," she said. "I am Miss Anatolia."

"Mawnin' miss," the girl said. "I am Suby Dyson. Dis my brudduh..."

"Len Dyson," the boy interrupted.

"Yes, Len. I met you on the road. What are you two arguing about?"

"She say we in da Newnited State," Len continued. "Uh says we in Monfort."

"You're both right," Anatolia smiled. "You are on Monfort Island, which is part of the United States. A big country like this has lots of small parts. Monfort is a part of America."

Suby wet her finger in her mouth and stuck it her brother's ear.

"None of that, Suby!" Anatolia scolded. "You sit in the second row, and Len, you sit in the first." The children did as they were told.

More children came in: Gog Culpepper, Mary Jones, Vernon Smith, Rayford Johnson, Violet Eames, and many more. Anatolia knew they would range in age from six to about eleven years old. Schooling on the island only went as far as fifth grade. Anatolia placed the students according to grade, starting with first graders in the first row and fifth graders in the last. She counted eighteen children.

Anatolia wrote MISS ANATOLIA on the blackboard. "This is how you will address me," she said. "Miss Anatolia."

"Yes, Miss Anatolia," the children said in unison.

Anatolia began the school day by giving all the first graders slates and having them practice copying letters and writing the numbers one through ten she had written on the blackboard. She gave the older children a reading assignment and gathered the second graders around her to read aloud to them.

She had felt bad in the morning but better as the day went on. Three in the afternoon came quickly, and Anatolia was surprised the first day had passed so easily and it was time to dismiss the students.

As the students filed out of the classroom, Reverend Smith appeared in the doorway.

"Reverend Smith," Anatolia said, "Good afternoon."

"I wanted to check up an' see how oonah fus' day gone."

"Very well. I can't believe the day is over already. Children were all well-behaved..."

"Dey a bit ska'yd still. Give um time. "'Spechially Suby an' Gog an' a couple others."

"I'll keep that in mind," Anatolia smiled.

"It's a Chanyberry tree down by de indigo thet's pretty dis time o' year."

"In winter?"

"Come ahead on... uh show oonah."

Anatolia hesitated. She wanted to refuse his invitation but saw no way to do it.

Smith led her to the sandy road that wound south toward the cemetery. He seemed awkward and self-conscious. He smiled at her nervously a few times but seemed at a loss to think of anything to say.

"Everyone has been so kind to me here," Anatolia said after an uneasy pause. "I can't express how grateful I am."

"Well... us sutt'nly knows 'bout de dark powers," Smith said. "Us nebuh los' touch wid dem. Not libin' de simple life as we pefer, close to God's simple purpose like us does."

"Yes, I see that."

"Us knows about ol' Plate-Eye an' how he work he mischeebus ways on sinners. He troubled us on dese islan' for two hunnert year."

Anatolia became quickly exhausted. She stopped walking. Smith looked at her with concern and invited her to sit on a cypress log fallen near the road to rest. A crash could be heard off in the thicket behind them, as if a dead tree had fallen. Smith looked out over the palmettos for a few seconds. He seemed satisfied there was nothing to see. He sat next to Anatolia.

"Uh doan want to be stiff-toned or unspecctable by axing you," he said... "if uh am, jus' say so. But de' bush-chile oonah carryin' is evil, Tendetta say. How did de debbil get to onnah like that? Wid de praisin' of God, onnah could hab..."

There was another crash behind them. A deep snorting sound followed and seemed to come from several directions at once. Anatolia got to her feet in terror as Smith stood, drawing a large revolver from his overcoat. The snort was heard again, and an enormous boar, bristling black and brown, charged out of the palmettos. Anatolia shrieked as Smith fired the pistol into the animal's face, shattering one of its huge, curving tusks. The boar stopped a second and shook its head as Smith fired a second time, and the animal fell dead on the pine needles. Its body quivered and shook for a few seconds, then was still.

"Thet Loomis' old boar got loose lash year," Smith said. "Dey go wild an' git dangerous."

Anatolia didn't seem to hear him. She was shaking uncontrollably and on the verge of tears. Smith cautiously put his arm around her shoulder.

"Onnah all right, Miss Anatoly. Uh got oonah now."

# CHAPTER THIRTY-SEVEN

*M*y dear Father Vannier:

      You will notice that I address you as "Father," not "Mister Vannier." This is because I decline to acknowledge the assertion made by you in your recent letter that you have left the priesthood, forsaken your ordination vows, and thrown your responsibilities to Jesus Christ and your parishioners, by the wayside.

      In your position, I would ask myself, how many souls are dependent upon my administration of the sacraments, of access to holy mass, and for general counsel and reassurance, which all pious Catholics routinely seek from their parish priest? How can I leave these responsibilities behind and abandon these poor souls? My answer, Father, would be, simply, I cannot.

      For years I have watched your progress with much satisfaction. You have served your flock and Holy Mother Church very well. You have been a model of humility, declining advancement in favor of remaining among your parishioners. Even when the Diocese of Belleville requested our help in administering the parishes of Kaskaskia, Prairie du Rocher, and Fort de Chartres, you volunteered for the assignment, to the great satisfaction of those congregants. I have been proud, and most gratified to read the reports of your ministry and management that come to me from those regions.

      For these reasons, my young friend, I have prayed over your situation and concluded, with the help of Our Lord, that whatever disillusionment or exhaustion you may be feeling at this moment is temporary. Your vocation is certainly a true one. To abandon it, even if you could do so without the loss of your immortal soul, would be a great wrong and a terrible mistake. I am certain it is one you would regret for the rest of your days.

      So, to repeat, I do not accept your resignation. I implore you, in the name of God and with deference to your sacred ordination vows, to pray over this rash decision and to quickly resume your responsibilities.

Yours In Christ,
Most Reverend,
Peter Kendrick
Archbishop of the Archdiocese of St. Louis

Vannier arose from the settee in Mrs. Zell's parlor. He neatly and respectfully folded the letter and dropped it into the fire.

"What is that you're *burning*?" Mrs. Zell placed a tray with coffee and toast on the table in front of the settee.

"Just an old letter," Vannier said.

Mrs. Zell sat. "Moira is *buried* tomorrow."

"Yes," Vannier said.

"Can you *manage* it? Will you be *able*?"

"I will. I can't say mass, but I know she didn't want that. We will meet in the great hall at the old school and commemorate her. She is to be buried next to Perdita."

"Yes, I saw *the* grave being prepared."

The day he mailed his letter to the Archbishop, Vannier had moved out of his basement room at the church and into Moira's old room at Mrs. Zell's Tranquille House. Vannier had some small savings, and he calculated that he could live independently for a year or more.

He set up a work area at Moira's old desk at the front window of the room, overlooking the street. He brought all the materials salvaged from the Cathar chest and began collating and studying them with an intensity his former priestly duties had made impossible.

Vannier was dismayed to find, when he first received it, that the reference book sent to him from the Carthesian Library had been damaged by water. In 1829, there had been a great fire in and near the library at the Carthesian University. Unfortunately, this necessary volume, *A Practical and Leisurely Phrasebook and Dictionary of the Ancient Occitan Language,* had been greatly compromised. Many pages were plastered together from moisture and could not be separated without obliterating the text within them. On other pages, print and illustrations were smeared, smudged, and illegible. Vannier spent most of a week trying to gently separate the pages with indifferent success.

At ten o'clock the next morning, Vannier, Mrs. Zell, and most of the New Phrygians gathered in the main hall at the Academy of Perpetua. Some of the native townspeople were also in attendance, though many more were kept away, apprehensive and suspicious that the service was just to be a memorial, not a funeral mass. Moira's simple casket had been placed on a makeshift bier, and six of the New Phrygian men had volunteered to be pallbearers.

A few minutes after ten, Vannier rose before those gathered and spoke.

"Friends old and new, this may not be the funeral service you expected for our dear Moira, but it is the one I know she wanted, or rather, *preferred.* Some of you here assembled, like myself, have known Moira since she came to Ste. Odile after the death of her dearest friend, Perdita Badon-Reed. The tragic events of those times shattered her, nearly broke her. But she was a woman of great courage and resolve, and more importantly, of compassion and responsibility to humanity. She saw a need in the town, an emptiness left by the passing of her friend, and without hesitation, she sought to fill it.

Many a young girl at the Academy of Perpetua has benefited from her knowledge and grown in character because of her advice, example, and counsel. I personally knew a special light shone from within her, and I am fortunate to have counted her as the greatest and closest friend of my life. Two great women transformed the character, ethics, and sensibilities of this old town. We bury the last of them today. I can hardly conceive of the emptiness of my few remaining years on earth... without her."

Vannier hung his head and composed himself.

"If any of you have anything to say," he continued, "please do so now."

Mrs. Zell arose slowly. "She was a *daughter*. Very truly a *daughter*. All our *bedeviled* little town, and especially me, are the *worse* for her loss."

Mrs. Heugyens stood with the aid of Susan, who was sitting next to her.

"I was privileged to have known Miss Parnell, if only for a short time. She was a protector and mentor of our dear Anatolia at a terrible time in her life, and for that, I, and I am sure all the New Phrygian congregants, are forever grateful."

As Mrs. Heugyens sat, Vannier walked in front of the casket. "All rise please, for a prayer for the dead," he said. Vannier bowed his head.

*Loving God our Father,*
*Your power brings us to life.*
*Your care guides our lives,*
*and by Your command we return to the dust from which we came.*
*Father, those who pass on still live in Your presence,*
*their lives are changed but do not end.*
*I plead in hope for my family,*
*relatives and friends,*
*and for all the dead known only to You.*

Vannier motioned to the pallbearers who assembled at the casket. He led the company in a slow procession out of the great hall and across the grounds to the old cemetery of the Sisters of Perpetua. The grave had been dug next to Perdita's monument, and the headstone, carved in white marble according to Vannier's specifications, read:

*Here once, through an alley Titanic,*
*Of cypress, I roamed with my Soul—*

As the coffin was placed over the grave, the congregants gathered around it. When everyone had found a place to stand, Vannier spoke.

"Moira thought little of ritual and not much of organized religion. Hence, so far, I have said only one prayer. For my sake and to get you all in out of this cold, I will read only one passage from Scripture. I will read from Paul to the Philippians, a verse which I think perfectly expresses the soul and nature of our departed Moira.

*Finally, brethren, whatsoever things are true, whatsoever things are honest, whatsoever things are just, whatsoever things are pure, whatsoever things are lovely, whatsoever things are of good report; if there be any virtue, and if there be any praise, think on those things.*

Vannier made the sign of the cross and prayed to himself for a few moments. The congregation began to move away as the coffin was lowered into the grave. A few of them thanked him for the service and expressed their condolences. Mrs. Heugyens and Susan stayed back and when most of the gathering had dispersed, approached Vannier.

"Uh so sorry for oonah loss," Susan said, taking Vannier's hand.

"Thank you, Susan."

"Yes," Mrs. Heugyens said. "So much loss has followed us. Now, I am afraid it will only be multiplied. I never thought to see the day."

"What is it, Mrs. Heugyens? What do you mean?" Vannier asked.

"Our dear Anatolia is lost to us. The heart and soul of our community. Set is lost to us. The center is gone, and all has fallen apart. I suppose it is understandable under these awful circumstances. Ste. Odile is seen as cursed, dark, and benighted. I will stay. I hope Susan will stay, but the New Phrygians are no more. My people are returning home. All are leaving Ste. Odile."

# CHAPTER THIRTY-EIGHT

*Anno Domini 1348, December*

"Let down your shift," I said, "let me see your back."

Seraphica did as I asked. As she stood, undraped in the freezing farmhouse, I examined her back, neck to pelvis. I saw no mark on her skin of any kind.

"No mark here, nothing." I helped her cover herself. "If these were pagan times, you would be thought a perfect sacrifice to Baal. Blemish-free."

"I wish I knew what all of this means," Seraphica said.

"So do I. Livilla, my teacher, made vague reference to such a woman who may appear once in a thousand lifetimes, but it meant nothing to me then. She didn't understand it herself, I think."

"Freezing in here," Seraphica's tone was sullen and sad. "I'm going to build up the fire." She threw more branches and twigs into the fireplace. She then rewrapped herself in her shawl and went outside to find more.

I placed a crock with ice in it on the hearth to melt. I thought to make some herbal tea and a soup from dried beef.

It seemed to me that the attempted attack on Seraphica had deeply affected, perhaps even changed her. There was something missing in her speech and manner and even in the way she looked at me. She was empty and hopeless now, without illusion or expectation. I hoped that in time, she would become herself again.

The door opened, and Seraphica dragged in the bundle of sticks she had collected. She stacked them near the fireplace and built up the fire even more. "It is exhausting being cold all the time," she said.

"I will be making some broth if you are hungry," I said.

She sat on the bed, pulling her shawl more tightly around herself. "It will be spring soon," she said.

"Yes. Not long. We will make it through."

"Of course, the pestilence may resurge in the warmer weather."

"Yes,"

"Yet... if we have no hope, no joyful expectation, how do we maintain the will to get through this?"

"We must have hope. You are right."

"On the road to Ribeauville, just north, there is a small apricot orchard."

"Yes, I have seen it. It borders a field of hops near an old church. A ruined chapel."

"The Chapel of St. Aldaric. The land was once owned by my uncle but is now abandoned. My parents were married in the chapel. On a holy day when I was very young, we visited there. It must have been Easter. It was warm and there was a grand feast. In the evening, the three of us sat in the chapel. Mother, Father, and I. I listened to the story of their wedding day... each exchanging individual memories. Soon the meaning of their words faded as I sat on Father's lap, and all I recall is the sound of their voices. A happy murmur, it was."

"Those things we truly value..." When she made no response to this, I turned and saw she had fallen asleep on the bed. It was only early evening, but I knew she was fatigued.

Some hours later, I made myself a bed on the cold floor.

I dreamt that night of *my* family—of old Thrace, of Lyon, of the Saturnalia and the rites of spring. I saw my brother and my parents on what I took to be the day before the soldiers came to arrest them. I awoke with a start.

A cold breeze swept across the floor of the farmhouse. I could see that the front door was slightly ajar. Sitting up, I saw that Seraphica was not in the bed, nor anywhere in the small house. I stood and looked outside. It was a cloudy, dark night. I called her name a few times, but there was no answer.

A sense of dread swept over me. She would not take an idle walk this time of night, suffering from the cold as she had been for the last few days. In her melancholy, almost hopeless recent state, her sense of distraction and preoccupation, I feared she would try to make her way to Ribeauville and the old Chapel of St. Alderic.

I wrapped myself as warmly as I could and made my way to the southwest on the well-worn road winding through the dormant grape fields. I hadn't been to the area in years, and it was much further than I remembered. After perhaps an hour of walking, I came to the spectral remains of the old apricot orchard and turned southeast on the lane. The ruins of the old church came quickly into view. I was surprised to see how deteriorated the old building was. It had only been abandoned for twenty years. It is an unfortunate fact, in these days of disorder, chaos, and lawlessness, that landowners and local peasants have taken to harvesting stone from abandoned buildings—even blessed and sanctified ones—for their own use., What will be left when this pestilence has gone?

All was darkness in the old church. As I approached it, I heard a cough, a wet-sounding, gurgling cough coming from inside.

"Seraphica?" I called. No answer.

The front door had long ago been removed for firewood or building material. I walked through the opening. In the darkness, I heard a gasp and another gurgle. As my eyes adjusted to the gloom, I saw a dark mound on the floor.

She was struggling for breath. I could just see that her face, her arms, and her skirt were blood-spattered. She seemed too weak to open her eyes to look at me. I shuddered and wept to think of my responsibility to her. How would I keep her alive? How would I get her to safety?

# CHAPTER THIRTY-NINE

Anatolia managed to teach five more days before she was too ill to go on. On the afternoon of the fifth day, she apologized to the children before she sent them home. She told them she could not come to the classroom anymore. Several of them cried and most stayed behind to ask her about her sickness and would she be back to teach them again.

Chester Williams, a second-grader, pressed against Anatolia's knee as she sat. "Was us mischeebus, Miss Anatoly?" he asked. "Was us bad?"

"No, Chester," Anatolia smiled at him. "All of you were very well-behaved, most of the time. I love being your teacher."

"What kinda sickness oonah got, miss?" Suby asked.

"It's something I will tell you all about someday. I won't tell you now, but someday you will know. I want you all to read on your own and I will arrange a way to have you visit me in small groups at Miss Tendetta's. It's the best I can do for now."

"Miss..." Suby continued, "Pa say ef us doan git eddycayshun, we nebbuh git out dis' islan'."

"Don't be so anxious to leave here, Suby," Anatolia said. "But, yes, you deserve an education. And you will get one."

The last two afternoons, Reverend Smith had stopped by the school at closing to walk Anatolia home. But today, as he sometimes did, he went out to Cooper Reef with St. Michael Culpepper in his boat at low tide to harvest oysters. Anatolia was slightly relieved he didn't come. It was not attention she wanted or needed, and she had a persistent sense that he considered her condition to be evidence that she was fallen and Smith's duty to Jesus was to save her. The walk home after school had become Anatolia's private time to think about Set and about how terribly she missed him. She shuddered to imagine how he had met his death and frequently had to put this thought out of her mind.

And she thought of her father. He had spent years struggling to make a good life for her, only to have it destroyed in a moment of violence and hatred. She had at least some sense of gratitude that he was not witnessing the horrific circumstances in which she now found herself.

By the time Anatolia reached Tendetta's porch, she was light-headed and depleted. She collapsed onto the rocking chair. The front door opened.

"No, no," Tendetta said. "Fetch on in de house. Too cold out cheer." She helped Anatolia stand and move inside. "Lay up inna bed. Uh gone draw oonah a baf. An' dis come today."

Tendetta handed Anatolia another telegram from Mrs. Heugyens and sent by Susan Henry.

*Dear Anatolia:*

*All of the New Phrygians have gone home. Our community is no more. Only Susan and I remain. We would certainly not be harmed by your pursuer if he still lives. We pray to see you again. We pray you will return to Ste. Odile.*

*M. Heugyens*

Anatolia sat slowly on the edge of the bed and then lay on her back. She felt pain all over her body and that she may have a slight fever. Looking down at herself, she could see her stomach had grown noticeably. She had no notion of how her condition compared to a normal pregnancy. She did not know if she would come to term in nine months or, it seemed more likely to her, less.

It seemed to Anatolia that Tendetta was gaining proficiency in her care. More accurately, it appeared that the old, wise woman was remembering a forgotten skill or acknowledging the dim familiarity of some newly confronted sight or sound.

A sudden queasy feeling came over Anatolia. She looked down at her stomach and, to her horror, saw a wave of motion under her blouse. She pulled the blouse up and gasped. Tendetta rushed into the room.

"Land 'o Goshen," Tendetta whispered. "It a tanglety sitchashun dancin' wif de debbil. Oonah sweet gal... de time es short."

Tendetta placed a warm cloth on Anatolia's forehead, and in a few moments, she drifted off to sleep.

In another twenty minutes, Tendetta had heated enough water that it filled the washtub she had placed on the kitchen floor. She then stoked up the fire in the stove even higher to warm the room more.

Tendetta gently awoke Anatolia and helped her sit up. Anatolia had the confused look of someone who had been disturbed during an intense dream.

"I was dreaming of my father," Anatolia said. "After Perdita died and Miss Moira came to Ste. Odile, my father came for me. I was a child. So many horrible things had happened by that time. My father was not much more than a stranger to me then. I hadn't seen him above three times in my life."

"Oonah was 'faid?"

"Yes. I knew that nothing was certain or permanent. Nothing could be counted on. I believed I could trust this man and was obliged to love him, but I didn't know him. And if I did trust him and love him, it seemed, like my dear Perdita, that he could be ripped away from me."

"Let git oonah in de baf, chile," Tendetta helped her stand.

"But the trip we made together back to New York was wonderful," Anatolia continued. "Everything melted away. We took the train."

"De trip on de strain berry nice."

"We crossed the great bridge in St. Louis and went across the country, through mountains and..."

"Let git oonah in de wadduh while it hot."

The kitchen had warmed up considerably. Tendetta helped Anatolia get undressed and step into the tub. She sat in the warm water tentatively, but grew slowly accustomed to it. After a moment, she glanced down at the soothing water and saw a whisp of red wafting away from her. She closed her eyes.

"Oonah rest and set still. Rest." Tendetta washed Anatolia's arms and face with a warm cloth. She hummed a soothing, quiet tune that Anatolia thought she must have heard in church long ago. The old woman washed the nape of Anatolia's neck and moved toward her back.

"Chile..." Tendetta said suddenly. "What dis mark on de back? Buthmark? I nebbuh notice it befo'."

"I don't have a birthmark. Set would have told me."

"Sweet Jedus!" the old woman exclaimed, "It change it shape!"

# CHAPTER FORTY

With a great deal of care, Vannier was able to separate most of the damaged pages in the reference book in the better part of two days. The damage to the text was considerable and inopportune in many instances, but he knew he had to work with the result as best he could.

When he had a workable reference book, he focused his attention on the Cathar document containing the heading *Es lo rituala destruccíon del díable*.

Approximately the first third of the reference book had sustained most of the water damage. The Romance Language roots of the text made it obvious to Vannier that these pages had to do with exorcism or control of evil spirits and demons. The passage consisted of several hundred words. Step-by-step instructions of the rituals were interspersed, he discovered, with long passages of scripture and apologetics. It seemed to wander off on tangents about the dual nature of existence, the province of evil on earth and its connection to the earthly god, and the inherent wickedness of material things.

After three hours of laborious translation, cross referencing, and guesswork caused by the incompleteness of the dictionary, Vannier concluded that these rituals were general instructions for exorcisms and were Catharic variations on the rituals of the medieval Catholic church. There was nothing specific here to the expulsion or destruction of the incubus.

There was a gentle knock on Vannier's door. Mrs. Zell stepped into the room with a tray containing a sandwich and coffee. "I don't believe you have *eaten* anything today," she said. "I took a *chance* that you were hungry."

"Thank you, Mrs. Zell," Vannier said. "Put it on the dresser. I will eat a little."

"Have you made any *progress*?"

"Only in eliminating irrelevancies. All of this so far is general. Rituals that existed from the beginning of the sect. I suspect that anything relating specifically to the incubus came later, after Bastide became one of them and his true nature was known."

"But *why* would Bastide have joined them? Why become *part* of an eccentric Christian religion?"

"It's hard to say. It would have been a perfect place to hide away if he were being pursued. He could have had some commonality with their philosophy, some sympathy and agreement with their concept of goodness. The human side of him, from what I have learned, did not wish to do evil. His two natures were at war with each other. That is also the Cathars' view of existence: the dark and the light constantly at war."

"Yes," Mrs. Zell nodded. "Perhaps then, these old papers are *useless* to you?"

Vannier shrugged. "It remains to be seen. I certainly hope that isn't true. The other indicators from the old chest suggest otherwise."

Mrs. Zell left the room and closed the door behind her.

Early in the evening, Vannier moved to the second page of the document. More than halfway down the page began a sentence: *Solament lo cambion...* The rest of the phrase, three more words, was indistinct. The first three words translated to, "Only the cambion..."

As he scanned down the rest of the paragraph, Vannier noted faded letters that he became convinced were parts of the word "incubus."

\*\*\*

Soon after dawn, there was another tapping on the door. Not waiting for a response, Mrs. Zell stepped in.

"My *goodness*, Father," she said, "have you been up all *night*?"

"Yes." He rubbed his face in exhaustion. He stood and stretched. "The creatures associated with Bastide and his victims..."

"*Le Vorace*," Mrs. Zell said.

"Yes, the Ravenous."

"The hellish, *unfortunate* spawn of the union. They aren't produced by *every* attack, but often are. They are then seen by the *potential* victim, who afterward knows she is chosen. They are verminous, *savage*. They can attack and *kill* at the will of Bastide."

"Yes... yes. But they cannot harm Bastide?"

"No. It is his spirit that *directs* them."

"And they do not live long?"

"No longer than a *damselfly*, if they have done him service."

Vannier collapsed back into his chair. "It seems there is more than one type of spawn," he said. "Once in a century, once in an eon, by chance, the offspring is something more. There is one who is attacked who comes to know she is unique. All depends on her. I remembered something I read in the journal of old Euphrosine. There will be a mark on her back. A new, living mark that indicates that the beast she carries is called the cambion. Cambion is the awaited issue of the incubus. It perpetuates the curse into the future. When it finally appears, it alone can kill its sire. If it succeeds, it replaces him."

"I am *confused*," Mrs. Zell frowned. "It was *thought* that to kill the host would kill Balphoroth, the demon."

"That doesn't appear to be true. Mrs. Zell, we need for Susan to get another message to Anatolia."

# CHAPTER FORTY-ONE

*Anno Domini 1348, Christmas Day*

At dawn, I stopped the death cart from Ribeauville on the road. The driver's name was Charles. He was returning from carrying the morning's bodies to the common grave. He agreed to help me place Seraphica in his now empty cart and to carry her back to the farmhouse.

She made nearly no response to me for any word or ministration for a day and a night. After twenty-four hours, she went into a type of delirium, developing a high fever. I kept her covered after bringing her temperature down, and in the middle of the second night she was able to take a little broth. I cleaned her and repaired her clothes.

I believed that after this attack, she would be in some measure, safe for a period of time. I grew to feel at ease leaving her resting for periods on her own as I hunted for tubers, bark, and other medicinal elements, or walked back to Riquewihr for dried meats, herbs, and other supplies. On one such trip back to my rooms I saw Celeste, a servant in Seraphica's father's house. I waved to her, but she did not see me, or recognize me. She seemed preoccupied with some grave thought.

On the third day of her recovery, Seraphica greatly improved. Her appetite was returning, which gave me great relief. Long before the attack she had eaten sparingly, or not at all, some days, and had begun to look drawn and emaciated. Twice that day she took soup and bread and a little wine. By evening she seemed less pallid and slightly more animated.

"It was so *foolish* of you to run away at night like that," I said to her as I cleaned her plate and cup. "By this time, you should more than know better. You could have bled to death before I found you!" I was surprised by my own anger.

"Yes, Mother," her voice was weak. "I am sorry. Deeply sorry. The chapel... It was the place, one place I could definitely remember in my life, where there was *joy*. I just wanted to remember joy."

Under the pretext of checking her for bedsores, I examined her back two or three times a day. The notation we had read about the mark on the back of she who was called the "holy woman," who could bring about the destruction of the incubus, was on my mind. This prospect both thrilled and horrified me. I thought it must somehow be a responsibility visited upon one of Bastide's chosen. I thought it could quite possibly involve the loathsome spawn of the union, and I was worried that my charge may have been thus infected.

Yet, it seemed likely that any such woman must be at risk of her life to fulfill such a responsibility, to execute such an office. I could not accept the thought of any such risk surrounding my dear girl. I had failed to protect her. It was a duty I set for myself, and I failed. I knew I must never let her out of my sight again.

After days of checking her, no mark appeared on her back.

Seraphica's revived appetite began to quickly fade again. Most of what she did eat, she vomited up, and for two days could take nothing but a little bread and wine in the afternoons. As I was serving these to her on the second day, she was sitting at our small table beside the western window. As the sun hit her face and a familiar scent arose from her hair and belly, I knew she had changed. I knew instantly that *Le Vorace* was inside her.

I said nothing but sensed she could see a darkness pass over my face. She must have suspected what I knew, but at that moment, we both seemed to choose to let the obvious, the dreaded truth, remain unspoken.

Seraphica fell into a great melancholy. She grew restless. She stood and walked more to regain her strength. Very little effort quickly exhausted her, but I could see some slight improvement, fueled by her own will.

"Mother," she said to me on the fifth morning after the attack, "you have truly been a mother to me, more attentive, more solicitous than my own mother. Yet... I miss her. I feel I must see her again. I want to see my house, see familiar faces. Do you think we could walk into town? Could we visit my mother?"

"I doubt you are up to it."

"I can make it, if slowly. I have a sense that this world is too wicked to persist, too contaminated, too rotten throughout. Who knows if we have a week or a month more before it is all righteously annihilated?"

"Very well," I said. "We will go in the morning."

The morning was bright and cloudless and a bit warmer than the previous week had been. Slowly and by careful degrees, Seraphica and I made our way back to Riquewihr. Four times we stopped to rest for a half-hour or so, and by late morning we had reached the town's north gate. We very quickly arrived at the door of Seraphica's family home.

Celeste was just dumping a chamber pot into the street as we approached. "Oh, Miss Seraphica, is that you?" she said. "What has happened to you?"

Seraphica shook her head and embraced the girl. "I will tell you all. But I miss my mother. I have come to see her."

Celeste sobbed. "We have just taken her to the hospital this morning, miss. She has the pestilence!"

Seraphica gasped. She hurried, as best as her depleted condition would allow, east toward the hospital. I tried to steady her arm. Her body was in such a weakened condition that I thought surely her legs must quickly give out.

The sisters at Perpetua's did not recognize their one-time benefactor as we entered the main room. Seraphica saw her mother on the bed marked St. Andrew. A dead woman lay next to her.

Seraphica sobbed into her hands. Her mother was in a momentary delirium. She was drenched in sweat and bursting buboes had erupted around her mouth. Her eyes were glazed, and for a long time she seemed to not acknowledge that her daughter was kneeling at her side. She wheezed a little and after a few minutes, tried to speak. Seraphica drew closer to her.

"Not too close, my child," she said. "It is a miracle that you have avoided this plague thus far. I do not wish to die knowing you caught the contagion from me."

"Mother, do not try to talk. We will pray over you."

"Prayer pays little dividend," the sick woman spat the words, so covered in bodily effusions were her lips. "So I have heard it said. But in the last hour of one's life, who does not fear to abide by such assertions?"

"Mother..."

"If God does not destroy the world, but only purifies it, if he lets it be reborn, my girl, you will be a rich woman."

"No... I don't care about..."

"A woman of property and position. Monsieur Roualt has a copy of the will. Pay your taxes, treat the servants well. Honor God and beware of suitors who would claim your property. If you marry, marry wisely."

"I have no intention or interest in marriage..."

"Intentions change. Listen to your feelings and common sense. Mother of Centuries will help you..."

"*You* will help me, Mother. We will live in the house together, and I will nurse you back to health."

"God love you, my dear daughter." She coughed, gurgled a shallow breath, and died.

# CHAPTER FORTY-TWO

"Oonah say de ole book oonah brung es writ by a wise woman?"

"It is," Anatolia said. "It was. I read through it before I left Ste. Odile. Moira thought I could benefit from it. I am not sure what she meant. My experience seems to be like that of countless others."

"Mebbe," Tendetta said. She found Euphrosine's old journal in the satchel containing Anatolia's few possessions, which they had been keeping under the bed. The old woman opened the book and skimmed through it. More than halfway through the book, she handed it to Anatolia. "Read up on dat top part," she said.

"'The world, wizened, old,'" Anatolia read, "'and so familiar to the powers of darkness and the earthly god, will not see the demon pass away. The world must be made anew and then will come a holy woman, marked on her back, who [indecipherable]. If she doth fail, never will the curse pass away.'"

"Oonah... *you* hab dat mark!" Tendetta said.

"Me?"

"Oonah is de holy woman. Dis duty fall to *oonah*."

Anatolia was incredulous. "We don't know that for certain."

"It fuh true. I knows it, I feels it. Set up, now."

Anatolia sat up and leaned forward. Tendetta opened the back of her blouse and looked at the mark.

"It change agin," Tendetta said. "It look sumpfin' like a crab befo', now it like a lizzrid or a sallymanter."

Anatolia buried her face in her hands. Tendetta embraced her.

"De ole world is de world across de salt, across de water. Dis place, dis land de new world. De Newnited State. An' oonah has de mark it talk about."

Anatolia shook her head. "What do I do about this? I don't want any part of this!"

"Doan know." Tendetta stood.

"What is different about me?" Anatolia said. "I know this has happened time and again over the years to so many women. So many young women. What is different now?"

"God will 'splain when de time come. It all tangelty now, but us onduhstan when us meant to. Heerd oncet 'bout de cambion. Uh was hopin' it not dat." Tendetta walked into the kitchen. "Uh make some okry an' rice. Onnah eat sumpfin?"

"No, I can't. I can't think about eating."

"'Nuthuh wise woman tolt me oonah feed de cambion or it feed on oonah!"

"We don't *know*..."

There was a gentle tap on the door. Tooney pushed it open and stepped inside.

"Oh, Tooney it's so good to see you!" Anatolia said.

Tooney embraced her friend. "I been worried about you, and Eva is more worried, still. How are you feeling?"

"Tell huh to eat somefin'." Tendetta called from the kitchen.

"Still very weak," Anatolia said to Tooney. "Seems like it's all coming to an end-point, and I don't know how to face it."

"You know you're safe here." Tooney sat next to Anatolia.

"I'm not sure what I know anymore." Anatolia said.

Tooney touched Anatolia's cheek. "Little bit of fever," she said. "Tendetta and me talked it over. Both of us gonna watch over you. Eva stayin' at the Culpeppers' for now..."

"Gal gone eat sumpfin'?" Tendetta entered the room carrying a small plate of okra and rice.

"I can't eat," Anatolia protested. "I need to get some of my strength back, but I can't eat. I need to get up. Walk around a little."

"Now she want git up out de bed," Tendetta frowned. "Oonah need git back de strent fus."

The front door pushed open. Reverend Smith stepped in with a bucket full of a gray and tan glistening mass. "Sorry fuh t'bust in ladies," he said. "Gots some oysters uh clean fuh oonah."

"Uh jus' done hankuh fuh erysters," Tendetta said. "Fetch um on in de kitchen,"

Smith carried the bucket into the kitchen, followed by Tendetta. He quickly returned to the front room.

"She ain't hungry but she want to walk. Get the blood moving," Tooney said to him.

"I do," Anatolia agreed.

"Well, how fuh oonah want to go?" Smith asked. "Uh walk a ways witcha."

"Not far," Anatolia said, "I can't go far. Maybe just the crossroads and back. I have been afraid to walk alone since the boar attacked us."

"It safe now. Ol' Loomis et' dat hawg!" Smith said. "Yent no mo' out der."

"I'll walk too," Tooney said, glancing at Anatolia. Anatolia looked back at her gratefully. Tooney knew her friend felt awkward walking alone with Smith.

Anatolia and Tooney wrapped themselves warmly and they joined Smith outside. Tendetta stoked up the stove to cook the oysters Smith had brought.

The sea breezes swept across the treetops, nearly muffling the sound of the surf on the eastern beach. The sky, visible above the town and above the south road, was dense and smudged with stars, which would soon be joined by the full moon rising over the dark Atlantic later that night.

"You feelin' any better at all?" Tooney asked as they crossed the square toward the south road.

"No. I would say no," Anatolia answered. "I would only expect it to get worse until it's all over."

"Dat fuh true," Smith agreed. "What happen when it obah? What become of oonah?"

"I don't know. I have thought about it, and sometimes it doesn't seem right to be here if I put anyone in danger. Whatever is inside me will surely do that. If it is *Le Vorace,* as has been shown so many times before, once it is out free in the world, Bastide will know it, and he will find me."

"But Tendetta says no," Tooney said. "She says it's somethin' else. She says she's sure of that."

Smith cleared his throat as they reached the crossroad and turned east toward the boat docks. "Dat bring up sumpfin' uh want to ax about, Miss Anatoly," he said. "Ebrybody know now oonah gots de mark o' de debbil on de back."

Anatolia stopped and looked at him in disbelief. "How is that? *How* is it that everybody knows that?"

"Well, it hawd to say..."

"I don't know what the mark is. Tendetta saw it, not me."

"I think Tendetta let it slip out to Edny. She didn't mean to tell her. Now the whole village knows," Tooney said.

Anatolia looked exasperated. "I should leave the island. I should go back to Ste. Odile and see this through there. No one left in the town anymore I would endanger. And I feel this is *supposed* to end there. Meant to end in Ste. Odile."

"How will you face it alone?" Tooney asked. "Tendetta and me will protect you."

"Tendetta is a frail old woman, and you, my dearest friend, have a child to raise. It would be unthinkable to put you in danger."

"Ladies... ef uh could continue," Smith interrupted. "Onliest point uh makin' is ebil has foun' oonah, Anatoly. Es de pastuh ob dis flock, it fall to me tuh stop it."

"No..." Anatolia objected.

"Some kinder way oonah let de debbil in," Smith went on. "'Ooman's has dat weakness. Jedus gone fix it. Us habe de shout on Sunday. Us baptize oonah agin, an' de whole billage pray de debbil away. Befo' oonah find det bush-chile, us purify it."

"Reverend, I don't think..." Tooney began.

"No, no, Reverend. I heard Wiley tell Tendetta that Mr. Post, Mr. Franklin Post, who first brought me to the island, is bringing the mail tomorrow."

"Reg'lar man sick. I heerd 'bout thet," Smith said.

A sound of breaking branches could be heard above the surf and wind sounds. Looking toward the southeast, the three of them could just see the moonlight glimmering off the surf through the trees in the distance. For a second, the light was blocked from view as a dark form passed across it. Smith removed his pistol from his overcoat and began to walk briskly back toward the main road.

"Ladies, please fetch on home," he said.

"What is it?" Anatolia asked.

"I don't know," Tooney said. "I don't know what it really is, but Reverend Smith thinks it's Old Plate-Eye."

# CHAPTER FORTY-THREE

"Was it *worth* it, Father?" Mrs. Zell had a look of deep concern on her face as she placed Vannier's plate before him. His appetite had faded drastically in the last few months, and when he took up residence at Tranquille House, he asked Mrs. Zell to only prepare him light meals—baked or boiled meats and a vegetable were all that he would require. Tonight, the meal consisted of a baked chicken leg and asparagus.

"I am now *Mr.* Vannier, not Father."

"Yes, of course. Old *habits*, you know."

"Yes, it was worth it."

"Well, it's none of my *business*, of course," Mrs. Zell sat at her place at the dining room table adjacent to Vannier, "but you gave up your *vocation*, your life's calling, to deal with the Cathar *mystery*, and that took only a few days, now..."

Vannier smiled at her. "There was more at work than that," he said. "I have tried to do my duty over the years to the faithful, to my parishioners. But my vocation has been fading for quite a long time. My friendship with Moira, my connection to her, showed me how fragile and even shallow that vocation was. I have nothing left to give of myself to the Church, to faith, or to those who look to me for spiritual guidance."

Mrs. Zell sipped her coffee. "Then... whatever will you *do*?" she asked.

"I spoke to the sheriff yesterday, and Mrs. Heugyens."

"Oh?"

"And to Mr. Purviance this morning."

"The lawyer?"

"Yes."

"Do you have a legal problem with the *archdiocese*? The archbishop must have objected *strongly* to your decision."

"No. I wanted to establish to everyone's satisfaction that no one has a claim to the Cathar documents."

"Mrs. Heugyens's group *retrieved* the chest and *brought* them here. The New Phrygians are all but gone now."

"Mrs. Heugyens lays no claim to them. Purviance told me in that case, since I have physical possession of them, they are legally mine."

"I see," Mrs. Zell seemed confused. "Then, what will *you* do with them?"

"I will make a gift of them."

"To whom?"

"My friend at the Carthesian Library will consider them a windfall. They will be a great addition to their collection of rare documents. And I have a reference volume to return."

"I am *certain* you are right. I am sure your friend will be *most* grateful."

Vannier had hardly touched his dinner. "And I wanted to tell you, Mrs. Zell, that I hope to win a position at the Library. I will be leaving Ste. Odile in a few days. Forever, I think."

Mrs. Zell's expression went blank. "Oh..." she said. "So, you must *leave*."

"Yes. I am sorry to leave you, but there is nothing for me here anymore. None of us know if Anatolia is still alive. We have had no indication. If she is, if she has truly disappeared, she is better off, safer now, I pray. Of course, I am not accustomed to acting only in my own best interests. That is not a vocation. But now, I am compelled to do so. There is nothing more I can do to protect Anatolia or destroy Bastide, if he survives. The power to overcome Bastide lies solely with Anatolia. May God help her. My thought is that neither of them will ever be seen in this village again."

Mrs. Zell arose and began clearing the table, saying nothing.

Vannier spent a restless night, his mind racing across all his years at Ste. Odile. He thought of Moira, of Perdita, Anatolia, old Father Condell, of the Sisters of Perpetua, and all the girls who had come and gone over the decades at the old Academy. He wondered if he was abandoning some moral responsibility by leaving the town. In the end, he knew he wasn't. It was truly Anatolia alone who could stop the great pestilence that had lain over Ste. Odile for nearly two hundred years.

In the morning, he carefully packed the Cathar documents in a portfolio he had purchased and gathered his few possessions. Mrs. Zell was waiting for him at the foot of the stairs with a cup of coffee. "I met Mrs. Heugyens on my morning *walk* just now," she said. "She tells me that the Academy property has been sold. It will become an *orphanage* very soon."

"Ah," Vannier did not know how to react to the news. He took a sip of his coffee and returned the cup to her. He gave Mrs. Zell a short embrace. "Thank you for everything, Mrs. Zell. Best to you here." He meant to say more but could think of nothing. Mrs. Zell patted his cheek and turned to walk into the kitchen.

Vannier walked north on Constantinople Street toward the Academy. At the great gate and the avenue of cypresses, he left his parcels against one of the tree trunks and walked among the gravestones of the old cemetery of the Sisters of Perpetua. Side by side were Perdita's monument and Moira's gravestone.

He knelt at Moira's grave and repeated the Prayer for the Dead. He crossed himself and stood. He kissed the top of the stone, then walked back and retrieved his luggage. Vannier then made his way toward Bosphorous Street and Vizir Packet lines to book his passage to St. Louis.

# CHAPTER FORTY-FOUR

*Anno Domini 1349, January*

The funeral of Seraphica's mother was small and scarcely attended, as are all funerals these days. It is unusual for plague victims to have a funeral; most are wrapped and thrown into common graves as this is thought to be an effective precaution against the contagion. Seraphica, however, insisted that her mother have the Christian burial she wanted and be laid to rest next to her husband in the St. Cyr churchyard. The mayor, the sheriff, and the priest all were persuaded to capitulate to her wishes.

I stood with Seraphica at the service and steadied her. Celeste attended, as did an older serving woman named Aurelia. The last two days had been warmer, and standing in the churchyard didn't seem as onerous as Seraphica's father's service had been.

When it was over and the sexton was filling in the grave, I walked my young friend back to her family home, followed by the two servants.

"I know you wish to keep watch over me," Seraphica said after a long silence. "If you wish to do so, I welcome it."

"Yes, I do."

"I wish, however, to live in my own house. I want to spend the rest of my days in my own home."

"I understand your wish, but remember you will be putting your servants at risk. Should you be attacked again..."

"I have already spoken to them. I told them under no circumstances, no matter what they may see or hear, to come to my aid in the night."

"Very well," I said, and touched her shoulder. "I think you will remain unmolested for a time. I will spend a night or so in my own house and put some things in order. Then I will join you."

Seraphica smiled warmly at me as she and her serving women stopped at her house. I continued to St. Engurrand Lane and my own front door.

My home was in good order. In need of a good cleaning but unmolested; no one had claimed it in my absence as happens so often in these desolate days. There was evidence of rats, but they are a constant pest even in the best of times.

A great exhaustion overtook me. I wanted to rest and perhaps nap a while before I undertook to prepare myself a meal and wash my clothes. I built up a fire in the fireplace, and when the room warmed a little, I lay across my bed and drifted off to sleep.

I awoke early in the afternoon. I ate a little dried beef and sat by my front window. I thought of Bastide and wondered when he would seek out Seraphica again. I thought of all the young women who came before her and how my best defense for them was in the beginning of their acquaintance with Bastide. I warn them, and if they heed that warning, they will be safe. If they do not, there is so little I can do to protect them. I can heal their injuries, listen to their stories, and physically intervene when I can because Bastide has only limited power to harm me. But their suffering is still great. I wish I knew what the passage we found in Bastide's farmhouse meant and how I could use it to destroy him.

I fell asleep in my chair. When I awoke, it was early morning. I heard roosters crowing at the east end of town and beyond the town walls. I opened my window. The air was cool but not frigid. I thought this would be the best time for me to keep an oath to a dead nun.

I wrapped and veiled myself and made for the north gate. I unlatched the postern and pushed it open. I made my way to the north road toward the foothills and the abandoned convent of Perpetua.

I passed two travelers on the road heading to Riquwihr; otherwise the road was empty. As I climbed the hill toward the convent and chapel, I saw that the foxes and ravens had returned to the empty buildings and were greatly displeased that I had come to disturb them. Two yipping foxes ran out of the ajar kitchen door, and a raven swooped down at me from above as if intent on tearing off my veil.

The rusted mattock I had used so often when Seraphica and I lived there still leaned against the outer wall. I grasped it as I walked by, continuing my way up the hillside to the tree line.

The mound of stones with which I had covered the dead nun we had found in the convent had begun to look like a natural mound. It was covered with branches, twigs, and blown leaves. I picked a spot next to the mound that was relatively level and hoped that the warmer weather in the last few days had warmed the ground sufficiently for me to dig.

Clearing away the brush and stones on the spot I had chosen, I was relieved to find the ground was pliant and reasonably soft. I began to dig.

This labor that I originally surmised would be quickly done proved to be more difficult the deeper I dug. There were buried stones and tree roots, and after an hour's struggle, it seemed as though I had made very little progress.

I rested. After a while, I resumed my labor and was relieved to find that below the frost line in the earth, the soil was looser and easier to remove. After another hour, I had produced a grave as wide as my own body and nearly as tall. I hoped it was large enough to respectfully hold the dead sister's remains. I thought it deep enough to deter animals from digging up the corpse.

Now my task was to recover the body. I started removing the stones I had piled on her and tossed them down the hillside. After a few minutes' work, I could detect a slight odor of corruption and rot. Soon I saw the edge of a tattered habit, then the bones of a hand with blackened flesh still adhered to them. The odor of decay was more noticeable now, and I dreaded the duty I had sworn to perform.

When I had completely uncovered the cadaver, I considered how I would deposit it into the grave. I did not want to touch it, as I knew it would likely come apart in my hands. As much putrescence as I have seen in this plague, I thought that even I could not bear that experience. Far removed from becoming benumbed by this pestilence, I found that I had become exhausted by death.

I decided to drag the body with the mattock. I positioned it behind the shoulder of the corpse and pulled it toward me. Immediately, the head separated from the body. I repositioned the mattock to the ribs, and as I dragged, the left arm separated from the corpse and fell free.

My gorge rose. I stepped away and turned to face the mountains to the west. It took a moment to collect myself. Then, as quickly as I could, while endeavoring to not look directly at the carcass, I dragged the remainder of it into the pit I had dug. In a very short time, I covered the body with dirt.

When I had mounded all the loose dirt onto the grave, I placed many of the stones remaining from the original pile onto the small tumulus.

I sat to rest a moment. I heard a small yip in the trees above and behind me. I turned and looked into the penumbra of the forest. It took me a moment to see the wolf, partially hidden by an oak tree, watching me. I stood and turned toward it.

The wolf never moved nor averted its gaze. Soon, I could see another wolf watching me behind the first one. Perhaps they had been watching me the whole time I had been moving the corpse. Perhaps they would dig it up when I had left. There was nothing I could do to stop this.

I threw the mattock in their direction, but they scarcely moved. I sighed at the futility of my efforts of the last couple of hours and began my walk down the hill toward the town.

As I approached the north gate, I could hear something of a commotion arising from behind it. I pushed open the postern and saw a group of townspeople surrounding old Ronsard the tanner as he roughly grasped the arm of the boy Abramet, the grandson of the Jew Belshom, who along with his partner in business, Milhaud, had been burned at the stake early last month.

The sheriff and two armed men approached the small crowd. "What is this?" the sheriff asked. "What are you doing to that boy, Ronsard?"

"That Jew, you mean!" Ronsard said. "We dealt with his grandfather, and now its him and more Jewish deviltry!"

"The boy has been living on his own since you townsmen murdered his only guardian!" I screamed.

"The hides I am getting are poor quality," Ronsard said. "Suddenly poor quality. I can't use them. This is revenge for his grandfather's death. Then only yesterday morning, my father-in-law saw this boy transform into a cat!"

"A cat?" The sheriff looked incredulous.

"That's not true!" the struggling boy protested.

"It's nonsense," I said. "You are willing to kill this boy on the testimony of a half-blind old man?"

"The court will decide that," Ronsard insisted. "All know that the Jews are likely bringing this pestilence on Christians."

"Yet it has never been proven except in cases of trial by ordeal," the sheriff said. "I have never approved of torture as a means to truth."

"So if the boy is a witch's familiar, as you are suggesting," I said, "who is the witch? A familiar must surely act on the commands of a witch."

"I don't know that," Ronsard mumbled. "But it will come out at trial."

I had confronted Ronsard before. He seemed to assume I was a practitioner in the dark and Satanic arts, and I let his imagination run astray with that idea. He was one who lumped witch and wildcrafter/midwife and pagan into the same category. He feared me and dared not challenge me.

"Am *I* the witch you are implicating?"

"No, not you," Ronsard blurted out. "I do not accuse you of witchcraft!"

"Turn over the boy to me," I said, "and I will see to it that he has left the town by this time tomorrow. Do you object to that, Ronsard?"

"No... not if you take responsibility for him."

"Does anyone here object?" I continued. No response came. The Sheriff smiled and, taking Abramet's arm from Ronsard, delivered the lad to me. The small crowd quickly dispersed.

"Come on, then," I said. Abramet followed me to my home.

"Thank you," he said, climbing my stairs.

"How have you been getting on," I asked, "since your grandfather died?"

"The Crown and the township took our property. I have been living in a hovel behind the old house."

"Have you been getting enough to eat?"

"No."

"Do you have family nearby?"

"An uncle and his family in Saint-Hippolyte."

"Would they take you in?"

"I think they would. I don't know the way, nor do I have any money, or I would have gone to them before now."

"I will get some food into you, and we will face your other problems in the morning."

The boy slept on my front chair. Before dawn, I awakened him. I gave him bread and a little wine. From the cabinet above my oven, I removed two coins which I slipped into my apron. "Come on," I said, "there isn't a moment to lose."

We made our way quickly down the stairs and along St. Engurrand toward the town square. There I found the personage for whom I was searching—Antoine, the death-cart driver. He was just lifting a shrouded body onto the back of the cart.

"Antoine!" I called.

He squinted at me in the early morning light. "Mother," he said. "Do you have anything for me this morning?"

"Two deniers if you will take this boy to Saint-Hippolyte. His people are dead here and he has family there."

"I think I can find my way once we are in the town," Abramet said. "I know it's near a church. I just don't know the way to the town from here. It's a far distance."

Antoine smiled. "For two deniers, I would take him to Strasbourg!" he said. He held out his hand and I placed the coins in it. "Climb on, boy," he continued. "I hope you don't mind the odor. We have a long ride."

As I walked back toward my house, I stopped at Seraphica's to look in on her. Celeste answered the door. She seemed to be in much distress.

"Miss Seraphica was very sick in her stomach last night," Celeste said. "This morning, she told me she was leaving everything she owned to the hospital and has resolved to work, to be of real service there."

"In her weakened condition, that is a death sentence!" I said.

"She is there now, Mother. She left in the night and sent word this morning." Celeste closed the door.

I retraced my steps hurriedly to the square and the hospital. I saw Seraphica as soon as I entered the colonnade. She was applying a damp compress to the forehead of a dying woman. Seraphica was pale, and sweat was apparent on her face and neck despite the coldness of the room. She smiled weakly when she saw me.

"It has happened, Mother," she said. "I have become another of the multitude."

"What has happened?" I asked, though by her look, I already knew the answer.

"I have the demon in me. I am carrying a demon. A ravening demon."

I could think of nothing to say. I reached to touch her cheek, but she withdrew.

"No," she admonished. "I am already afflicted. I have the symptoms. I am contaminated."

"Oh, my dear girl!"

"This is left to me as I see it. I alone will control these circumstances.

I have left everything to the hospital. I will leave this benighted earth in my own way, on my own terms. I defy the evil one by meeting my end doing some good in the world." She staggered against the bed near her. A nun standing nearby caught Seraphica's arm and steadied her, guiding her toward the curtained chambers at the rear of the room. A stifled gasp and moan as the curtain closed behind me was the last I ever heard of her.

*The end of Euphrosine's Journal.*

# CHAPTER FORTY-FIVE

A natolia had gathered her few possessions into her satchel as
Tendetta slept. She wrapped herself in her shawl and stepped out
the front door as quietly as she could. The night before, as she
and Tooney waited for Reverend Smith to return, she decided that
those who cared for her on the island would object to her leaving. Since
she was certain that for her to stay would put others in danger, she felt
that telling no one she was going was the best course of action. When
Reverend Smith did not return and a search party found no trace of
him, she was convinced that her decision was in the best interests of
everyone. She wrote Tooney and Tendetta brief notes explaining
herself and left them on the threshold as she left the house.

She hurried to the crossroads and then east to the fishing boat docks.
As she hoped, she saw a familiar bateau tied up to the dock.

"Mr. Post?" she said. "Mr. Franklin Post?"

"I'm here," the old man said, dropping a mail sack on the dock. "Oh,
it yuh, um... Anatolia."

"Yes. I heard you were running the mail today. Can you take me
back to the mainland?"

"Well... sho'. I kin do it. But I gots to go to Savannah dis mawnin'.
Gots to be in Savannah by midday. S'pose to pick up some packages
fo' a lady."

"That's fine. Savannah would be better. I only have twenty dollars
left."

"Aw, I'm goin' anyways. Keep yuh money. Git in de boat. I take dis
mail sack up to de' sto'."

The morning was especially cold. Franklin kept close to the coastline
as the breezes arose. He tried to carry on a conversation with Anatolia
about why she was leaving Monfort and where she was headed, but she
had little to say. They had been on the water an hour before the sun
started to rise.

A few lights flickering on the shoreline defined a dark space that
looked like the mouth of a river.

"Savannah River," Franklin shouted. "Twenty more mile."

The breezes were brisk, blowing in from the sea. In another two
hours, the lamps and streetlights of Savannah began to appear on the
south bank of the river. Franklin steered the boat up to a small, private

dock far east of what appeared to be a large area of commercial docks where larger boats were loading and unloading. He tied the boat up and helped Anatolia step out onto the platform.

"Yuh all right, gal?" he asked.

Anatolia shook her head no.

"I hates t' leave yuh. Yuh don't know nobody?"

"No. I just need to get home. No place else to go."

"Yuh gonna find a baby here direckly. Shouldn't be on yuh own."

"I'll get home. Mrs. Heugyens is there... No place else to go."

"Yuh runnin' like somefin' after yuh. Travel safe..." Franklin nodded to her and smiled. "I'll pray fuh yuh."

Anatolia walked west toward the larger piers and docks. A line of brick warehouses under construction bordered the riverfront. She sat on a stack of bricks, facing the river, to watch the activity on the levee and think of what she would do.

An elegant schooner was berthed just opposite from where she sat. Food and other provisions were being loaded aboard by four stevedores. The sound of a wagon approaching from the east attracted Anatolia's attention. A buckboard carrying several brightly painted trunks was followed on foot by six well-dressed black women. Driving the coach was a regal-looking, attractive black woman of about forty. As the wagon passed, Anatolia saw the words, *Vulpinatrix LaFemme and her Exotic Revue* painted on it. She smiled. The driver of the wagon suddenly drew in the reins and stopped the horse pulling it.

"Are you amused by the name of my company?" the driver asked.

"Well, yes," Anatolia said. "I like it very much"

"Good. That's the idea. It's my stage name. I had to think of something memorable."

"I think you succeeded."

"Are you idling here, young woman? You look a little lost. And more than a little pregnant."

"Yes. I am trying to get home. I need to get to the Mississippi."

"We are getting on that boat for New Orleans. My serving girl just quit. Ran off with a porter at the hotel. Do you want a job?"

"Oh, yes, I do!" Anatolia stood. "That would help me so much!"

"It was providential then that you chose that spot to idle. Climb up."

Vulpinatrix's real name was Violet Fortner. She and Anatolia were to share the small stateroom, while the six women of her company, the Vulpettes, shared the three remaining cabins.

"The boat was sent for us by Mr. Prentiss, the owner of the Rialto Opera House in New Orleans," Violet said. "Have you heard of it?"

"No, I haven't," Anatolia said as she helped to unpack Violet's trunk.

"He has engaged us for two months after our great success in Richmond. Two months!"

"What kind of show do you perform?"

"It's low comedy—dancing, singing, naughty jokes. They expect it."

"I am so grateful you have employed me," Anatolia steadied herself against the bureau.

"You don't look well."

"No... I'm not. I'm sorry."

"Do what you can. We just need a little extra help with things. Just... do what you can. How did you get in this state, if you don't mind the question? Is the father gone?"

"I was attacked, while my... husband... was away. It's been a difficult time."

"Happened to me, too. When I was fourteen. Where is your husband?"

"He was killed."

Violet took Anatolia by the shoulders and pressed for her to sit on the edge of the bed. "You'll have good days and bad days. Two of the ladies with me I found on the street. Charity is the greatest beatitude. My mother taught me, and I have always lived as such.

"It's an eight-day trip. Can you make it?"

"Yes, I think so."

"Do what you can for us."

After the first day at sea, Anatolia felt a little better and was more able to assist Violet and the other women of the company. She pressed some of their dresses and costumes and trimmed the hair of the sisters Riva and Dolores.

On the fourth day, the seas were rough. A squall blew in from the northwest, and Anatolia could scarcely leave her cot until the weather calmed. On the fifth day, the schooner rounded the tip of Florida and entered the Gulf of Mexico.

The day before landing, Anatolia was weak and feverish but insisted on helping the Vulpettes varnishing their nails. Their first performance was to be the evening of the day they landed.

As the sloop made port on the morning of the eighth day, and the company gathered and repacked their belongings, Violet took Anatolia aside. "Do you feel well enough to be on your own from here?" she asked.

"I'll make it. I must make it."

"How much money do you have?"

"Twenty dollars."

"Here's another forty. This will more than get you home and feed you on the way. Steward will show you to the train station. Train will be faster for you." She hugged Anatolia. "I think you have bigger troubles than you have told me. Be safe, and trust in God."

# CHAPTER FORTY-SIX

The new train station serving the St. Louis and Southern Railroad was many blocks north of the Port of New Orleans. Anatolia hired a hansom to take her there, as she felt she didn't have the strength to walk. At the station, she was relieved to find that the first train of the day heading north would be leaving in forty minutes.

The ticket agent told Anatolia that her trip to the station at Belgique, the nearest one to Ste. Odile, would take twenty-two hours. She decided to pay the eighteen dollars for a sleeping chair at the rear of the Pullman car. She settled into her seat and found it extremely comfortable. In another thirty minutes, the train pulled away from the station.

Her stomach was unsettled, and she felt slightly feverish. As she tried to relax in her chair, she realized a tension in her body that she must have been carrying all day was fading.

There were only five other people in the car: two prosperous-looking white couples sat near the front and a young Negro girl, who sat at the rear across the aisle from Anatolia. The girl glanced across at Anatolia with what seemed to be a concerned look on her face. Anatolia knew she was now ill enough that she would start attracting attention to herself.

Anatolia watched an almost alien landscape rolling past her window. Lush river bottoms gave way to impenetrable thickets, then to live oaks whose branches were grotesquely splayed and dripping with Spanish moss.

Between Baton Rouge and Vidalia, she saw many ruined plantations with fields overgrown and mansions burned out. Many of these expansive properties appeared to have been divided into smaller working farms.

In the late afternoon, the train stopped at Vidalia. The station had a refreshment saloon, and from her window, Anatolia could see second-class and emigrant car passengers scramble off the train to eat as much of a long-overdue meal as they could manage in the twenty minutes that the train was scheduled to stop.

A news butcher, a boy of about twelve, stood shivering on the platform just outside the Pullman coach, selling newspapers, magazines, and candy. Anatolia removed a silver dollar from her coin purse and stepped out into the vestibule, then out onto the platform. She bought a copy of *The Sentinel*, a journal of literature and opinion she had often seen in Mrs. Heugyens's house. She told the boy to keep the change from the dollar.

Anatolia returned to her seat in the coach as the conductor stepped out onto the platform to warn the passengers that the train would be departing soon. She opened her magazine and tried to read from it. She glanced through a tale by Joseph Sheridan Le Fanu about a spectral monkey and smiled to remember that Tendetta pronounced the word "monkrey." She read an essay on the scientific and anecdotal evidence that the earth is hollow. She then closed the magazine and set it aside.

After the engine had taken on fuel and water, the bell was sounded, reminding passengers of the train's imminent departure. Just as they had scrambled off the train twenty minutes earlier, the lower-class passengers rushed out of the refreshment saloon and back on board, many with their mouths and pockets full of food.

As the evening progressed, Anatolia read through the rest of her magazine. Reading combined with the movement of the train made her more than a little queasy from time to time, but she found she could control this condition to an extent by putting down the magazine and closing her eyes for a few minutes.

By ten o'clock, she was exhausted. She dreaded the prospect of attempting to sleep in her reclining seat. She remembered as a child, Moira telling her of accounts she had read of transcontinental train trips. She considered how much more uncomfortable the emigrant car passengers must be, cramped together on poorly upholstered benches, with their coats and jackets draped over them or bunched up to serve as pillows against the oak bench backs or armrests. The discomfort, coupled with the snoring and coughing of the other passengers, plus the wailing of children, inconsolable in their weariness and sense of displacement, made the probability of rest unlikely for any but the soundest sleeper, Anatolia imagined.

She lowered the back of her chair by a few inches and settled in, prepared to make the best of what promised to be a futile attempt at even the most intermittent sleep. Turning her head toward the window, she was entranced by the moonlight on the hillsides and fields, and by the silvery bands of rivers, partially frozen, winding off into the dark forests. After a few minutes, her eyelids grew heavy.

She nodded off. When she awakened, it was nearly eleven. She realized she had been dreaming of the night she was attacked and of the dark figure on horseback she had seen on the docks as she and the New Phrygians were boarding the *Seneca Princess* in New York. She had dreamt, too, of Monfort Island, of Tooney and Tendetta and the specter they had seen in the forest. She assumed Reverend Smith must have been killed. She hoped her women friends were still safe, since she left Monfort to protect them. And she had dreamt of Set.

She remembered him as a boy, shyly stopping to talk to her as he passed the Negro School. She remembered his devotion to her, his belief in her. She remembered his delight in discovering, because of their connection, his talent for numbers and organization, and his opportunities as her reputation grew to use them to do good in the world. There would never be anyone like him in her life again.

It took several hours for Anatolia to drift off again. She slept a deep, dreamless sleep, awakening only when she felt the sunlight on her face. She sat up. The girl sitting across the aisle from her was looking at her and looked away, embarrassed, as Anatolia awakened. She decided to speak to the girl.

"My name is Anatolia. Since we are on a long trip together, I thought I would introduce myself."

The girl nodded and smiled a little. It took her a moment to respond. "I am Louise Norman."

"Where are you from, Louise?"

"New Orleans."

"And where are you going?"

"St. Louis. My mamma was trying to raise five of us, and she found me a job in St. Louis through her cousin Merle."

"I see."

"I get room and board, so I'll send my money home."

"That will help out, I'm sure. I haven't seen you eat anything, Louise."

"No. Wasn't money for that. I didn't know seats were different prices. I paid too much."

"You must be hungry?"

Louise shrugged. Anatolia opened her coin purse.

"Here. Here is ten dollars," Anatolia said, giving the coin to the girl. Louise's face went blank, and she was speechless for a moment. "Thank... you." She took the coin and looked at it in disbelief.

"We will be stopping at Lake Josephine soon," Anatolia said. "Get something to eat. That should feed you as far as St. Louis."

Louise shook her head yes. "Thank you," she said again.

The conductor, a tall, slim man in blue, passed through the car. "Lake Josephine in ten minutes," he said.

Anatolia did not feel rested. She lay back in her chair. She was starting to cramp, and a pain was developing behind her left eye. She felt light-headed and breathless and had a sense that Louise's eyes were on her. A sudden cramp seized her stomach painfully, and as she watched in horror, a sharply-angled wave of motion kneaded itself hideously under her dress and across her stomach.

She looked across at Louise, who was watching her in disbelief and disgust. The girl jumped up from her seat, grabbing a small satchel on the floor. She hurried into the vestibule at the rear of the car. Anatolia could hear the door lock. When the train stopped at Lake Josephine, Anatolia saw Louise run into the station. Through the narrow building, she saw the girl run out the front door and disappear into a crowd.

In twenty minutes, Louise had not returned, as Anatolia had foreseen. She mentioned to the conductor as he passed through that the girl was missing, and he responded that the train could not wait.

Anatolia had no appetite and resigned herself to insomnia. Tendetta had warned her against starving the cambion, if that was what was inside her. "Starve de cambion an' it feeds on oonah," she said.

But Anatolia was beyond caring. She no longer cared what would become of her. She only wanted now to protect others and end this curse if it were in her power to do so. By tomorrow night, she would be in Belgique, and then she would walk on to Ste. Odile.

She felt much pain that night, trying to rest in her seat. All the next day, she felt feverish and terribly thirsty. An hour after the sun went down, the train pulled into the station at Belgique.

Anatolia was the only passenger to step out onto the platform. Exhausted, she dragged her bag toward a bench she could barely make out in the dark. She collapsed onto it. In the gloom, she could just see two coach lamps shining some distance away on the road opposite her. As she looked, she could make out what seemed to be a maroon Rockaway coach. A stocky black man stepped down from the driver's seat and approached her.

"Miss Anatolia?" he said.

"Yes. How do you know me?"

"I've been sent for you."

"Who sent you?"

The man smiled as if her question was an ironic one. Anatolia stood.

"Very well," she said. "The time has come. I feel the time has come... and is providential. I will come with you. What is your name, sir?"

"I am Jean-Joseph."

# CHAPTER FORTY-SEVEN

The two chestnut geldings pulling the Rockaway clopped along the cobblestone streets in perfect unison. As the Belgique Road turned into Bosphorous Street at the southern edge of Ste. Odile, the few streetlights that merchants could afford to burn were being lighted. At the same time, the lamps and candles that illuminated private homes, large and small in the old town, were flickering out for the night. But as the carriage continued north and the black stain that was Jardin Noir could be seen on its looming prominence high above all else, Anatolia could see lights burning in its tower windows.

The Rockaway turned west on Mal Ardents Street and then north again on Thermopylae. The carriage soon left the paved road behind as it climbed the hill toward the great house. Anatolia was jostled uncomfortably as she held onto the hand grips inside the compartment. She felt as though the remainder of her life could be counted in minutes, not years. She considered this possibility with complete indifference. All that remained now was the justice that she felt many dead awaited, and to accomplish the thing that needed to be accomplished, regardless of the cost.

Soon the rocking of the coach caused Anatolia's back to pain her severely. She felt her gorge rise and thought she may vomit or choke to death. A great cramp overtook her, and she felt fluid on her inner thigh. She knew she must be bleeding again. She drew up her skirt to see what had happened. In the darkness she could tell little, but she could see that what was glistening on her leg was not blood.

She felt a change come over her as if she were transitioning from one truth to another. In a few more minutes, she saw the grounds of the great estate opening before the coach. An enormous, gnarled oak tree with fantastically splayed branches like those she had seen in the south could just be made out in the darkness, as could a large and grotesque fountain that dominated the weedy lawn. Beyond these stood the ancient house, a foreboding mass just starting to be touched by the illumination of the rising moon. A dim light flickered behind a high oriel window on the first floor.

Jean-Joseph circled the drive and stopped the coach at the mansion's front door. Anatolia tried to compose herself as Jean-Joseph opened the coach door. She stepped out.

"I am to wait for you here," Jean-Joseph said. "I'll take you wherever you are staying... afterward. Do you want to leave your bag with me?"

"No. I will keep it."

Jean-Joseph pulled open the heavy front door for her. She stepped inside. As she crossed the threshold into a dark vestibule, she felt a strange sense of loss, dread, and isolation pass through her. The vestibule opened onto a large, pentagonal room, lined with dark wainscoting, off which radiated several rooms and hallways. A large round table, dust-covered, dominated the room. The table was piled with books, papers, bones, minerals, and fossils.

Beyond the table was a large oak staircase that rose to a landing featuring a window some twenty feet high. Several niches in the entry hall on either side of the staircase were populated by stone statues from antiquity. A pharaonic figure and ibis-headed god represented Egypt, marble figures of Eros and Psyche bespoke the Classical world, and bearded, winged bulls of basalt recalled Nineveh and the court of Ashurnasirpal.

Large pocket doors just to Anatolia's right were ajar. A faint light shone from within the room. Walls lined with books told her this was the library. She looked through the parted doors, and she saw him.

Bastide stood facing the fireplace across the expansive room.

He was unusually tall and painfully thin. Facing away from her and at a great distance, it appeared to her that his left arm was misshapen. His hair was long and white and in wild disarray. He wore a black frock coat that looked fifty years out of date. The only light in the room aside from the fireplace was a moderately-sized oil lamp on a nearby table. In the dim light, she was aware of, though barely noticed, thousands of books on the walls, paintings, antique statues, bones, and other natural objects.

"You are here," a deep but wet-sounding voice said.

Bastide turned to face her. She gasped. His face was haggard and drawn, gray in color, and looked as though it was covered in thinly stretched, dead flesh. His lips were an unnatural red, and the teeth behind them were long, thin, and set in purple gums. His right eye was missing, leaving only a black, weeping socket with withered eyelids sagging over the gap. The left eye was hideously round, artificially held open by wire, just as the story had passed down to Anatolia. His left arm was twisted and hung uselessly at his side.

"I felt after everything, I had to meet you as soon as you arrived. I wanted to finally talk with you face to face. Pointless for you to keep running. You will be taken wherever you want to go in the town as soon as you wish to leave. Forgive the great latitude I have given myself in sending a coach for you," he said.

"You have allowed yourself a far greater latitude than that, as you can see." Anatolia answered.

"I am of two natures... as you know. The master and the host. The host is loath to harm you, but the master will have his way."

"Always at a terrible cost."

Bastide took a few steps toward her. Her body tensed. He stopped. "You can see what your mentor, Miss Perdita Badon-Reed, did to me. Shattered my arm, pierced my eye. As the ages pass, the host body has diminished ability to heal itself."

"A small thing compared to what you did to her. I thought your two natures were fated to live and die together."

"Euphrosine was mistaken about that. I always told her that her power would fade away. When it did, it was the end of her."

"Euphrosine didn't understand everything she needed to understand. I believe I do."

Bastide took a few more steps toward her. "You have been in my mind for twelve years."

"Since I was a child."

"Yes, since you were a child. You were like no other, by all accounts. An image implanted itself in my spirit and that of the master, and it has never left."

"It's an abominable thought."

"I, we, gave you a gift. A gold Aureus, which you accepted. Then a connection was established. Wherever you went, given time, we, the master and host, could sense it and find you."

"Why did it take so many years then?" Anatolia asked.

"My physical self was nearly destroyed. I resisted the will of the master as long as I could, knowing the harm that would come to you. I did *not* want to harm you. It took time."

"And now?"

"You are grown. The harm has been done. *Le Vorace* must proceed from you. Soon they will die and you will be free of them."

"*Le Vorace*..."

"Yes. The worst has happened already. But there is still my compulsion for you—my need for concordance, however brief, that two millennia of effort have not provided before now. Something at last that Balphoroth the master cannot end."

Anatolia felt an urgent pressure in her abdomen. "I almost pity you," she said.

"Pity?"

"You were a victim too, as Perdita, Solana, my Set, and so many others were. That doesn't absolve you, though. My time has come, and I know a thing you do not know."

"What is it?"

"I am the one with the mark."

"Mark?"

"The one who has been awaited. It is not *Le Vorace* I am delivering. It is the cambion."

Bastide looked at her, expressionlessly. After a moment he remembered and understood. "I knew nothing of the mark," he said. "But the cambion...!" Bastide returned to the fireplace and grasped a brass poker.

Bent over in pain, Anatolia scurried across the library toward a door standing ajar in the shadows. It was the cellar door. She slammed the door shut. She was relieved to find it had a bolt on the inside. She pushed the bolt across and secured the door. She collapsed onto the floor. Wave after wave of pain passed through her, and she thought she must surely faint. She felt the irresistible urge to compress her muscles as Bastide began pounding at the door.

"I'll kill it!" he screamed. "*I must kill it.*" He began pounding on the door with the poker and tearing at the door handles.

A sense of release came over Anatolia. Fluid expelled from her, followed by a squirming black mass that flopped hideously on the floor. As the thing moved, its black flesh began to turn gray. It was almost hairless except for a few coarse strands on the top of its small head and growing down its bony neck. Flesh sagged into folds under its neck and thin arms. Its eyes were orange and seemed too large for its face, which was slightly prognathous and appeared wizened and terrified. Its teeth were triangular and gleaming white.

Its look of terror seemed to dissipate as it looked upon Anatolia. She felt as though she was in shock and didn't know if she could move or acknowledge the horror lying next to her as real. She looked into the face of the creature and saw an expression she could only define as deference or affection pass over its face.

Anatolia struggled painfully to her feet. With what little strength she had remaining, she pulled open the bolt.

The door swung open. Bastide fell backwards in surprise. With a single-minded but emotionless sense of purpose, the cambion was upon him. The creature tore at Bastide's withered arm. In an instant, half the arm was severed and skidded uselessly across the floor like a dry tree branch. Bastide growled a deep, guttural cry and struggled to pull the creature from him.

Anatolia fell to the library floor in a swoon. She could not focus her eyes on the terrible confusion she was hearing. She thought she saw a form, liquid and dark, arise from the struggling figures, hover at the high corners of the room for a second, then disappear back into the bloodied, gaunt anatomy that was Bastide.

Hearing the noise, Jean-Joseph rushed into the slightly ajar front door. He rushed to Bastide's aid but seemed unable to grasp the creature. "Outside! Outside!" Jean-Joseph screamed.

Anatolia rose to her feet. She picked up the small oil lamp from the library table and made her way out the front door.

She could hear a great crashing and screaming coming from the library. It appeared, from her limited vantage point, that something had caught fire in the house. In another instant, Jean-Joseph emerged, shaken, from the house, supporting the severely injured Bastide.

"Into the carriage! Into the carriage quickly!" Jean-Joseph cried. Bastide climbed in, and as Jean-Joseph lashed the geldings, a dark, glutinous mass burst from the house and into the coach. As the horses reared and began to run, Anatolia threw the oil lamp against the carriage lamp nearest her. The lamp exploded against the Rockaway, engulfing most of the front of the coach in flames. The horses bolted in terror and ran across the front grounds toward the edge of the high prominence overlooking the river.

Jean-Joseph's pant legs were aflame, but Anatolia saw him reach down below his seat as if he were trying to operate a mechanism. In an instant, the geldings broke away from the carriage shaft and veered away to the north. The momentum of the coach, though now completely engulfed, drove it on its original trajectory and over the edge of the precipice. It crashed into the leafless winter trees as it fell down the steep hillside, and flames arose whose upper reaches were visible from the lawn.

Anatolia collapsed onto the ground.

The flames continued to burn for a long time. She could also plainly see now that books were burning in the library. The house might be destroyed, but she still did not have the energy to move away to safer ground.

She saw a flicker of movement out across the dark lawn. The movement was approaching her. Her head cleared a little, and she was able to make out the cambion scampering toward her. It was dragging something in its mouth. As it neared, she could see that it had a tattered rag of flesh in its teeth—an ear, part of a cheek, and a shock of long, white hair.

The creature dropped its prize before her. It looked at her a moment and then scampered off toward the south, toward Ste. Odile or the river, the forests, or the salt marshes beyond.

The pain of the delivery seemed to be subsiding. Anatolia would have to make her way down the hill and back into town, somehow. If it took all night, she still knew she could manage it. She would reach the town and Mrs. Heugyens, Susan, Mrs. Zell, and whoever were left of those she held in her heart. Surely the nature and hopes of the town would change now. The privileges of comfort and even complacency could be afforded. The cost was her childhood, her security, the peace of her memories, and the terror of all who came before—the suffering and the seeping gray corruption of centuries of the dead.

# ABOUT THE AUTHOR

John S. McFarland's short stories have appeared in numerous journals, in both the mainstream and horror genres. His tales have been collected with stories by Stephen King, H. P. Lovecraft, Robert Bloch, and Richard Matheson. His work has been praised by such writers as T. E. D. Klein and Philip Fracassi, and he has been called "A great, undiscovered voice in horror fiction." This novel is the sequel to *The Black Garden*, and his short story collection, *The Dark Walk Forward*, contains tales connected to the small town of Ste. Odile. Both are available through Dark Owl Publishing. His young reader series about Bigfoot is in print in three languages and is being reprinted by Dark Owl Publishing with illustrations by McFarland, starting with *Annette: A Big, Hairy Mom* in October 2022.

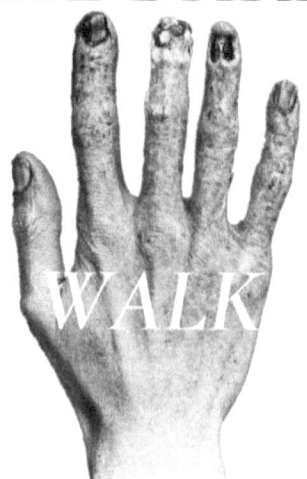

A little boy gets lost in the big woods.
His parents are so worried and are trying to find him.
He gets found, but by the most unlikely of creatures,
and she becomes the most unlikely of friends.

# ANNETTE
## A Big, Hairy Mom

### Written and Illustrated by
### JOHN S. MCFARLAND

Available in paperback and on Kindle
October 15, 2022
from Dark Owl Publishing, LLC
www.darkowlpublishing.com